NOT ALL BODIES
STAY BURIED

A Novel

by Garth Jeffries

CHAPTER ONE

Six years ago

It was a beautiful evening to bury a body.

The moon, viewed through wisps of fog, was just a slight sliver in the western sky and shedding very little light as it prepared to set. A high overcast thinned the stars. The evening was warm and damp, the moisture clinging to the scrub brush, sedge, and heather on the edges of Coskata Pond near the island's northeast tip. Despite the calendar, it did not feel like fall, more like late summer. She would have loved this weather, he thought. And chuckled.

The Boston meteorologist had called for a Nor'easter to strike late tomorrow with strong winds and heavy rain. The timing could not have been any better. The storm would erase any traces of his presence here. All evidence of her grave would disappear from the world. Only he would know where she was buried. The thought brought a wry smile.

Beads of water trickled down his face, and a shock of his salt and pepper hair dropped over his gray eyes. He leaned over and plunged the shovel into the sandy soil. The blade, scraping a shell, sounded out in agony as the steel violated the earth. He turned and emptied his effort onto the small pile of tailings he had created— the swish of soil over metal.

Plunge. Scrape. Swish.

He stopped and rested on the handle. He was not a young man anymore, and despite his daily walks, he simply did not have the stamina for hard, manual labor. Fortunately, he had never had to do any hard, manual labor in his life courtesy of wealthy parents and a substantial trust fund. The most challenging work he faced was writing checks to the landscapers, maids, and maintenance teams that tended to him and his large home on the island. It was a good life, and he intended to keep it that way.

This would work, he told himself, as long as his story was clear and consistent for when he would talk to the police. Given the circumstances around the First, he would be better prepared. Much better.

The First had gone for a swim after having a few cocktails. They had been at the beach to watch the sunset and had had one too many. It was a warm evening, and she had wanted to take a quick dip to cool off. Despite her intoxication and the heavy rip tide, they had questioned him intensely on why he had not tried to stop her. Why would he let her swim in that situation? Why didn't you go after her? They did everything but accuse him of pushing her in on purpose.

Which, of course, he had.

She had slipped into the water easily, helped along by the valium he had mixed into her drinks. He was pretty sure that she was still breathing when the currents carried her out to sea, where he thought nature would take its course. And it did to some extent. But she eventually washed up on the island's south shore a few weeks later and was discovered by a young couple walking the beach. Thanks to exposure and sea life, there wasn't enough of her left to determine a precise cause of death. The certificate he had submitted to claim her life insurance had stated accidental drowning.

He had been devastated.

As he rested on his shovel, the damp breeze blowing the flaps of his yellow rain slicker, he thought about his upcoming discussion with the police.

Yes, they had fought, and she said she was done. Leaving for good. I said fine and grabbed my fishing gear to find some peace and do some thinking. I love to fish and often set out in the evening to catch the right tides at Great Point. Yes, it was late. No, there wasn't anyone at the guard house when I drove by. Mostly blues, but also hoping to potentially land a striper or even a bonito. Yes, it was a couple of hours but didn't have much more than a few strikes. And no, I didn't see any other fishermen. I was trying a new spot off Coatue and was alone in the surf the entire time. I returned before daybreak and discovered she was gone when I got home. I was devastated.

He was quite good at being devastated.

But this would require more effort. She couldn't be found this time. With all of the lingering suspicion from the First, finding the Second would prove to be too much. If not outright jail time, at a minimum, it would cast a dark shadow on his life, which would have harsh negative impacts both professionally and socially. The First had generated wary sympathy. Although they never told him to his face, many of his friends no doubt wondered why he had let her swim. What would they think of the Second? He shuddered at the thought. He would probably need to leave the island. No, she could not be found.

Plunge. Scrape. Swish. The hole grew.

Making her disappear physically was one thing, but how to make her disappear from the electronic world? That had proved easier than he thought. He had purchased a ferry ticket off the island in her name and had given that ticket, along with her phone, credit cards, and several thousand in cash, to a transient he had met while partying at a popular bar on the island. She was a beautiful, wealthy college dropout that claimed she wanted to see the world. He saw it more like seeking revenge for poor parenting. But it didn't matter to him, she had turned out to be great fun in bed, and they enjoyed several evenings together. But like many travelers, she was anxious to move on, itching to make her way to the West Coast. All he asked was that she use the phone and the credit cards along the way and dump them when she arrived. And, oh yeah, please spend money like a pissed-off wife out for revenge.

The final step would be to establish her as unstable with the police.

Yes, detective, she has had a history of mental illness, although she never sought treatment despite my pleading with her. Before we were married, she often went on alcohol-fueled manic binges that would last days, if not weeks. Yes, I tried to get her treatment, but she refused. I think our marriage helped immensely, though. The stability and comfort improved her mental state. Yes, very concerned that this fight and separation might have triggered another episode. God knows what she might do. No, not sure where she would go. She grew up in California, so maybe? What can I do to help?

It was a pretty thin story, but the digital traces would lead them away from him and Nantucket. Not the perfect solution - with murder, what is - but enough for plausible deniability. Yes, he would still get suspicious stares from his neighbors, and his friends would likely keep a quiet distance for a while. But it would pass. Bad news always does. And he would help it along, nurturing it with carefully curated snippets of information. He had ensured she had only superficial relationships with those on the island, so interest would wane quickly. And with her parents dead and no kids, there wasn't anyone to continue to drive the investigation or even care about her disappearance. Eventually, it would just slip away like a low tide.

The cry of a seagull in the distance startled him from his thoughts, and he looked around guardedly. The breeze rustled the low bushes of the moors as they swayed in cadence in the dim light. There were no signs of people or cars. The sound of the surf, just a few hundred feet away, soothed his nerves. With the closest person at least a mile distant and the terrain accessible only by an off-road vehicle, he knew he would see someone coming from a long way away. He relaxed and turned his attention back to the job at hand.

Glancing down, he saw he was nearly there, the depression a couple of feet deep. Thankful for the loose sand, he dug his shovel in again, and his pile grew, now almost waist high.

He had killed her in a fit of rage. She could be such a bitch sometimes and just didn't know when to back off and shut the hell up. He certainly hadn't planned it, not like the First. He knew, eventually, it was going to happen. He was slowly losing control and having a more challenging time managing her. He wasn't sure what triggered it, but she was fighting back more and more. And it was unacceptable. When she threatened to leave and expose his abuse, he, of course, had to take decisive action. He was a well-known and respected member of Nantucket society. He was a generous philanthropist and served on several boards and foundations across the island. Exposing him would risk it all.

Her attack had briefly caught him off guard, but he deftly fended it off and leveraged his size and bulk to overpower her. Within minutes of that threatening comment, she was gone. It had given him a strange sense of satisfaction, much more so than the last time. It was good. Total control.

Satisfied that the grave was sufficient, he retreated to his ancient Land Rover and opened the rear hatch. He had been careful to turn off the interior lights before he left the garage and could just make out her shape under the weak moonlight. He grabbed her body and pulled her out, dropping her onto the sand, still partially frozen from the time in the freezer. Grasping her ankles, he dragged her off the main path and into the scrub. Her long, light brown hair trailed behind her, leaving faint tracks in the sand, much like the seagrass when it blows in the wind. The tracks followed her into the hole.

Breathing heavily from the exertion, he paused and looked down at what he had done. She looked as if she were sleeping. He would miss her. She had been a decent cook, and the sex had been satisfactory and convenient. She had also looked good on his arm at the island's high-end social events and fundraisers. He sighed. He knew he would struggle a bit until he could find the Third. He was reasonably attractive and very wealthy, so finding another would not be a problem. He just wasn't sure what he wanted. A blond? Brunette? Maybe even a redhead? He had several prospects in mind and knew that once the dust settled and an adequate mourning time passed, he would be back in a relationship and back in control.

Patience, he told himself. Patience.

He plunged the shovel into the pile, turned, and dropped it on her face. He felt a surge of power flow through him. Bitch.

Plunge. Scrape. Swish.

It took nearly an hour but finally the last of the sand filled the hole, leaving a slight rise in the terrain. He casually brushed out the edges and his mass of footprints around the grave, knowing that the coming storm would do the real work.

He slowly backed out of the scrub, smoothing the evidence as he went. Making his way to his car, he closed the hatch, got behind the wheel, and started the engine. He lowered the window and took a deep breath of the salt-tinged air. He dropped the car into gear, put some Coltrane on the stereo, and accelerated slowly across the sand toward home. Life was good.

It had been a beautiful evening to bury a body.

CHAPTER TWO

Present day

R ob McGlynn still couldn't believe he had buried his wife.

It was early afternoon on a rare summer-like day for early October in Hyannis, Massachusetts. A sky of deep blue was spotted with large, puffy white clouds floating gently above the harbor. Standing on the docks below, he waited alone for the car ferry to take him to Nantucket. Sarah, the love of his life, wife of over ten years, and the woman he planned to grow old and die with, had been in the ground for six months. Just thirty-four, the years of being without her stretched out in front of him like a prison sentence.

He leaned an elbow on the railing and looked out over the water, his blue eyes squinting in the bright sun. The breeze tickled cats' paws on the water, and small waves lapped on the pilings below him. Even though they had never been here together, Rob thought of her everywhere he looked. They had talked about coming here together, visiting Cape Cod and Nantucket, maybe Martha's Vineyard, but had never made the trip. Things would crop up and get in the way, and they would put it off. They were young and had plenty of time.

They had plenty of time until they didn't.

Sarah had been a very successful marketing executive with a well-known consumer products company and was the primary breadwinner for the family. Her success allowed Rob to start his own small business, running a handyman repair franchise out of their home in St. Louis. He didn't make much in the first few years but enjoyed the work and helping people. Together they were pretty comfortable and very happy.

When they married, they both agreed they didn't want children; too much work, too expensive, not for them. But over time, that changed, and on their 10th anniversary, at dinner on a rooftop with a spectacular view of downtown St. Louis and the Arch, they surprised each other by confessing that their feelings on parenting had changed. Rob had cautiously raised the topic first, carefully feeling out Sarah's response and fearful of how she might react. But upon hearing him voice his desires, Sarah let out a little scream and jumped up in excitement. She leaned over and hugged him hard, whispering, "There is nothing more I want in life than to have your baby."

They celebrated with a bottle of Veuve Clicquot and a rich chocolate dessert before heading home and getting to work on having a child. Despite being young and healthy, they were unable to get pregnant no matter how hard they tried. The collection of store-bought pregnancy tests grew, as did their frustration.

After nearly a year of failure, they went to the doctor. Rob checked out okay, but an exploratory ultrasound for Sarah revealed the worst; a large mass in her abdomen. The shock was quickly followed by more appointments and more doctors. Despite having excellent health insurance and access to some of the best hospitals in the country, the answer was always the same; weeks, not months. The mass was too big and complex for surgery, so they had explored a multi-modal approach of radiation and chemotherapy. The treatment wreaked havoc on Sarah's body but did little to stop the spread of the disease. Sarah endured many more rounds of chemo, but the cancer was aggressive, and she passed away quietly one night, just a few months after her initial diagnosis.

Rob was heartbroken. Life lost all flavor and meaning. His business helped distract him during the day, but when he returned to the home they had made together, he was brutalized by the memories of their life and all that had been taken from them. Finally, Rob could handle no more of the pain and put their house on the market.

The life insurance through her employer had been extremely generous. Combined with the equity in their home, with careful investments and frugal spending Rob would be comfortable for many years. He would need to work eventually, but the financial cushion gave him the freedom to do whatever he wanted, wherever he wanted, at least within reason.

* * *

"I want to write a novel," he had said to her one night, just a few months after the wedding. They were in bed after making love, and he was on his side, leaning on his elbow, and looking at her. Sarah was on her back, her head on the pillow. Her green eyes widened in surprise.

"What!" Sarah said and giggled. "You've never told me that."

"I know. I've been reluctant to admit it. I wasn't sure what you would think."

Sarah rolled onto her side, smiled, and cupped his cheek in her hand. "I think it's wonderful, honey. I want whatever you want. If it makes you happy, then it will make me happy as well."

Rob smiled and looked down.

"What is it?" Sarah asked.

"Do you think I can do it? Write a book, I mean?"

"Oh, Rob. You are such a talented man. I know you can do whatever you put your mind to. And I know you are a good writer; you just need a good story."

"Humph"

"What's that for?" she asked.

"A good story. I've been trying to think of a good story for years, something unique and different. It's impossible."

She looked at him intensely. "Give it time, Rob. It will come to you, and when it does, I know it will be a hell of a good book."

Rob smiled. "You've always been my biggest fan."

She smiled back. "And I always will be. Don't forget that."

He leaned down and kissed her gently on the lips. "I love you," he whispered.

"I love you too," she replied and then giggled. "Ooh, is that what I think it is?"

Rob chuckled. "Maybe? Are you interested?" he said with a wink.

She smiled warmly and pulled him close.

* * *

Looking out over the harbor, Rob caught his first glance of the car ferry as it rounded a spit of land and made its way toward the dock. She was a rounded-off box like an old-fashioned refrigerator lying on its side. Standing three levels tall, she had a gaping hole in her bow to accept vehicles and a matching one in her stern to discharge them. Painted a fading white with flaking black trim, rust stains were visible up her short bow and down her flanks. A small cabin on the top level was set back from the bow, and Rob could just make out the officers there, carefully navigating the ship toward her berth. In block letters on the bow, he saw her name. *The Eagle.*

He chuckled. The Eagle? The Brick would have been a better choice.

For a moment, Rob thought about backing out. Hop in the car, turn around, and head back to St. Louis. Why was he even going to Nantucket? He had never been there. He only knew it by reputation and by reading the notes version of Moby Dick in high school. He had stumbled on the decision quite by accident. He had been cleaning out the basement, preparing the house for sale, and dispensing the accumulations of their life together. Going through one of her boxes, he had found a brochure on Nantucket and Martha's Vineyard and remembered their conversation. On it was a yellow sticky note with a handwritten comment from Sarah. *Maybe Nantucket for our 15th?* They had talked about the trip as being a great way to celebrate their milestone anniversary. Unfortunately, that milestone never came.

They had agreed to go so why not? It was as good as any other destination. And with it, he was going to give his dream a shot and try and finally write that novel. At worst, he hoped he would at least be escaping the grief, the hole he felt every day. There would be no memories of Sarah on Nantucket. His only memories of her would be the ones he brought with him.

On the advice of a friend who had visited the island, he rented a small cottage in the village of Siasconset. Just until April, while the off-season rates were so attractive. The tour books described it as a charming old fishing village perched on the Atlantic on the east side of the island. The pictures he saw online showed quaint cottages, some with bright roses covering their roofs, streets covered in shells, and manicured hedges everywhere. He had no idea what to expect other than it should be quiet and peaceful. It was mainly a summer place with most of the houses unused during the off-season, hence the cheap rents. The official Nantucket tourism website stated that there were only a few dozen residents in Siasconset during the winter months.

A few dozen plus one.

The ferry approached the dock, and Rob walked back to his car. The crew deftly managed the large boat into its berth and set about securing a steel ramp to her bow. From the gaping square hole at the front of the boat, Rob heard a big diesel engine come to life and was shocked to see a full-size tractor-trailer emerge and descend down the ramp and across the parking lot. It was followed by several more trucks before he started to see cars appear. The cars must have been from the seasonal visitors as they were stuffed full of baggage and covered with all of the equipment needed for a summer on the island; fishing poles and surfboards on the roof, beach chairs, and bicycles on racks off the back. They were closing out their time on the island, heading to their destinations to wait out the winter until they could return.

Rob's old Jeep Wagoneer was one of just a handful of cars in line to board the ship. He had not planned on buying the old Jeep but had been surfing an online car auction site one evening. It probably didn't help that he had already downed several bourbon and waters. Shopping while drunk - especially for cars - was never the smartest of choices. What had caught his eye was that it looked just like one his parents had had when he was growing up, complete with the navy blue paint, tan interior, and fake wood grain down the side. The listing claimed less than fifty thousand miles and a great maintenance history. His drunken self thought it would be a perfect car for the island and escalated the bidding until he had crushed the competition. Now after having driven it for a few weeks and halfway across the country, his sober self was happy with the choice despite the premium they had paid.

When the last vehicle rolled off, the crewman waved his hands for everyone to start their vehicles. The big trucks went first, loaded with supplies to keep the island stocked with food, alcohol, lumber, and other essentials of life. Then one by one, like ducklings following each other across a spring pond, the cars made their way aboard. Coming to the top of the ramp, the crew directed them either left or right down the tight alleys on the port and starboard sides of the ship. When those filled, the remaining vehicles went down the middle and parked alongside the commercial trucks. It was far from full, and within minutes the ship was loaded and ready to go.

Rob locked his car and stepped out to explore the ship. Taking the steps to the first level, he was surprised to find rows of comfortable chairs and a snack bar. Not luxurious by any stretch, but certainly nicer than expected given the exterior appearance of the ship. He was also surprised by how few people he saw. Just a handful in the seats and a few navigating their way down the aisles. He continued up the stairway to the top passenger level and stepped outside, and leaned over to look out over the Hyannis harbor. He was nervous. This would be a new chapter in his life, and he really didn't know what to expect. Would he like the people? Would they accept him? Could he put the pain behind him and be happy again?

For the hundredth time of the day, he thought of Sarah. He closed his eyes and saw her smile, her eyes, and the face that had taken his breath away. He raised his head and turned to feel the warm sun on his cheeks. Rob sighed sadly.

A vibration shuddered through the vessel as the ship's engines came to life. Black smoke belched from the large stack midway down the boat, and slowly the ship began to back out of the berth, the crew tossing the mooring lines as she went. The boat reversed and rotated until she was perpendicular to the dock. After a brief pause, the vibration swelled, and the propellers kicked up the water at the stern. The Eagle began to accelerate and slowly made her way through the harbor. She was not a fast vessel. The thirty-mile trip, due south to Nantucket, would take over two hours.

Rob stayed on the top deck, enjoying the warmth of the afternoon sun and the incredible beauty of the sea around him. He was fascinated at how the water changed color depending on the angle of the sun, the depth of the water, and the occasional cloud that would block the sun. From a grayish green to a deep blue, even black at times. It captivated him. An hour into the journey, he realized he could no longer see Cape Cod behind him and ahead, towards Nantucket; all that was visible was the broad expanse of the ocean. He was truly out to sea, like the old-time whaling ships he had read about, and it made him very uncomfortable. He didn't have much personal experience on the water, just water skiing behind small boats on the lakes around St. Louis.

The feeling of isolation didn't last long, as he could see land emerging from the sea ahead of them. At first, he could just make out a blurred line on the horizon, but slowly he could start to make out the larger man-made structures. A lighthouse on a spit of land to the east, a water tower, and several tall radio antennas, their lights pulsing white. It wasn't long before he could make out houses on the shore and perched on the shallow hills that stretched to the west. Soon he could see the entrance to the harbor and, beyond it, dozens and dozens of gray-shingled homes lining the water.

Nantucket.

They passed the buoy marking the entrance to the harbor, its bell clanging loudly as it rolled lazily in the swells. Seals were sunbathing on the long rock jetty as gulls circled overhead, squawking in protest as the boat passed under them. The ferry slowed and approached another lighthouse. It was small, white, and had a large American flag stretched across its side. A slowly blinking red light was contained in the small glass room at its top. The wake from the ferry rolled up on the sand at its base as a few people dressed in shorts strolled the beach. They looked up at the ferry and waved. Rob waved back.

Rounding the lighthouse, Rob caught his first glimpse of the town of Nantucket and felt as if he had been thrown back in time. The harbor was lined with gray shingled buildings of simple shapes and varying sizes. Past them, he could make out a number of larger brick buildings, and beyond them and up a hill, the tall white steeples of two churches. It was then that he realized what he didn't see; commercial signs, billboards, power lines, or other indications of modern life. If he didn't know better, it could easily be mistaken for the 19th century.

The Eagle proceeded toward its berth as the captain gave a long pull on the ship's air horn to announce their arrival. Rob made his way back to the Wagoneer. Waiting patiently, his hands tapping at the rim of the steering wheel, Rob felt the ship bump into the dock. He could just make out the shouts of the crew and the screech of winches as the bow was lined up and the ramp secured. A few minutes later, a crewman emerged and whistled, his hand waving in the air. A diesel engine roared to life, and a trailer truck crawled its way up to and down the ramp. After a few more trucks, the crew pointed at the car in front of his Jeep and waved it forward. Rob followed, navigating the Jeep carefully down the narrow side of the ferry and heading slowly toward the main door. Waving at the crewman who had given him the thumbs-up, Rob drove the Jeep through the doorway, the tires thumping lightly as they crossed the threshold where the dock met the bow of the boat.

Butterflies stirring in his stomach, Rob drove the Jeep down the ramp onto Nantucket and away, he hoped, from his grief.

CHAPTER THREE

R ob made his way through downtown Nantucket taking in the sights. He had plugged the address of his rental cottage into his phone's mapping program and relaxed, knowing the app would guide him when necessary. Freed from worrying about directions, Rob turned his attention to the buildings around him and tried to get a feel for his new temporary home. Along the street to his left were small shops offering ice cream, bicycle rentals, snacks, and food. Essentially everything the tourist needed to spend a day on the island. Looking to the right, he saw a large brick building with a white cornice and a sign that read Whaling Museum.

That looks interesting.

"Prepare to turn left on Water Street," the English-accented female voice said.

Sarah had once teased him about his choice of voice for his navigation app, claiming that perhaps he had a thing for English women.

"Okay," Rob had replied, laughing, "Then why is your voice some Australian guy who sounds like a baller?"

"No comment," Sarah had replied, and they both laughed. It had become a running joke between the two of them as they would occasionally respond to the other's question in their best interpretation of their preferred navigation voice.

Rob sighed and made a mental note to change the voice to something blander. Something that wouldn't remind him of Sarah and better times.

He made a slow turn onto Water Street passing the police department on his right and what looked to be a wonderful old-fashioned-style movie theater on his left. A few blocks later, the pavement turned to cobblestones, and the nearly forty-year-old suspension of the Wagoneer creaked and protested as tires bounced over the large stones. Rob caught a glimpse up Main Street and was pleased to see the tree-lined street with its beautiful old buildings. Like everything else he had seen so far, it looked to be straight out of the 18th century. A handful of people were walking about enjoying the beautiful October afternoon, many carrying bags loaded with recent purchases.

The body of the car swayed heavily back and forth one last time before the road returned to relatively smooth pavement. Rob thought he could almost feel a sigh of relief coming from the old bones of his Jeep. Passing a huge compass on the side of a building, he noted his destination was only 7 ½ miles away.

"Continue down Washington Street," the English voice said.

The road paralleled the harbor, and Rob could look out across the blue water. Being so late in the season, he wasn't surprised to see most of the moorings empty. But a few boats, remnants of the summer, floated serenely at anchor.

The navigation system had him make a couple of turns, the first to the right and then quickly another to the left. Soon he found himself at a rotary and completely unsure of what to do.

"Proceed through the rotary and take the third exit to the right," said the voice.

Third exit to the right?

Rob slowly made his way around the rotary and, counting the streets, veered off on the third one.

"Continue on Milestone Road for seven miles."

Rob relaxed his hands on the wheel and forced his shoulders to drop. He had become so tense, the reality of the situation washing over him. Here he was in a new town, thirteen hundred miles away from his home, alone and not knowing a soul on this island. For the second time today, he was tempted to turn the car around and head back. Maybe this was a mistake. Maybe he should just try and forget about ever being happy again. He dismissed the thought and instead opened the big sunroof of the Jeep. It squeaked as it retreated, but soon he had blue sky overhead and the sun streaming in. He took a deep breath and sighed, feeling a little better. The smells were foreign to him. He could just make out a touch of salt but also what he thought must be heather, the scrub pines, and the moors.

Paralleling the road was another narrow stretch of pavement with a buffer of green grass in between. It took a mile or two before Rob realized that it was a bike path. He passed several packs of bicyclists along with several runners. One attractively shaped young woman was skating down the path on rollerblades, her small dog trailing behind her on the leash and struggling to keep up.

When he had driven through New York, Connecticut, and Massachusetts on his way to the Cape, he had been blown away by the colors of the trees. The bright reds, deep oranges, and vivid yellows had been amazing, much more intense than what he was used to back in St. Louis. But driving along Milestone Road, he was disappointed to see just hints of muted color. The island must be weeks behind the mainland as it still looked like summer.

Once again, his thoughts turned to Sarah. Fall had always been her favorite season. And so many of their personal milestones were set in the fall, October in particular. They met in October. Married in October. And set the events in motion that would discover her cancer in October. He tried so hard to let those memories go, but they continued to gnaw at him. Nothing had been right since that day.

A sight to his left caught his eye and pulled him out of his reflection. The landscape had switched from scrub pine and brush to what looked like the savannas of Africa. He half expected to see a pride of lions or a herd of gazelles. But then he let out a chuckle as he saw life-size wooden forms painted to look like lions, giraffes, and even an elephant. Clearly, someone had a sense of humor.

His mood brightened a bit as the road climbed a small hill, turning slightly to the left at the top. Across the moors, he could make out a large white lighthouse with a red band at its middle. It was a stunning sight and so alien to what he was used to in the midwest. The butterflies stirred again in his stomach.

The road descended, cutting off his view. He then realized that he hadn't seen a single house or structure since he had left town. The drive had revealed nothing but the moors, scrub pines, and the bike path bordering the road. Shortly, the land around him opened up again, but this time was just high grass with a solitary house sitting well back from the road.

Passing along a small golf course, houses began to emerge from the landscape, all uniform in their gray shingles and white trim. The road angled upward, and the old Jeep downshifted as they started to climb a long, shallow hill. The speed limit dropped, indicating to him that he must be getting close to Siasconset. There certainly weren't any signs announcing the fact. As he crested the hill, the landscape changed as if someone had flipped a switch. Large majestic trees lined the road - a stark contrast to the moors he had been traveling through the last ten minutes, as well as beautiful old homes set well back from the street. Fronting them were white picket fences and broad expanses of lawn. And everywhere he looked, he saw the manicured hedges that he had first seen in the travel photos.

"Prepare to turn right," said the voice.

Rob ignored the voice and continued straight, following the street slowly as it now descended into the small village.

"Recalculating"

"Shut up," said Rob. He grabbed his phone and quickly exited the mapping app.

He was not yet ready to reach his destination. In some way, Rob thought his arrival at the cottage would mark an end to a major chapter in his life. His time with Sarah. He wanted to stall that milestone for as long as possible, delaying it as if it could change his past. Or pause his future.

At the bottom of the hill stood another rotary, this one circled by a two-foot-high painted wall. In the inner circle were pruned hedges and flowering bushes. At its center stood an impressive mast-like flagpole flying a huge American flag. On a pair of yardarms connected just above halfway, red and green lanterns hung, the red to the west and green on the eastern side. A black arrow at the top declared the wind was from the northeast.

Behind the rotary sat several shingled structures, with the road giving him three options. Knowing his cottage was to the right and seeing the very narrow lane that sat across from him, Rob chose to go to the left. He maneuvered the Jeep around the rotary - counterclockwise, of course - and drove slowly past the post office, then a small market clearly closed for the season. A small brick-paved park with benches and bike racks sat next to the store, an old, gnarly tree keeping watch in one corner.

Three streets opposed the park, all one way, two in his favor. He decided to try the one farthest at the end and turned onto the narrow street slowly. The Jeep idled along at walking speed while Rob peered out the windows like a kid at the zoo. The homes were packed tightly together and looked like they had been here for centuries. All shingle covered, many leaned clumsily, and all with the front door just a few feet from the street. But they were far from ramshackle. Clearly well maintained, the owners likely wanted to keep the historic feel and charm of the old structures while providing for some of the modern necessities of life.

A curtain parted in one of the houses, and Rob saw a face looking out at him. He smiled, but the face withdrew quickly without responding to his gesture.

Must be one of the other dozen residents.

A few cars were lining the street, but most of them looked like they had been parked for the winter. With that one exception, these houses looked to be closed for the season.

At the end of the street, just a few hundred feet after he turned onto it, the street curved and rejoined an opposing lane. Pulling to the side of the road, Rob called up the mapping app on his phone to get a sense of where he was relative to his rental cottage.

Zooming in on the screen, he saw that he was pretty close to the large lighthouse he had seen across the moors just minutes before and decided to head that way. Taking the first turn, Rob followed the street and quickly came up on an old Victorian house that was clearly past her prime. Unlike all of the houses he had seen so far, the graceful old structure had clapboard siding and gingerbread trim. It sat on a huge lot facing the ocean and looked like it hadn't been lived in for years. The handyman in Rob looked past the missing trim and fading paint and saw the beauty and the bones of the elegant design. He smiled sadly at the thought of all the summers this house must have seen, the laughter it must have heard, and the love that it had once enjoyed.

Reluctantly he continued past the old Victorian and followed the road as it meandered along the eastern bluff of the island. The houses here were different from those in the village. They were larger and spread out from their neighbors. Most had substantial lawns, and some sported sizable garages, impressive outbuildings, tennis courts, and other trappings of wealth. And between them, he could just catch the occasional view of the Atlantic, its water a rich greenish-blue, the sun reflecting millions of diamonds across its surface.

The street widened and ended a few hundred yards from the lighthouse. A short stone wall faced him on the left, while a wide wooden gate sat to the right, open and inviting. He moved the transmission to park and turned off the Jeep. He stepped out of the car, and his feet touched Nantucket for the first time. Making his way up the gravel path, his steps crunching as he walked, he soon came to a set of circular benches with the graveled paths diverging in several directions.

"They really like their rotaries here," he said out loud, chuckling at his own humor.

Hearing Sarah in his head mimicking the English voice of his mapping app, he followed the path to the right that rose to the edge of the property bordering the water. He climbed a short but steep hill to a chain link fence and, leaning his arms on the top rail of the fence, looked out across the expanse of water.

Wow.

It was an amazing view and one that gave him the chills. The water, a rich blue, stretched as far as the eye could see. Perhaps from being from the landlocked midwest, Rob had always been intimidated by the ocean. He thought of all the men who had sailed out there looking for adventure and trying to put food on the table for their families. And the many, the thousands, who had died in that quest. Rob had gotten nervous on the ferry just being out of sight of land for a few minutes. He had always been in awe of the courage and drive those men and women had had to carve a life out of the sea.

He turned his back to the water and gazed at the lighthouse. It was a graceful structure, its shape elegantly tapering as it reached towards the sky. Painted white, a large red band circled it at the middle and was topped with a black, windowed canopy, the lantern just visible within and turning slowly. A metal gallery circled just outside the glass, likely giving the lucky visitor an amazing view.

Sarah would have loved this.

Rob turned his attention from the lighthouse and noted that the sun was nearing the southwestern horizon. With only an hour or so to sunset and not wanting to arrive at his cottage in the dark, he walked back to the car. Taking in one long last look at the lighthouse, he opened the door, started the car, and made his way back down the lane towards Siasconset.

Navigating back to the heart of the village, he followed the directions from his phone, skirting the rotary, and drove slowly up the main road back toward the top of the hill. There the voice told him to turn left, and he proceeded carefully, navigating his way past a couple of landscaping trucks. Three men in overalls were trimming a six-foot-high hedge. Its lines were so crisp, and straight Rob thought he could have used it as a straight edge on one of his construction projects.

He was several hundred feet down the road when the voice spoke again.

"Turn left on Starbuck Lane."

Rob turned onto the shelled street, his tires crunching on the unusual surface. The cottage was the second on the right, and he pulled onto the grass bordering the street.

"You have arrived at your destination."

Rob reached down and turned off the car. Looking through the side window, he surveyed the cottage, his home for the next six months. It was smaller than he expected; the pictures he viewed online had not clearly reflected its diminutive size. Set back from the street, an old fence extended across the width of the property. A few pickets were missing, others leaning, and the entire fence was in need of fresh paint. A gate short stood just offset to the right of center and neatly lined up with the front door of the cottage.

To the right of the front door was a small wooden plaque noting the name of the house.

The Shanty

The rental agency claimed it was a historic cottage, built in 1880, and to his eye, it looked like it had indeed been built over a century ago by builders who didn't possess a level or a straight edge. It wasn't much more than a box that had a few additions over the years, covered in gray shingles and white trim, also in need of some attention. It was all a single story, its roof taking different angles depending on which part of the house it was covering.

Rob assumed the door entered the original part of the house and was likely what led to the name of the place. It looked like a lean-to with walls and windows, the roof sloping back to front, ending just above a narrow doorway. That door was bordered on both sides by multi-pane windows, painted white with small window boxes underneath holding some late blooming flowers.

He sighed as he opened the car door. It was time.

Rob stepped out of the car and closed the door. A movement caught his eye, and just down the street, a lady on a porch a few houses down waved to him. He smiled and waved back.

Maybe this will turn out alright.

He walked towards the gate in the fence and opened the latch. He looked down the street again but noticed the lady had disappeared. Sighing, he pulled the key from his pocket and thrust it into the lock. He turned the key, opened the door, lowered his head, and stepped inside.

CHAPTER FOUR

T he first thing that hit him was the smell, stale and musty with an earthy undertone, almost of rot. The house must have been closed up for a while, and the lack of ventilation had taken its toll on the air quality. He left the door open.

As his eyes adjusted to the dimly lit space, he realized that the cottage was much bigger on the inside than he expected. The front door had entered into a generously sized room with a brick, wood-burning fireplace centered on the wall to his left, flanked by small, double-hung windows. Set to the left of the fireplace was a large brass tub filled with split and seasoned wood ready for burning and several old newspapers for starting.

Across from the fireplace was a large and comfortable-looking sofa. It looked perfect for watching football and taking Sunday afternoon naps. A smaller chair that matched the design of the sofa sat perpendicular to the space. Mounted above the hearth was a large flat-screen TV.

So not totally historic.

Turning to his right and so close, he almost bumped into the frame, a door led into a very small bedroom. A twin-size bed was tucked under the slope of the roof, and crammed between the bed and the wall, was a small desk. A window in front of the desk looked out onto a green hedge and blue sky. It wasn't a big space, but it would be perfect to set up his laptop and try to do some writing.

Walking through the main room, a second doorway opened into the center of a long hallway. In front of him sat a small bathroom with an old plank door, its frame slightly twisted and the white paint flaking. Peeking in, he could see that it was so narrow he would have to twist himself to get past the toilet to the claw foot tub built into a little nook in the wall. There was no showerhead.

Stepping back, Rob turned and walked down the hallway to his right and into the kitchen. It was nowhere as big as the main room but large enough to satisfy his modest needs. A wall of white cabinets sat on the far wall, the sink centered under a window looking out on another green hedge. The space thankfully looked to have been updated at some point with newer appliances, including a dishwasher and microwave. A stainless steel coffee maker sat on the counter.

He turned and headed back down the hallway past the tiny bathroom. Rob was more than a little worried that he would be bumping shins all winter against the toilet and clumsily bathing in the archaic-looking tub. The rental listing had claimed two bedrooms and two bathrooms, so he silently prayed that the yet unseen bedroom and bathroom would be larger and more modern.

At the end of the hall, Rob was relieved to find a much bigger bedroom fitted with a queen-size four-poster bed. Windows on three of the four walls ensured the room was filled with the golden light of sunset. It was on the smaller side but looked cozy and comforting to his eye. It would work.

On the far wall of the bedroom, a small arched doorway led to a short hall with a closet. Opposite the closet, a door opened out onto a brick patio. Peering out the door's window, Rob could see the patio was nicely sized and had a large teak table with four chairs and a pair of Adirondack-style loungers. The space was framed with a tall wooden fence for privacy from the nearby homes, and a large maple tree provided much-needed shade.

Satisfied, he turned and followed through the final doorway into a much more modern bathroom. Rob was happy to see that although still fairly small, it at least had a roomy walk-in shower along with a toilet and a single-sink vanity. Nothing fancy, but it would serve his needs and save his shins.

Rob made his way back to the car and started to unpack. Not knowing what to expect on Nantucket in October, he had stopped at a grocery store in Hyannis and purchased enough groceries to last him a week. He had also secured a couple of bottles of his favorite bourbon.

His supplies were minimal. Aside from the food, he had two suitcases of clothes, his backpack, and a box of office supplies. When he had sold the house, much of the furniture and all of Sarah's clothes had been donated to a local charity. He had also sold off all the equipment and tools he had used to run his business. What was left, which was mostly the personal effects of their life together, he had sealed up in some plastic tubs and left those in the basement of a friend.

He wheeled in the two big roller bags and unpacked into the chest of drawers and the closet. Movement out of the corner of his eye drew his attention down the long hall to the kitchen. He thought he saw a shadow but dismissed it without another thought.

Retreating to the Wagoneer - and taking special care as he made his way through the narrow front door - he grabbed his backpack along with the box which he brought into the smaller bedroom, his new office. From the box, he pulled a silver framed picture of Sarah he had taken on their honeymoon. They had been in New Orleans and had gotten caught in a sudden rainstorm. Soaked through and laughing, they had taken refuge in the narrow doorway of the Clover Grill in the French Quarter. Sarah was leaning on the frame of the doorway, her hair sodden and rain running down her cheeks, smiling back at the camera, her green eyes sparkling in amusement. Rob stared at the image and smiled sadly at the memory of the week they had spent in the Big Easy.

He placed the picture on the right side of the small desk. From the box, he pulled his Chicago Manual of Style - a gift from Sarah on his birthday - and laid that by her picture. Next came a few more books on writing and storytelling which he stacked on the left side of the desk. Finally came the office essentials; a couple of reams of paper, a stapler, binder clips, spare batteries for the mouse, and a few thumb drives for back-ups. The paper he stacked next to the desk while the rest he organized neatly in the top drawer. He cracked open the laptop and fired up his browser. His email had just one new entry from the realtor with a few links to local island resources as well as offering her availability for any questions he might have. Navigating to an office supply site, he ordered a printer and spare ink to be delivered. Satisfied, he closed the laptop and pushed the chair back.

Time for a fire and a drink.

Making his way back to the fireplace, Rob stacked a few logs on the grate and checked to confirm the flue was open. He reached into the bin for some newspaper, where he found a fairly recent copy of the local paper, The Inquirer and Mirror. He pulled a few sheets, crumpled them up, and slid them under the grate. He lit the newspaper and watched as it engulfed the wood.

He was putting the remaining paper back in the bin when a picture caught his eye. It was of a tall, well-dressed man handing an oversized presentation check to a young boy and girl. All three of them were smiling. He pulled the section closer to read the story.

Boys & Girls Club Receives $1.5 Million Donation

Jack Reiner, Nantucket's well-known philanthropist and community supporter, has done it again, donating $1.5 million to the Nantucket Boys & Girls Club to fund the construction and long-term maintenance of a new sports complex. Long an advocate of youth sports, Mr. Reiner is shown here handing the check to Eliza Macy, 11, and Orlando Coffin, 10.

As our readers know, Mr. Reiner has a long history of supporting the community. Just in the last few years, he has donated in excess of $4 million to causes across the spectrum of island needs, including affordable housing, hospital expansion, land conservancy, and of course, the Boys & Girls Club.

"I have never been blessed to have children," said Mr. Reiner, "So for me, this is the next best thing."

Mr. Reiner's wife, Emily, was unable to make the event.

Construction is set to begin in the spring, with the facility to be open and ready for use by next fall.

He folded the paper up and put it back in the bin.

Maybe that could be a story? Well-known philanthropist with a dark side?

With the fire now blazing and throwing heat into the room, Rob retreated to the kitchen. It took him a few minutes to find the glassware, but he settled on a nice highball glass with an image of a lighthouse and filled it with ice. He poured a couple of shots of Weller's and added a splash of water. Grabbing a bag of pretzels, he walked back into the living room and settled on the couch facing the hearth. He leaned back and took a sip of his drink. Looking around, the reality hit him.

What am I doing here?

Coming to Nantucket was his Hail Mary pass at trying to get his life back on track. The past six months since Sarah's death had been nothing short of brutal. Not only had he lost his wife, but his future had been totally derailed. The plans that they had made together were worthless, and his mental survival became a day-by-day challenge. Rob knew he was drinking a lot more now to deal with that and hoped that this new experience and the challenges it presented would help him overcome that looming dependency.

He finished his drink and made another.

Returning to the couch, his thoughts turned to writing. When he had confessed his dream to Sarah, he had fully expected her to cast a questioning eye his way, but, typical of Sarah, she had fully supported and encouraged him. But what business did he have in writing a novel? His only experience was from his days as a reporter for his high school newspaper and from a short stint as an assistant marketing manager straight out of college. But deep in his heart, he knew he could write. And now, with Sarah's loss, he felt he had to follow through not just for himself but also for her. He knew it would make her happy, and that would make it all worthwhile.

Despite the fire, the room had chilled with the sunset. Rob went back to the bedroom to grab a sweatshirt. He found the top drawer of the bureau open. He went to close it but noticed an impression in the drawer bottom he hadn't seen before. Etched in the soft wood, scrawling and old, was a name and date. Lisbeth Hopper, 1900.

Hmm. I wonder who she was?

He closed the top drawer and opened the bottom one. He pulled out his favorite sweatshirt. It was a ratty black one that Sarah had borrowed a lot while she was working on the nursery. They had always maintained a positive attitude about getting pregnant and planned to make the smallest of their three bedrooms into a farm-themed nursery. That project ground to a halt immediately following Sarah's diagnosis.

Rob pulled the sweatshirt to his nose and took a deep breath. He could still smell her perfume, her essence, and found it comforting as though she were not really gone. He slipped the sweatshirt on and went back to the couch.

Staring into the flames, he started to cry.

CHAPTER FIVE

H is scheme to make the Second disappear had pretty much worked flawlessly.

The Nor'Easter had struck as planned and scrubbed the land free of any traces of tire tracks, footsteps, or the swell of a grave. Out of curiosity, a few weeks later, he had driven out over the sand to do some surf fishing and made a point to stop by the Second's resting place and inspect its condition. He struggled to even locate the site of the grave and left confident that she would never be found.

His transient girlfriend had also exceeded his expectations, although it had cost him dearly. But compared to jail, it was a worthy expense.

She had crossed the country, spending thousands along the way on high-end hotels, expensive dinners, and the best alcohol, and he suspected, based on the substantial cash withdrawals, drugs that money could buy. With stops in New York, Chicago, Kansas City, Denver, and of course, Vegas, she had nearly maxed out the thirty-grand limit on the card. Still, she had laid a paper trail leading from Nantucket all the way to Los Angeles. And there, as planned, the trail stopped, leaving the authorities to wonder what had happened to Jack Reiner's second wife. Had she committed suicide? Had she been a victim of foul play? Had she shacked up with some rich asshole? Or had she just disappeared, intentionally starting a new life under a new name?

Jack feigned intense interest all along, frequently calling the sheriff and the detectives and pleading for them to work harder and try and find his beloved wife. But after three months without any new leads, they gave in, citing much more pressing matters. Jack was devastated at their decision but reluctantly agreed. He would still call them every few months, just to check in and keep the case alive, but few thought this missing person would ever be found.

His cleverness pleased him. Unlike the First, suspicions about the Second didn't follow him around town like an unwanted stray. His friends felt genuine anger at her for leaving him, for covering up her illness, and for not trusting him to be able to help her through her difficult times. Jack became a target of their sympathy instead of their misgivings.

Three entered his life a little over a year later.

He had been back in New York for a long weekend and was attending a fundraiser for The Met. The idea of finding a Third hadn't yet solidified in his mind - he feared it was too soon - and the craving for control hadn't quite struck yet, but when his eyes first landed on Emily, that all went out the window.

She was easily thirty years younger than him and had a classic beauty that captured his interest. Her sculptured features, high cheekbones, thin nose, and strikingly large hazel eyes framed by a burst of auburn hair reminded him fondly of the First. Just a couple of inches shorter than his six-foot frame, she had a figure to match her beauty with long legs and a generous bust. He had been taken immediately.

Almost nothing excited him more than the game. From the moment he saw her, he knew he had to have her. His desire to obtain her increased after he spent some time getting to know her.

Beyond her beauty, her background and personality suited what he desired. She was recently divorced and childless. She had caught her first husband in bed with the maid not once but twice and refused to tolerate his serial infidelity. Thanks to a prenup, the divorce was straightforward, if somewhat lacking from a financial perspective. Although her settlement was well into the six figures, that wouldn't last long in Manhattan, especially in supporting the lifestyle she was accustomed to. Knowing she would need longer-term support, she too had been on the chase.

Emily had been flattered when he approached her at the Met, but she was used to being wanted. Although she was rather good at turning men down, something about Jack made her hesitate. He charmed her in a way her ex-husband never had. Despite clearly pressing on sixty, he still had a handsome, rugged face that reminded her of the explorers she had read about in boarding school. He was trim and active, and while he was clearly wealthy, it never seemed to be flaunted the way she was used to in New York. In the pensive moments after sex, he had confessed about his wife leaving him, and the trauma of her disappearance.

In those seemingly candid acts of confession, she could sense his loneliness. And if it was one thing Emily knew, it was loneliness. She had been an only child and, in many ways, had been her own parent as well. Her mother was an alcoholic whose attention turned to her daughter only when she needed another drink. Her father traveled constantly, and she never really knew if it was for work or pleasure. Regardless, he was rarely home.

She escaped her pathetic excuse of a family by leaving home at twelve to start seventh grade, and Emily quickly learned to fend for herself at an exclusive all-girls boarding school in Connecticut. Vacations were often spent at friends' houses or at summer camps.

She worked hard, achieved good grades, and left for college without looking behind her.

It all became blindingly clear on Christmas break from her junior year of college. Her mother, hungover as always, sent her to the local pharmacy to get something to alleviate the headache. While looking for the off-brand pain relief her mother requested, she heard her father's laugh. She peered around the corner to see him lovingly kiss the forehead of an attractive blond woman. Holding her hand was a tow-headed boy not much older than five that looked surprisingly like her father. As she watched, her father leaned down and ruffled the boy's hair with a look of love and adoration she had never seen or experienced. Years later, however, she'd still find herself questioning if it was her mother or the fact that he wanted a son that drove the wedge between them.

A year later her mother died, having asphyxiated on her own vomit after drinking almost a full handle of vodka. Her father made it home for the funeral, as did a few distant relatives who hadn't had to bear the full brunt of her disease. It was a cold and raw winter afternoon, the weather closely matching the emotions Emily felt for a mother who had never been there. Following the graveside service, she exchanged a few uncomfortable words with her father before they parted ways. Emily hadn't talked with him since.

Jack Reiner was not her father. He wanted to be with her and seemingly cared about her thoughts and feelings. Several months into their relationship, he looked at her across the pillow after a particularly vigorous lovemaking session and proposed. She didn't hesitate before saying yes, and they married a few weeks later. Neither saw the need to wait or have an expensive, formal ceremony. After all, they had both been there before. In the end, it was just the two of them, a few of Jack's friends from his club, and the minister. For a moment, Emily contemplated inviting her father, just so he could suffer the embarrassment of her marrying someone his age, before deciding against it.

They had left almost immediately for their honeymoon, three weeks of bareboat sailing in the Caribbean. Leaving most of the hard work to their chartered skipper, they hopped from island to island, sleeping mainly on the boat, skinny dipping in the warm waters, making love under the stars, and enjoying delicious meals prepared by a Michelin-starred chef Jack had flown in for the occasion.

It had been a wonderful trip and had truly swept Emily off her feet. Jack had been loving, charming, and witty making her laugh harder than she had in years. His intensity of devotion and constant caring filled a hole in Emily that she had lacked all her life. With that, her feelings for Jack grew stronger, and she eagerly looked forward to their life together.

Reluctantly, they left the islands of the Caribbean to return to the island of Nantucket. While Emily had tired of New York, living on a small island thirty miles out to sea hadn't been on her list of places to move. She had never visited but knew many within her circle who had and read all about this haven of the one percenters who had deemed themselves "too good" for the Hamptons.

Having known quite a few people who boasted about having houses on the island, she had expected the arrogance of The Hamptons combined with the scenery of Cape Cod and was completely taken aback by the sheer beauty of the landscape and the lack of any real commercial development. There were no billboards, no glitzy signs, no fast food places, just gray-shingled buildings, windswept moors, scrub pines, and charming rose-covered cottages wherever she went. It was as if she stepped back a hundred years when she married Jack. At first, the homogeneity of the architecture and the muted colors made her a bit uncomfortable, but she quickly warmed to the island, much as she had with Jack, and let herself be seduced by the raw beauty and charms of the place.

Despite having been married for almost a month, Jack insisted on carrying her over the threshold of his island home. It had been in his family for years, and Jack was the fourth generation to steward the property. The house, known as Gratitude, was built in the late 19th century and featured five bedrooms, four bathrooms, and several acres of land shaded by a number of old trees. It was gorgeously landscaped with climbing roses, hydrangea bushes, and a formal cutting garden. To the north lay magnificent views of Polpis Harbor, while cranberry bogs bordered the house to the east and west. To the south, down the driveway a few hundred yards, was the only means of escape, Polpis Road.

Moving in, Emily had commented on the name of the house and thought it admirable that his family recognized how fortunate they were to have the means to build such an elaborate and beautiful home. She was grateful that Jack had come into her life right when she needed him. Jack had snorted and responded that it was nothing of the kind. His ancestors had been far from humble or thankful for their position. The house had been named after their most successful whaling vessel. Gratitude had sailed the waters of the Pacific for over twenty years slaughtering whales, rendering oil, and making a fortune for his family. The original figurehead, an intricately carved image of a large-breasted woman with flowing hair, now hung in the library.

Those first few months had been wonderful for Emily. Jack's devotion, thoughtfulness, and concern for her continued as if they were still on their honeymoon. Breakfast in bed, romantic dinners out, and his constant attention made her feel truly loved and cherished for the first time in her life.

That devotion and attention seemed to wane as they approached their first anniversary. She began to notice subtle changes in his moods and behaviors. At first, she thought it might be stress - or, heaven forbid, the onset of some sort of dementia - but his brain seemed as sharp as ever. He had just become more and more particular about how he wanted things and much less tolerant when he didn't get his way. He had stopped laughing at her gentle teasing and began to control more of what she did and how she acted when they were around his friends.

By their second anniversary, she began to feel that she was nothing more than someone to hang on his elbow and make him look good at social events. He was more critical of the way she dressed and had a negative opinion of everything she did or said. No longer was she consulted on where they should go out or how they should spend their weekends. He rarely asked about her feelings or inquired about her moods. She struggled when he put her on a very restrictive allowance but accepted it thinking that he must be having some financial pressures. But when she realized he hadn't stopped spending, she began to feel angry and hurt, as if he didn't trust her to be a good steward of his money.

And his controls over her and her time increased.

She had never been a social person. Growing up, she realized the only person she could count on was herself, so what friendships she had tended to be superficial. The only friends she had made on the island had been his to begin with. But even the few acquaintances outside of him she had made on the island seemed to have raised his concerns, and he began to question her intensely every time she left the house. Where did you go? Who did you see? What did you talk about? The interrogations wore her down, and eventually, she stopped going out for even the simplest errands; the only time leaving the house was when Jack needed her to accompany him for one of his many social functions.

A week before their third anniversary, he hit her for the first time. They had been at a party at his club, and she had shared what she thought was a sweet story about him.

He was enraged and screamed at her, spittle flying in her face. "You know how much I wanted to be part of that committee, and now they must think I'm an idiot. A pussy whipped, incompetent asshole thanks to you." Despite being drunk, his eyes were gleaming as if he had found some sort of treasure or purpose in his anger.

The charming and kind man she had once known now looked at her as if she was dog shit on the bottom of his shoe.

She looked back at a man she no longer recognized, her eyes filled with tears. "I thought it was such a sweet story about you. Showed a side of you that most people wouldn't see. I didn't mean to embarrass you."

Without uttering a word, Jack raised his hand and slapped her hard across the face.

Raising a shaking hand, she put her palm against her left cheek. It was hot to the touch and wet. She realized she was crying. Looking at him, she pleaded, "Please, don't hit me. I love you. I'm sorry." Surely this was her fault; she knew she should never have told that story. Her mother, in a rare moment of sobriety, had told her she could never read a room.

She felt a gentle finger against her chin, and it guided her face up until she made eye contact with Jack. It was then that he hit her again. "You dumb bitch. You should have known better than that. I don't know why I even married you," he said as if scolding a child.

Emily sobbed heavily and collapsed into an upholstered wingback chair. "I'm sorry, I'm so sorry. I would never want to hurt you. Please forgive me."

"Don't talk to me for the rest of the night," he said coldly and walked out of the room.

Emily sat in the chair, hugging her legs to her chest, and cried. She slowly rocked back and forth as the tears came out. She was in shock more than anything. Her husband, the man she thought she would live out her years with in joy, had disappeared and been replaced by this monster.

She felt a flood of shame wash over her. She was reminded of one of the last times her father had ever spent at home. Her mother had been drunk, and her father had the same blame in his eyes that Jack did. What is wrong with me? Why don't men love me?

Her entire body protested as she slowly made her way to the guest bedroom and climbed under the covers. She watched the moon rise outside her window through swollen eyes and questioned what was wrong with her for the seemingly millionth time since that first slap made contact with her cheek. Staring out the window, she resolved to give herself only a few more moments before she had to pull it back together and prepare the kitchen for breakfast. She didn't want to know what he would do if the coffee wasn't ready for him when he woke up.

CHAPTER SIX

After a fitful night's sleep in a strange bed, Rob woke just after sunrise. He rolled over and instinctively reached for Sarah, his hand finding nothing but air. Despite her being gone over six months, he still felt the punch in the gut when the reality hit him. It was a horrible way to start the day.

Shuffling slowly down to the kitchen, Rob was thankful that he had included coffee in his initial provisions. He found filters for the coffee maker and filled the grounds to the brim. Adding water, he clicked it on. The maker snorted a few times, and then coffee began to drip down into the pot. As soon as a couple of inches were visible, Rob pulled it out and filled a mug with the steaming brew. Adding a splash of cream, he retreated out of the kitchen, walked to the other end of the house, and out onto the brick patio.

He made his way to one of the Adirondack chairs, sat down heavily, and wrapped his hands around the mug. It was a cool morning, and he watched, fascinated, as the steam rose from his cup. It was a beautiful fall day, the sky a deep, cloudless blue, and just a hint of breeze tickling the remaining leaves in the trees. His mind wandered to the day ahead and whether he would be able to start the novel. And of Sarah.

This was not where we wanted to be.

Wistfully, he finished the last of his coffee and carried his mug to the kitchen. He could make some breakfast later. For now, he wanted to go for a walk and get some fresh air.

Ducking under the frame, Rob stepped through the front door and made his way out the gate and onto the street. The air was crisp and carried the sharp scents of fallen leaves, the tang of salt air, and a hint of sweetness from late blooming hydrangea.

He walked down Starbuck Lane, the shells crunching under his feet, and turned onto Morey Lane. He followed that slowly, taking in the unique sights and sounds of his new home. He had walked about a half mile when the street ended at a stop sign. Straight ahead was scrub brush and sand while another road extended to his left and right. The street sign read Ocean Avenue. He was trying to figure out which way he wanted to go when he looked out.

Oh my god.

In front of him, across a few hundred feet of sand dunes, lay the great expanse of the Atlantic Ocean, its blue waters shimmering in the sun. Waves danced back and forth, colliding, collapsing, reforming, and then coming onto shore. He could just make out the faint roar of the waves as they reached the shallows and started breaking, the whitewater a vivid contrast to the deep blue. Past the shore, the water went as far as the eye could see all the way to a perfect line where it met the horizon. Rob had never seen anything like it in his life, the sheer beauty, the magnificence of the ocean. It made him feel small.

Forcing himself to move, he turned to the north and walked along the lane as it meandered along a shallow bluff. The houses to his left were much larger than his cottage but still covered in gray shingles and white trim. They had everything needed to capture the amazing views to their east - large porches, grand patios, huge windows, and for a lucky few, roof decks. To his right, rosehip bushes and grass bordered the roadway before the bluff descended into a broad stretch of sand spotted by scrub pine and clumps of beach grass.

An older man with a black and tan beagle on a leash was walking toward him. He looked to be in his seventies and had a long gray beard and an old-style sailer's cap well worn from years at sea. The dog, upon seeing Rob, strained at the leash to reach him. Rob smiled and knelt down to pet him.

"Good morning," said Rob.

"Morning," said the man, somewhat cautiously.

"What's his name?"

"Boomer."

Rob rubbed the dog's head. "Hi, Boomer." The dog promptly laid down and rolled over onto his back, exposing his belly.

"What a sweetheart." Rob rubbed his belly.

"He can be. But mostly, he's just a grumpy old man, like me."

Rob stood up. "Do you live here?"

The old man nodded. "Lived here all my life."

"Well, nice to meet you. I'm Rob McGlynn." He extended his hand.

The man took his hand and immediately brightened. "William. But you can call me Will."

"Nice to meet you, Will."

"And you."

Rob knelt back down to rub the dog's belly. Clearly, Boomer was enjoying the attention. "I've just arrived and am settling in. I'm staying on Starbuck Lane. In the Shanty. My plan is to be here through the spring."

"I'm two streets down from you. On Lily."

"That's great. Are there many others in the village?"

"Aye. A few. But it is a very lonely time to be here."

"I'm ready for some peace and quiet."

"Well, if that's what you're after, you'll find it here." Will looked around. "It's best that we get going."

Rob stood back up. "Nice to meet you, Will. I hope to see you around."

The old man nodded and shuffled along. Boomer reluctantly followed.

Rob watched them walk away and then turned. He continued down Ocean Avenue until he came to a narrow, white bridge that spanned a gully two hundred feet wide. It was built like the wooden trestle bridge they had built for the railroads a century ago. A sign in front requested riders to please walk their bikes.

A bridge for bikes and walkers? How cool is that?

He maneuvered past a waist-high cement pole meant to slow more aggressive bikers and made his way onto the bridge. Stairs to the right descended down to another street that led toward the beach. Straight ahead, the bridge extended a hundred and fifty feet, elbowing its way between two houses. The house on the left, its first-floor level with the bridge and a good twenty feet off the ground, had a large sundial mounted on its southern side. The shadow falling across the roman numerals suggested it should be nearing nine. Rob looked at his watch and was surprised to see it was just a few minutes past that time.

Following the bridge, he emerged onto a narrow, shell-lined path and walked between closely spaced cottages before emerging next to a lovely little park, paved in brick and peppered with teak benches and a few picnic tables. On one corner grew an old scraggly maple that looked as if it had been there for centuries. Much younger trees were planted in beds surrounding the patio, ready to assume the shade duties when the maple finally succumbed to time. It was charming.

To the north, three roads intersected with a wider street that paralleled the park. He remembered these from the day before and decided to follow the same street as he had driven. At this slower pace, he was able to get a much better look at the houses and was impressed that his initial impressions from his car were pretty much spot on. These were old houses, some with signs dating to the 18th and 19th centuries, but all were well taken care of and clearly loved by their owners. And each carried a name - Mizzentop, Snug Harbor, Sans Souci, Nonantum. Rob wondered how they were named and marveled at the stories they could probably tell. A movement in a window caught his eye, and he saw a man emerge from a curtain and look out. As before, Rob waved, but the face retreated before responding.

Not very friendly.

He continued down Broadway until it intersected with Shell Street, which despite its name, was paved with asphalt. Turning left, he followed the narrow one-way lane back toward the center of the village. He emerged from Shell Street back at the small market and made his way across the park, down the narrow path, and back out onto the bike bridge. He stopped about halfway across, leaned on the railing, and soaked in the view.

Next stop, Europe.

The sound of footsteps broke him from his reverie. He turned his head to see an attractive woman walking slowly across the bridge toward him. She was older, maybe in her forties, with long, light brown hair. Her skin was a pale white, almost translucent, and she had a sad, almost plaintive, smile on her face.

She stopped a few feet away and then turned toward him.

"Good morning," she said.

"Good morning," Rob replied.

"Are you new to town?"

Rob paused for a moment. "Why, yes, I just arrived last night. I've rented a small cottage over on Starbuck Lane for the winter."

"Ah, I thought so. I believe you are my new neighbor. I saw you arrive yesterday and move some things in. I'm just a couple of doors down from you."

Rob recalled seeing her wave to him as he was unpacking the Wagoneer. "That's right," he said. "Thanks for the wave yesterday. I needed it. I'm Rob McGlynn.

"Deirdre Collins. But my friends just call me Dee." She didn't extend her hand.

"Nice to meet you, Dee."

"Nice to meet you as well. Have you been here before?" she asked.

Rob smiled. "No, it's my first time. And to be honest, it feels very unusual to me. I'm from the midwest, St. Louis, so this whole thing makes me feel a bit uncomfortable," he said as he swept his arm out over the water. "But it is beautiful."

"It certainly is. And I understand your discomfort," Dee replied. "I'm from western Pennsylvania originally, and it took me a while to get accustomed to being on a small island."

"So you've been here before?"

"Oh yes, I used to live here with my husband. Now I just visit from time to time."

"You used to live here?" Rob asked, surprised at the thought of someone choosing to live here year-round.

"Yes, for several years. Now that took some getting used to," she said with a melancholic laugh. "Coming from the Pittsburgh suburbs to this sandbar in the Atlantic." She paused. "But in the end, I really did love this place and missed leaving it."

"Why did you leave?"

"I, um, separated from my husband," Dee said and looked down.

"I'm so sorry."

"It's okay, but I'd rather not talk about it," Dee said and turned the question back on him. "What about you? Are you here on your own?"

"Sadly, yes."

Rob was quiet, not sure how much he wanted to share with a woman he had known for less than ten minutes. But she seemed genuinely nice and caring. And if they were going to be neighbors for the next few months, it would probably be better to be more open than closed.

"I lost my wife six months ago."

"Oh, Rob, I am so sorry."

"Thank you. Me too." Rob paused and looked out over the water, his eyes squinting against the bright, late-morning sun. "That's really why I am here, to escape my old life, my old life with her."

Dee looked at him thoughtfully. "I understand that. In some ways, I'm here to escape my old life as well."

Rob wondered how coming back to where her husband had essentially dumped her was a way to escape her old life. He wanted to ask the question but instead just smiled and said, "Then I guess we are here escaping together."

Dee returned his smile. "And what is it you do, Rob?"

"Well, I guess you could say I'm in-between positions at the moment," he said. "I am fortunate that I can take a little time off to grieve and think about what I want to do with the rest of my life." He paused and then added, "without her."

"I understand."

"And I have always wanted to write a book."

"Really?" replied Dee, surprised. "Now, that is something I don't hear every day."

"I'm not sure why I told you that," Rob said quickly. "I really haven't shared that with anyone."

"That's okay. People often tell me things like that; I think it's because I'm a good listener."

He smiled at her.

"You know," Dee continued, "if you need some inspiration or are just looking to wile away a cold and gray afternoon, I highly recommend our public library, The Atheneum."

"Really? I was not aware that Nantucket had a library."

"Oh yes, and it is wonderful. It's in town, just a block or so off Main Street. You can't miss it; it is a large classical white building with a wonderful Greek revival facade. Trust me, you will love it."

"Hmm, sounds interesting. I'll have to give it a try."

Dee smiled at making another convert. "Excellent."

Suddenly she turned and looked back over the bridge and down Ocean Avenue as if someone were calling her. She turned back to Rob. "I'm sorry, but I really must go now. It was very nice to meet you."

"Nice to meet you as well, Dee. I am sure we will be seeing more of each other in the coming weeks."

"Yes, I'm sure we will." She nodded and turned. Rob watched her walk away, her hair shimmering in the sun, her pale skin almost glassy. A slight shiver went down his spine.

Sighing, Rob turned back to the water and thought of Sarah.

God, I wish she was here.

CHAPTER SEVEN

S arah's room at Barnes-Jewish Hospital in St. Louis was bright and cheery even though it was in the middle of the cancer ward. The walls were painted a soft shade of white, pale blue curtains hung around the bed, and a large window facing Forest Park brought in a lot of natural light. Wires and tubes from the host of medical equipment snaked in and around the covers to connect to Sarah. Every so often, one of the many machines would beep, interrupting the quiet and reminding them where they were. Her bed paralleled the window allowing her to look out on the life she would never again be able to experience.

Outside, it was a cool, early spring morning, just a few days into April. They had spent the better part of the winter meeting with doctors, dealing with treatments, and suffering the agonizing knowledge that they were losing. They had enlisted the best doctors and explored every treatment option, but the cancer was just too far along and too aggressive. The disease had been relentless and had run essentially unchecked through her body.

Rob sat on the edge of the bed, holding her hand, and looked out the window. The grass, celebrating the end of its winter dormancy, blazed a vibrant green, its rich blanket meandering through the park, occasionally interrupted with splotches of color from clumps of daffodils and tulips. The trees were emerging from their winter sleep and sported fresh, bright green leaves, made all the more so by the contrast with a sky of deep blue, the only blemish a contrail from a plane high overhead taking its passengers eastward. At any other time, they would have embraced the day and maybe gone for a picnic, a bike ride, or just a walk. But not today.

Their oncologist, a heavy-set, older man with bushy eyebrows and a disheveled mass of gray hair, had just delivered the news they had dreaded: despite all their efforts and the advances of modern medicine, there was nothing more to be done.

Sarah was quiet, letting the information sink in. She looked up at the doctor, her eyes red and brimming with tears, and asked, "So, how long do I really have?"

The doctor looked down kindly at her, knowing the impact his words would have. "Sarah, I need to be honest with you. At best, we may have a few weeks, but based on my experience with this type of cancer and where we are..." his voice trailed off.

"What?" asked Sarah.

The doctor reached out and placed his hand on her shoulder. "I'm afraid to say it could just be a few days. Your body has been fighting this cancer for months, and it's just too weak to take much more. I'm sorry; I know this wasn't the outcome we were all hoping for."

Sarah looked up at the doctor. "Thank you for your honesty and for everything you have done for us."

The doctor nodded, smiled wanly, turned, and left the room.

Sarah turned to Rob. He was hunched over, sobs wracking his body. She squeezed his hand. "Rob?"

He sat up and looked at her, his eyes swollen and his face covered in tears. "I don't want to lose you," said Rob. "I wish that I could go too so that we could be together."

Sarah smiled up at him through wet eyes and squeezed his hand. She said softly, her voice barely above a whisper, "I know. But you are young, Rob. You have a life to live, and I know that we will be together again someday."

Another sob wracked him. "I don't want to live without you."

"Oh, Rob, I know, but you must," she replied, her voice quivering.

Rob tried to gather his emotions to be strong for her. He needed to support her as well as she had supported them over their years of marriage. He asked hoarsely, "What would we have named the baby if we had been so fortunate?"

Sarah smiled weakly. "If it was a boy, I would have named him after you. We would have called him RJ, for Robert, Junior."

Rob smiled sadly and adjusted his grip on her hand. "And if it had been a girl?"

"Svea."

"After your grandmother," Rob said.

"Yes. She was such a sweet lady, and I always admired her."

Rob squeezed her hand again and smiled bravely. "Two really good names, although I so wish we could have had a girl, one that would look just like you." Tears started flowing down Rob's cheeks again at the thought of what they would never have.

"Rob," she whispered.

Rob sniffled. "Yes, babe?" he said and looked deep into her eyes. The cancer had not been kind to the face he loved so dearly. She had lost much of her hair, and the weight loss had accented her cheekbones in an unkind way. But the fire in her green eyes still sparkled.

"You will need to find someone."

Rob pulled back, shocked. "There is no way anyone could ever replace you!"

Sarah smiled sadly. "I know that hon, but you are a young man. You have many years ahead of you, and I do not want you to live them alone."

"Oh, Sarah, I couldn't, I can't. It just isn't right."

Sarah squeezed his hand and tried to lift herself off the pillow. "But it is right, hon. I want you to be happy, to share your life with someone. To live the dreams we had. You must promise me."

"Promise you? That I'll replace you?" he said, tears streaking down his cheeks.

"No, sweetie," she said softly. "I don't want you to replace me. Or forget me. But I do want you to find a nice woman, someone who you know I would like, and marry her. I cannot die in peace if I know that you'll be alone for the rest of your life."

Rob looked deeply into her eyes and cupped her cheek in his hand. "I promise then if it will make you happy now."

"It does, Rob. I'm heartbroken that I won't be there to share it with you but happy knowing you won't be alone."

Rob leaned down and hugged her, his body convulsing with sobs. Sarah stroked the back of his head and whispered into his ear.

"Kiss me."

Rob pulled up and tenderly kissed her lips.

"I love you," he said.

"I love you too, hon. With all of my heart. Thank you for making my life so wonderful."

Sarah fell asleep, her remaining hair splashed on the pillow, her face calm and peaceful. She would not wake again.

CHAPTER EIGHT

R ob woke to the sound of rain pelting the window of his bedroom. The wind whistled through the sashes, and he could almost feel the old cottage creaking around him. It was his fourth day on the island, and he felt like he had barely seen the sun since he arrived.

Dressed, he made his way down the hall towards the kitchen, pausing a moment to look out the window and take in the morning. The air was thick with fog, and the rain came down at an angle driven by the wind. The trees swayed in the gusts, and every few moments, a shower of leaves would cascade down, covering the grass and clogging the gutters.

Ugh. What a crappy day.

Sighing, he continued down to the kitchen and turned on the coffee pot. As the machine belched and burped, he dropped a couple pieces of bread in the toaster and slid the arm down. Returning to the fridge, he grabbed some cream, the butter, and a locally made jam he had purchased the day before. He filled his mug, plated the two pieces of bread, and sat down at the table. Smearing the butter and jam on his toast, he thought about the day ahead. Unless he wanted to dress up like an old lobsterman going to sea, any outdoor activity was pretty much off-limits. Maybe it was finally time to put pen to paper and start that book.

And if he was honest with himself, the thought made him very nervous. Ever since he had admitted to Sarah that he wanted to be a writer, he had felt pangs of anxiety. Who the hell did he think he was to write a book? He had never written anything creative since high school, and even then, he had barely made a B in the class. What has changed? Did eleven years of running a handyman business make him any more creative? Or a more capable writer? Why did he think he could do it now?

Because I made a promise to Sarah I would try.

He chewed his toast slowly, lost in his doubts. A wind gust rattled the metal storm window by the kitchen table and tore him from his thoughts. He finished up his toast, stood up, and put his plate in the sink. He refilled his coffee mug and carried it through the house to the small bedroom where he had set up his writing station. Settling down in the chair, he looked over at the picture of Sarah. Sadness gripped him again, and he fought back the tears. The rain and gloom of the day were doing little to help his spirits.

Rob opened his laptop and fired up the word processing software he had purchased explicitly for writing the book. The website had claimed that it was the #1 choice of fiction writers, and while it might help with his grammar and punctuation, it would do nothing for his storyline. On the screen, a box appeared with a prompt with two options: Open Existing. New Document.

He moved the mouse over and clicked on New Document. The screen flashed briefly, and then a white box appeared with a flashing cursor in the upper left. Across the top, a number of menu options were available intended to help him write the novel of his dreams. But what was he going to write about? The flashing cursor was daring him to write something. Anything.

Since sharing his dreams with Sarah, he had been more focused in thinking of ideas for storylines. He thought of them while installing new windows, fixing plumbing, and replacing rotted trim, all of the odd jobs that made his handyman business so interesting. When ideas came to mind, he would try and flush them out fully as he worked; the characters, the plot, twists and turns in the storyline, and the final denouement. At the end of the day, if the idea still held his interest, he would capture as much as he could remember in an antique leather-wrapped notebook that Sarah had given to him for their second Christmas together.

On the inside cover, she had written a short inscription. *To Rob. I believe in you. Believe in yourself.*

Coming up with ideas had not been an issue. He did have a creative mind and, with his work, had a lot of free mental time to leverage that creativity. Over the years, he had generated several dozen storylines across multiple genres, from action and adventure to crime thrillers and even fantasy.

He sat at the desk, the notebook in his hand, and thumbed through the pages at the years of work he had captured. Creating the foundation of a novel had seemed so simple when he was hammering a nail, but now that he was serious, they were quickly falling apart. He couldn't get past the basics to even write the first word. His head felt full of cotton. The cursor continued to blink, taunting him.

As he scrolled through the ideas, the same doubts cropped up with each. Not believable. Too predictable. Weak characters. Done before. He continued flipping through the pages at all of the ideas he had laid out. Surely one of them would work. But with each idea, as soon as he started to lay out a more formal outline, he would hit some barrier that he couldn't get past.

He reread the inscription from Sarah.

Putting his notebook aside, he looked at Sarah's picture. What about a love story based on our life? Would anyone be interested in that?

He turned to his laptop and started to type, thinking about the day they met at the laundromat, both fresh out of college and living in the same old neighborhood in St. Louis. But after just a few minutes, his eyes filled with tears, and he lowered his face into his hands. It was just too painful. Her loss was too fresh. He highlighted the words he had just struggled to write and hit the delete key.

I need to get out of here.

He slid back in his chair, the feet scraping the old wooden floor. He found the keys to the Wagoneer, pulled on a windbreaker, and headed outside, his body leaning into the wind. He unlocked the car and jumped in, his hair dripping water onto the old leather seat. In minutes he was on Milestone road heading to town, intent on taking up Dee's recommendation for the Nantucket library, the Atheneum. Maybe surrounding himself with books and doing some reading would help free up his mind and inspire his writing. It certainly couldn't hurt.

The Wagoneer lurched side to side as Rob turned onto the cobbled Main Street. He found a parking spot quickly and angled the old Jeep into the space. Looking at the mapping app on his phone, he noted that the Atheneum was just a couple of blocks away. He hopped out of the car and, stumbling a bit on the old cobblestones, made his way to the brick sidewalk.

He stopped briefly as he turned the corner of Main and Federal street and took a few moments to read through all of the ads and notices on the Town message board. Everything from help wanted signs to those advertising their skills as a nanny, dog walker, or caretaker. One notice that caught his eye was for a bereavement group that met monthly at the Unitarian Church. He pulled out his phone and snapped a picture of the announcement.

Putting the phone back in his pocket, Rob continued walking and soon found himself at the Atheneum. Dee had certainly been correct in her description. It was beautiful. The large white building had a lovely Greek revival facade, its corners sporting fluted pilasters while two large Ionic columns framed the front entrance. In engraved gold lettering above the entrance and below an elaborate gable with an inset pediment, read ATHENEUM. As if to emphasize the point, a large gold period completed the statement. A courtyard in front of the building was surrounded by a simple yet elegant white fence. A small opening, capped by a metal archway, led the way to the main door.

"I think I found it," Rob muttered to himself. He crossed the street and made his way under the arch. He climbed the steps and opened the front door.

As he walked in, he felt that same thrown-back-in-time feeling he had first felt when he had driven off the ferry. If he ignored the phone in his pocket and the lights overhead, he could easily be back in the mid-18th century. Tall white bookshelves capped with stained crown molding lined the space. Large models of old wooden sailing ships encased in glass frames and busts of prominent authors topped the bookshelves. Underfoot, old wide plank pine boards were worn with years of trodden steps and covered occasionally in what looked like antique oriental rugs. Scattered about the space were overstuffed sofas and Windsor chairs encouraging people to stay and read a bit. A gentle hum from the heating unit barely disturbed the silence as it worked to keep the old building warm and dry on this very damp day.

"May I help you?" a voice said.

Startled, Rob turned to his left and faced the circulation desk. It was white, with recessed panels, and generous in size. On the wall behind the desk, row upon row of shelves, contained books, magazines, and other materials being held and waiting to be claimed by library patrons. Standing behind the large glossy wood countertop, an attractive young lady looked back at him.

"Um, yes. I've just arrived on the island and am interested in checking out some books. Can I do that? I'm not a resident."

"You sure can. Are you looking for a temporary library card, or will you be staying longer?" Her large brown eyes sparkled with energy.

"Well, I'm planning on being here through the winter."

"Then I suggest we get you a full-time card. Do you have an island address we can use?"

"Yes, I do." Rob fumbled with his phone and pulled up the email the realtor had sent him a few short months ago. It took him a minute to find the address. "I'm at 11 Starbuck Lane, in Siasconset." He pronounced the last word slowly, uttering each of its four syllables. Sigh-ass-conn-set.

She laughed brightly. "You haven't been on the island before, have you?"

"No, this is my first time. How did you know?" asked Rob.

"Well, we usually just call it 'Sconset.'"

Rob blushed. "Okay. Thanks for letting me know." He looked down at his phone and read the address again. "In Sconset," he said with emphasis and looked back at her.

She smiled and laughed. "Well done. You are almost a native."

Rob smiled back at her. "Do you need anything more from me?"

"Just some ID we can use to confirm you are who you say you are. Do you have a driver's license or passport?"

"Sure." Rob pulled out his wallet, fished out his driver's license, and handed it to the librarian.

"Missouri?" she asked, somewhat surprised. "We don't usually get many people from the midwest here."

"Glad I can be a bit different then," Rob said and smiled again.

She returned the smile, accepted the license, and said, "I'll be right back." She disappeared through a door next to the desk into what looked like the main office.

As he waited, Rob's eyes wandered around the library, taking in the design and decoration of the interior. Given his business, he was used to working in old buildings, and the craftsmanship expressed in both the materials and design impressed him. The joinery of the paneling and moldings, the high ceilings with elaborate and detailed coffers, and the elegant dimensions of the space all combined to bring a sense of quality, timelessness, and style. Only the drop ceiling with the acoustic - and likely fireproof - tiles gave any hint of modernity.

"Here you go!"

He turned to see the librarian holding out his license as well as his new library card.

"Thank you," said Rob, taking the materials from her.

"Of course! That's what I'm here for. Now that you have your card, can I help you find anything in particular?"

"Um, where is your fiction section?"

"It is right over there," she said, pointing. "It takes up the eastern half of the first floor and is listed alphabetically by author."

"Thank you." Rob turned and walked through the shelves. He found a couple of authors he enjoyed and selected a few books. Two he had read before and thought reading again would be fun. He added a few new ones that looked interesting based on the cover blurbs. He returned to the circulation desk and checked out using his newly minted library card.

"There you go." the young librarian said and handed him his books. "I hope to see you again."

"No doubt about that," said Rob. "And thank you again for your help. I really appreciate it."

"My pleasure. And stay dry out there in Siasconset," she teased, emphasizing the first two syllables.

Rob laughed. "I will." He turned and walked out the door, the clutch of books under his arm.

CHAPTER NINE

The rain finally cleared, bringing chilly temperatures and a deep azure sky lightly sprinkled with wisps of cirrus clouds. Rob had been up for several hours, having woken from a fitful sleep. Images of Sarah had invaded his dreams and killed any further effort for rest.

He had gotten up, made some coffee, and tore into one of the novels that he had selected at the Atheneum. It was from a familiar author whose protagonist Rob knew very well, having read over a dozen of the series about the midwest detective. Like the others, it was fast-paced with witty dialogue, and before he knew it, he had finished the book and nearly an entire pot of coffee. He was also starving.

Rob stood and stretched, the book held high in an outstretched hand. Sighing, he lowered his arms and brought it in closer to read the blurb on the back cover. Probably less than 150 words, it was straightforward and highlighted the key parts of the story he had just read. And it made it seem so easy that he should be able to do the same. He walked over and placed the book on the stack he had borrowed from the Atheneum and made a mental note to return it later in the week.

Carrying his empty coffee mug into the kitchen, Rob pulled some deli meat and cheese from the fridge and made himself a sandwich on the locally baked Portuguese bread. He pulled a glass from the cabinet and filled it with water. Adding some chips to his plate, he sat down at the kitchen table and tucked into his lunch.

Chewing, he thought about a writing class he had taken, which had spent an entire morning writing a blurb. At the time, he had thought it was a silly and wasteful exercise. That changed when he read an article by one of his favorite writers who claimed that with every novel she wrote, she started with the blurb. It was her way of hooking herself into the story as well as testing the strength of her characters and the tension of the storyline. If she couldn't write a good blurb, then it probably wasn't a good story.

Maybe I should follow her lead and start with the blurb and see if I can make that work.

Rob finished his sandwich and put the plate in the sink. He refilled his water glass and proceeded to the small bedroom at the front of the house, where his writing station waited patiently. Easing into the chair, he cracked his laptop, settled his fingers on the keyboard, and waited for the words to come.

As before, the cursor blinked on an empty white screen, provoking him. And, like yesterday, his mind seemed incapable of creating a single word. At least today, though, he had an idea of what his story was going to be.

A few years before Sarah had died, he had completed a project for one of her colleagues. He was a senior executive in the company and lived in a large Georgian mansion in one of the finer St. Louis neighborhoods. He was father to a young girl, and to assuage his guilt over the long hours and frequent business trips that kept him away from her and the many milestones of her life, he had engaged Rob to build her a playhouse for her fifth birthday.

Rob had spent several weeks on the project and, in the end, had constructed an adorable playhouse complete with a small porch, kitchenette, and enough room for a play table and chairs. It was trimmed and painted to match the main house and designed to grow with her in the future. The girl, excited and impatient, had visited him daily to check progress and pepper him with questions like where could she keep her imaginary pony and how many of her friends could she invite to a tea party.

But during one of her visits, she had looked at him and said in a very serious tone, "Have you seen any of the tree fairies today?"

Her imagination had made him chuckle, but when he realized she was serious, he dialed it back and returned her serious gaze with his own. "I'm afraid I have not. Do you see them often?"

She nodded furiously. "I do. They live in that tree," and pointed to a large silver maple whose branches arched high above the building site. "But they are sad."

"Why is that?"

"Because there are mean fairies in that tree," she turned and pointed to an old walnut tree that looked as if it were in its final stages of life. "Those fairies want to take over and kick them out of their home."

"Really?" Rob had asked, the depth and detail of her imagination impressing him but more likely a reflection of the insecure life in her own home.

"Yes. And I wish there was something I could do to help them."

"I'm sure you do," Rob said.

"Gotta' go," she had said suddenly, turned and, pigtails bobbing up and down, ran back to the house, the trials and tribulations of tree fairies forgotten for the moment.

As Rob watched her go, an idea formed in his mind. When he wrapped up for the day, he stole a few minutes in his truck and briefly outlined a story in his notebook about tree fairies, a dying tree, and a battle among the sprites for the future of their respective communities. He thought it might have potential as fantasy fiction targeted at the young adult crowd. And maybe even had the legs for a series of books all based on the same characters but facing new and different challenges.

Rob took a sip of his water and stared at the outline in his notebook written years before, his mind churning but producing no forward progress, like a propellor cavitating in the water. It seemed like such a rich idea at the time, but he was struggling to kick-start it into something more than a figment in the imagination of a five-year-old and a few hazy thoughts of a handyman carpenter.

A few words came, and his fingers awkwardly typed them. Minutes passed, and then a few more. The cursor, waiting patiently, blinked in anticipation. He looked at the clock on his desk. Almost four o'clock. Over two hours in and he had produced a grand total of ten words. At this pace, he would complete his novel sometime in the next century.

Frustrated, he slammed the laptop shut, pushed back his chair, and went to the kitchen to dump his water.

I need a walk.

Rob grabbed his coat and sunglasses and headed out the door, ducking his head against the low jamb of the door. He paused at the gate and took in a deep breath. There were many scents in the cool, salt-tinged air, some that seemed foreign to him and some, like the smell of drying leaves, that brought him comfort and reminded him of happier times.

He turned to his right and strolled down Starbuck Lane, the old quahog shells used to pave the street crunching under his feet. He passed Dee's house and noticed it was quiet, the lights off and the drapes closed. A chill ran over the back of his neck, and he pulled his collar up tightly and continued.

Reaching Ocean Avenue, he paused and admired the stunning sight ahead of him, the sea a light bluish gray contrasting with the deeper blue of the sky. A young couple, holding hands, was walking the other way. Rob raised his hand in greeting. The man, startled, touched the brim of his cap and nodded.

Rob turned his attention back to the water. The rip churned just offshore, the waves building, crisscrossing, and breaking, their white faces rippling forward until they faded out, only to be followed by another. They were louder today, their sound helped along by the eastern breeze. Mesmerized, Rob just stood and watched the waves dance.

The cry of a hawk broke his reverie. Tearing his eyes away from the spectacle in front of him, Rob turned and headed down Ocean avenue toward the village center. Always a creature of habit, he followed his usual walking path along the water, across the bike bridge, and down the narrow lane that emerged at the small brick-paved park. Things were quiet in the little town; the only signs of activity were a few lone bicycles nose first in the rack by the post office and the flag atop the mast at the rotary waving gently in the breeze. Movement caught his eye, and he noticed a seagull flapping its wings as it settled on the ridge board of a nearby house.

He continued hands in his coat pockets, proceeding slowly through the narrow lanes and the cluster of old houses. He had walked this way many times since first driving down the street when he had arrived, and the slower pace let him have a far better appreciation of the old buildings. Many had been built in the 18th century, some on-site and some which claimed to have been moved from other locations on the island.

Reaching the end of Front street, he noticed a narrow lane off to his right, running between two old cottages. His first thought was a driveway, but then he saw it go past the houses and then turn to run parallel to the sea. Curious, he followed the lane around the house and came to a sign that announced the entrance to the Bluff Walk.

Bluff walk? Interesting.

Rob followed the arrow of the sign and soon found himself on a grassy path, narrow and rambling between the backs of homes on his left and the bluff on the right. Ancient trees bent and stooped from years of fighting the wind, arched over the path while their roots, intent on tripping him, coiled below. Groves of hobbled trees would give way to lush green grass, like walking through someone's backyard, and just as quickly, he would find himself back among the old trees. It was almost magical.

Every few hundred feet, a staircase would appear, built down the side of the bluff with wooden walkways extended between the scrub pine and beach grass to the sand and eventually the water. Each sported a gate, most of a simple design and a few more intricate, but all with a notice that they were not available for his use.

Emerging from a tangled canopy of branches, the space opened in front of him. The trail he had followed for over a half mile changed from a grassy footpath to a formal concrete sidewalk, each side lined with freshly trimmed grass. To the right, a row of native rose bushes lined the walk, while to his left, a large expanse of grass led to a large Victorian home. Resplendent in gingerbread trim, it stood proudly with nearly every window ablaze with light. People inside were walking about, drinks in hand, while a few sat on the large front porch, enjoying the coming dusk and talking animatedly. No one looked in his direction.

Where have all these people come from?

He had spent the better part of an hour walking through the village and hadn't seen anything more than a couple of seagulls. Were they visiting from Town? Were they residents of the house and staying here? Regardless, it seemed a bit odd to be having such a big party at this time of day and this time of year.

Rob's focus shifted from the people to the building. He stared at the old structure marveling at the intricate detail of the design; the carpenter in him was impressed with the exceptional quality of work. It took him a few moments before he realized that this was the back of the house he had driven by when he had arrived on the island the week before.

What? It looked like the place was falling down.

Confused, more questions flooded his mind. Did they restore the back of the house but leave the front alone? Maybe this was an active restoration project that was only partially complete? Perhaps he could find some work here and get back to using his hands and help bring this old beauty back to her former glory. Would they hire a stranger from Missouri who had been on the island less than a week?

He thought about approaching the party and trying to find out who the owner was to learn more about the project. He also thought about cutting through the lawn to the front of the house to get a better look and see if his memory was correct and how much more work remained. After a few moments, he decided that he would save that for a future date. He didn't want to interrupt the party - hell, he certainly wasn't dressed for it - and with the light fading, decided to head back home.

Turning, he made his way back through the canopy and carefully navigated his way back down the path. He was somewhat surprised now to see lights on in nearly all the homes he passed. In some, where the curtains were open, he could peer in and make out the design and decoration, while others had shutters closed and drapes pulled tight. Where he could see in he often saw people milling about, drinks in hand, and clearly having a good time. It was almost as if there was a coordinated block party - bluff party? - going on.

There are a lot more people here than Will made it sound.

Fascinated, Rob checked out each of the houses he passed as he walked back into the village. Some were dark and clearly deserted, but most had some signs of life. Lights on, sounds of music, peals of laughter, all of it clearly at odds with what he had heard from the realtor. He had been promised that the village over the winter was quiet and secluded. What he was seeing was anything but. It was like half the island was here partying away on the Sconset bluff.

He navigated back to Front Street, made his way over the bike bridge, and then found himself on a very dark Starbuck Lane. The last light remained in the western sky, a smear of purple along the horizon melting into a velvet black sky above him. A blanket of stars had emerged in the clear sky. His street was devoid of streetlights, and with none of the houses lit, he was carefully navigating up the lane squinting in the low light to avoid walking head-first into one of the many trees that lined the street.

"Hi, Rob."

Rob paused and peered into the darkness. "Dee?"

He saw a figure stand and approach him.

"Did you have a nice walk?" asked Dee.

Rob could just barely make out her face, her glassy, white skin almost glowing in the dim light. "I did, thanks."

"Good. Are you settling in okay?"

"I am, yes. And by the way, I went to the Atheneum yesterday. What an amazing building and wonderful resource. Thank you for the suggestion."

"Of course," replied Dee. "I'm happy to help. If you need any more recommendations, please let me know. Having lived here for so many years, I know the island well and what she has to offer."

Rob couldn't see her smile but sensed she was pleased. He started to turn but paused. "I do have a question, Dee."

"Sure, Rob. What's that?"

"I just did the Bluff Walk. Really cool, by the way."

"It is one of my favorite spots," replied Dee.

"The thing is, I was told that there are very few people in Sconset over the winter, that I would almost have the place to myself."

"Yes, it usually is very quiet during the off-season."

"But just about every house I passed seemed to have a party going on."

"Really?"

"Yes. Not that it bothers me, I'm just curious as everyone told me it would be quiet, yet seems to be quite the opposite."

Rob couldn't make out Dee's expression, just the outline of her face in the darkness.

"I'm not sure I can answer that one, Rob."

"Hmm, okay." Rob shuffled on his feet from side to side. "Well, good to see you, Dee. Enjoy the rest of your evening."

"You too, Rob."

Rob watched her turn and walk toward her cottage, her figure dissolving into the darkness.

The cool air sent a chill up his neck. Rob turned and headed for the Shanty.

CHAPTER TEN

T hree hours. Seventeen words. Nearly a week into the project and he barely had a paragraph to show for it. The cursor blinked menacingly at him from the comfort of its white screen.

At this rate, I'll finish the damn book when I'm ninety.

Frustrated at the glacial progress and tired of the cursor tormenting him, Rob slammed the laptop shut and looked out the window. It was late morning, and the fog he had woken to remained, shrouding the trees and neighboring cottages in a gray embrace. It was certainly not the idyllic blue sky fall day that the tourist websites promised.

Rob got up and headed into the living room. A fire crackled in the hearth, warming the room and his mood. He walked over to the fireplace, threw a couple of fresh logs on top of the burning embers, and settled in on the couch to finish the novel he was reading. It was the last of the books he had retrieved from the Atheneum earlier in the week and had just a few chapters remaining.

He read the chapters on autopilot, his mind stuck thinking of the cursor and laptop screen and his pathetic progress. What was wrong with him? His mind could see the story, but it seemed to get lost on the way to his fingertips. Maybe this whole idea was just a waste of his time and energy. Maybe he should just pack up and head back to Missouri.

He finished the book, barely recalling the climax and denouement, his mind still focused on the question of fight or flight. Closing the cover, he laid it on the stack of others on the side table and thought about his choices; pack up and head back to St. Louis, return to battle against the dreaded cursor, go for another walk, or what?

Thinking of the aisles and aisles of books and the very attractive librarian, he decided to reload his reading stack. He stood up, grabbed the clutch of books, and headed to the old Wagoneer. With his mind looking forward to talking with the librarian, he forgot to duck as he exited the house and smacked his head on the door frame. "Damnit!" he cursed out loud, his hand going to the now swelling bump on his forehead.

Head throbbing, he started up the car, the wipers doing their best to clear the heavy moisture from the windshield. The trip to town was impeded by the fog, at times forcing Rob to slow to barely a walking pace to make out where the road ended, and the grass median started. At one point, he found himself face to face with a beautiful twelve-point buck standing in the middle of the road. Had he been going the speed limit, it likely would have been an ugly meeting. But at this crawling speed, he was able to quickly bring the car to a stop and watched, entranced, as the deer made its way slowly off the road and into the scrub brush.

His mood boosted by the sighting, he navigated his way through town, over the cobblestones, and found a parking spot across from the Atheneum. He locked the car, tucked the books under his arm, and walked in. The interior was inviting, warm, and dry. A dozen or so patrons were spread out across the room, curled up in the various reading nooks with books in hand.

Rob turned and made his way over to the circulation desk. He was happy to see that the young lady who had helped him on his last visit was behind the counter. She had short brown hair, a mocha-colored complexion, a heart-shaped face with high cheekbones, and a button nose. He must have been very distracted before, not noticing just how beautiful she was. Today he found her absolutely stunning.

She looked up as he approached her and smiled. "Good to see you again. Did you enjoy those books?" she said, looking at the bundle under his arm.

Rob stumbled. "Oh, yes, they were enjoyable, if a little predictable. I had read a couple of them before but wanted something tried and true."

"Oh, good." She looked at him carefully. "Are you okay?"

"Am I okay?" Rob asked, surprised.

"Yes, that bump on your forehead. It looks like it hurts."

"Oh, this," Rob rubbed the bump. "That's what I get for renting an old cottage with short doors." He smiled.

"You need to be more careful." She returned the smile and changed the subject. "Are you ready for some more books?"

Rob smiled back nervously. "Yes, but I think I'm more interested in non-fiction, especially anything about Nantucket. I'd like to learn more about this place."

She let out a low chuckle. "Well, you've come to the right place. We've got lots of books on Nantucket! Is there any particular part of the island's history you are interested in?"

"What do you mean?" asked Rob.

"Nantucket has been inhabited for hundreds if not thousands of years. There are books on the original native Americans who prospered here, the settlers who joined them in the 1600s, whaling, and even more recent books on the rise of tourism, architecture, and design."

"Hmm, tough choices, especially for this Missouri boy. What would you recommend?"

She thought for a minute before responding. "If I were you, I'd probably pick whaling to start. It's really at the core of identity for modern Nantucket, and it is an absolutely fascinating part of our history."

Rob stared into her sparkling brown eyes and, for a moment, forgot where he was.

"So what do you think?" she asked.

"Oh! Sorry. I was lost in thought there." Rob blushed slightly. "Let's go with whaling."

"Excellent choice!" she said and laughed. "And the first book I would recommend is Moby Dick."

"Moby Dick?"

She smiled. "Yes, I know. But it really does accurately reflect the life of whalers and the island. And it is based on a true story from one of the whaleships of Nantucket."

Rob replied, "Really? Definitely add that to the list. I was supposed to read it in high school English class, but in the end, I just read the notes version of it." He smiled sheepishly.

She chuckled again. "I get that. I did the same thing!"

Rob smiled back. "By the way, I never did introduce myself. I'm Rob McGlynn."

"Nice to meet you, Rob. My name is Eliza Macy, but everyone calls me Pip."

"Pip?"

She smiled. "Yes, speaking of Moby Dick, my dad was a huge fan. I was a real tomboy growing up and actually jumped out of a sailboat when I was five because it was leaning way over, and it scared me. I got tangled in an anchor line and nearly drowned. My dad said it reminded him of the character Pip in Moby Dick, and the nickname stuck."

Rob smiled and extended his hand. "Okay then, Pip. It is nice to meet you."

"And you as well." Pip shook his hand. "Can I help you find any other books?

"Well, maybe. I'm trying to find out more about someone who I think stayed in the cottage I'm renting."

"Is this someone recent?" Pip asked.

"Oh no. From 1900."

"That's curious. What was the name?"

"Lisbeth Hopper"

Pip paused. "Lisbeth Hopper?"

"Yes. Are you familiar with her?"

"Well, yes, sort of. She's part of island lore."

"Really?" asked Rob excitedly.

"Growing up, we heard all sorts of ghost stories about people who died that some believed still walked the island. Captains who died at sea, people who drowned in the ocean, and..."

"And?"

"Murder victims."

"She was murdered?" Rob exclaimed. "Really?" He felt a unique combination of intrigue and dread. Was he living in the house of a murder victim?

"The legend is that she was found washed up on the beach in Sconset. Apparently, she had been assaulted sexually and hit in the head with a rock."

"What about the murderer?"

"Never caught. There was a man who they thought was guilty, but they didn't have enough evidence to convict. He claimed it was consensual and that she had fallen and hit her head."

"Interesting."

"Yes. And some of those stories we heard growing up, mostly at summer camp, you know, said you could occasionally see her ghost walking on the beach, dressed in her finery."

A chill spread through Rob.

"A ghost. Really?"

Pip chuckled. "Yes, if you believe in those things. Actually, we natives have a term for them. We call them winter residents."

"Winter residents?" asked Rob.

"Well, we have lots of summer residents, thousands of them. But when they go home and the houses are empty, weird things tend to happen. It's probably just our overactive imaginations caused by the cold, gray winters, but we like to blame them on the winter residents. So if you think you see a shadow moving out of the corner of your eye or hear a voice in the wind, we like to think it's one of them." Pip smiled and continued. "Legend has it that they are the ghosts of people who never want to leave Nantucket.

They return from wherever dead people go once the summer people depart."

Pip looked at him, her face bright with energy. "Anyway, enough about children's stories. If you really want to learn more about her, though, we can certainly help. We have a digital archive of all Nantucket newspapers going back to the early 1800s. And it's all online, so you can do it from the comfort of your cottage. And who knows, maybe Lisbeth will be looking over your shoulder." She winked at him.

"That is not funny," Rob said. "I'm not sure how comfortable I'll be in that house knowing what I know now."

"I'm sure it's fine. And if you do investigate her, I'd love to hear what you find out. Maybe we could grab a coffee sometime?"

Rob replied, startled, "Um, sure. That would be great. It's just that I, um…"

"As friends," said Pip.

"Okay," answered Rob, recovering his composure. "How about this Friday? I tend to work better under deadlines."

Pip smiled. "Friday it is."

Rob smiled, turned, and started to walk out of the library. He stopped and looked back at Pip. "I'm such an idiot."

"What is it?"

"I haven't gotten any books yet," said Rob and laughed nervously.

Pip smiled. "Well, Moby Dick is that way," Pip said, pointing down an aisle. "And once you have that, the Nantucket historical section is upstairs, directly above us."

"Thank you," said Rob.

"You are welcome."

Rob smiled and headed down the aisle in search of the Melville novel. Passing a window, he noted that the fog had lifted, and breaks of blue sky were visible above. His mood echoed the weather, and he noted he felt much more optimistic than before his trip to town. He selected a modernized version of the classic and then took the steps to the upstairs history section, where he grabbed a handful of books on whales, whalers, and the whaling industry. Satisfied, he made his way to the first floor and headed to the desk.

Pip was nowhere to be seen, and an older man, hair gray and face aged from years of living on the ocean and in the sun, helped him complete the checkout process. He thanked him, took a long survey around the first floor in hopes of spotting Pip, and, disappointed, headed out the door.

Thoughts of Sarah clouded his mind as he walked to the Wagoneer. In some ways, Pip reminded him a bit of Sarah; her outgoing personality, her sense of humor, and her spirit. As he hopped into the car and closed the door, he found himself looking forward to Friday.

He returned to the cottage and immediately fired up his laptop. Within minutes, he was searching the Atheneum's digital archive site and learning a lot about Lisbeth Hopper. Soon he was lost in her story.

CHAPTER ELEVEN

The Empire Theater, New York City, 1900

"Wow, I think that might have been our best performance yet!" exclaimed a heavily perspiring John Bleak, one of the leads in the production of *The Story of Richard Carvel*. He toweled his face rigorously and turned to face his fellow actors. "We need to celebrate! Especially since this is our last performance until after the summer break."

Lisbeth Hopper, one of the female leads, stared back at him with large, hazel eyes sparkling with energy. "Absolutely!" she cheered. She was a young woman with fair skin and short, curly brown hair and was frequently stared at by friends, acquaintances, and strangers alike for her sheer, captivating beauty. She scanned the room to capture the attention of the entire troupe. "Who's game?"

Choruses of "I am" from the dozen or so performers returned to her ears.

Smiling, she turned back to John, "So, where should we go?"

"To the Tapper, of course!" John made a formal, exaggerated turn and started to march out of the room, an imaginary baton keeping time to his steps. "Follow me!"

The Tapper was their usual post-show haunt. It was in the basement of a brick office building just a few blocks from the Empire at the corner of Broadway and 39th street. John led the group down the steps and into the smoky room. As usual, it was busy and packed with actors from some of the other local theaters as well as dozens of stagehands and hangers-on. They made their way through the crowd to their reserved space in the corner and settled into the upholstered couches.

A waiter approached. "Champagne all around!" shouted John to the cheers of the actors.

Soon, champagne was flowing freely, and the group broke down into more intimate conversations.

"So, what are your plans for the summer break, Lisbeth?" asked Percy Barnes, another of the female leads and a well-known beauty in her own right.

Lisbeth looked up from her flute of champagne. "I'm not sure. Probably head north to the Catskills. Or maybe Newport."

"Not sure? Oh then, you absolutely must come with us!" Percy exclaimed.

Smiling, Lisbeth looked at her fellow actor and friend. "Where are you heading?"

"We are going to Nantucket! To a little village on the east end of the island."

"Really? Sounds rather dreary to me."

"Not at all!" exclaimed Percy. "For the last 20 years or so, many of the leading actors from New York have headed there during the summer break. They have a wonderful time together. The air is cool and crisp, the beaches beautiful, and we stay in the most charming cottages. I went there for the first time last summer and loved it!"

"Hmm," said Lisbeth and took a sip of her champagne. "I'm not sure."

Percy reached out and grabbed her arm, "Oh, you must! You will love it, I promise. You can room with me and two of my friends from the Opera House. They are not as pretty as you," she smiled at Lisbeth, "but they are fun to be with, and I know you'll enjoy it."

Lisbeth paused, taking another sip of champagne. "Ok, I'm game."

Percy screeched in delight and raised her glass. "To a wonderful summer on Nantucket!"

Lisbeth raised her glass to meet Percy's, and they clinked. "To our summer on Nantucket!"

They emptied their glasses.

Percy looked at Lisbeth mischievously and said, "Now that that is settled, let's have some fun!"

* * *

The week before July 4th, Lisbeth found herself on a steamer bound for the island of Nantucket. It was a beautiful day, puffy white clouds dotting the deep blue sky. She and Percy were sitting at the stern, enjoying the sun on their faces and the promises of fun and adventure that lay ahead of them. The ship swayed softly from side to side in a light swell.

"Tell me more about the cottage and where we are staying," said Lisbeth.

"Well, the village is known as Siasconset - we just call it Sconset - and it's on the east end of the island. We are staying on the southern side of the village in what they call the Actors' Colony."

"The Actors' Colony? It's really called that?"

"It is! There are a dozen and a half of the most charming little cottages. They were built in the 80s and are actually modeled after the old fishing shanties of the village from a hundred years ago."

Lisbeth looked a little skeptical.

"And don't worry," said Percy clutching Lisbeth's arm. "They have modern conveniences such as freshwater cisterns and are fully outfitted with furniture and linens."

"Well, I guess they do sound, um, interesting."

"Oh, stop that, Lisbeth," said Percy, playfully slapping her shoulder. "No, they aren't too fancy, but they are quite nice and agreeable."

"What about our cottage?"

"It's probably the most charming of all of them!" said Percy. "It's called the Shanty, and it is all sloping roof and nooks & crannies. We only have two bedrooms, though, so we will need to pair up. But, it is cozy, and you will be very comfortable."

"I hope so," said Lisbeth. "I'm beginning to rethink my decision."

"Well, maybe this will change your mind. I heard from one of my friends that Anne Gilbert will be there. All the way from London!"

"Anne Gilbert? I didn't realize famous people were going to be there," said Lisbeth excitedly. "Who else?"

"Certainly, you'll see a lot of familiar faces from the New York acting scene. And, of course, a lot of wealthy people usually summer there from New York, Detroit, and Baltimore. Who knows, maybe you'll meet a handsome, rich man who will sweep you off your feet," Percy said teasingly.

Lisbeth blushed slightly, "You know I'm an old-fashioned girl from the farm."

"Uh-huh," said Percy and winked. "I know you are."

A long blast of the ship's whistle interrupted them.

"We must be coming into the harbor," said Percy. Let's go to the bow. I want you to see the view."

They two walked forward, the arms hooked together, their long flowing dresses swaying in the breeze. As they rounded the bridge, the harbor unfolded in front of them.

"Oh my gosh, it is so quaint and beautiful!" exclaimed Lisbeth.

"Yes, it is," said Percy. "You and I are going to have a summer to remember!"

* * *

True to her word, Lisbeth found the Shanty to be quaint and snug. She and Percy were sharing a bedroom with her small bed tucked under the sloping roof. She had to constantly remind herself to mind the rafters each time she got out of bed so as not to bang her head. And they were having fun. Dinner parties at night, sunning on the beach during the day, and late-night soiree's that often had her out well into the wee hours of the morning.

It was after one of these late nights that Lisbeth found herself down the street on the patio of another cottage sitting with a half-dozen fellow actors from New York. Most, like Lisbeth, were nursing hangovers, and several had not seen their bed that night.

"Are we ready for our new production tomorrow night?" asked Irving Bell, a character actor best known for his vaudevillian comedy.

The group had been rehearsing for weeks to perform in a new building in Sconset called the Casino. A wealthy group of summer residents had had it constructed to be the new social center of the village, and after two years of planning and construction, it was finally ready to open its doors. The entire Actor's Colony had been involved in preparations for the inaugural performance and were excited to be the first to perform in the elegant new structure.

Lisbeth peered through red-rimmed eyes, her head hurting from the many, many glasses of champagne she had enjoyed the night before. "Not with this hangover."

"No drinking for you tonight, young lady," chided Irving playfully. "You are our star of the show, and you absolutely must be ready!"

Lisbeth smiled ruefully. "I'll be ready, I promise."

Opening night came, and the Casino doors opened to the largest crowd the small island had ever seen. A mass of people swelled at the entrance as ticket holders fought their way in to get the best vantage point for the upcoming performance. Some later claimed that their feet had never even touched the floor; they were just carried in with the crush.

The production was a huge success and was a mixture of song, dance, and comedic numbers. Lisbeth concluded the evening with a soliloquy based on Joan d'Arc. She brought the house down to a standing ovation. After changing out of their costumes, the performers joined the patrons in a large tent filled with tray upon tray of food and a seemingly endless supply of champagne. A small band was set up in the corner and playing some ragtime to a group of dancers.

Percy and Lisbeth each picked up a glass from a passing waiter and toasted their performance.

"Well done, Lisbeth. As usual, you were captivating. I think you may have won the hearts of every man in the audience."

Lisbeth was about to respond when a voice interrupted.

"I can attest to that."

Lisbeth turned to the voice and stared into deep-set blond eyes.

"You were indeed captivating this evening, Miss Hopper."

Lisbeth smiled. "Well, thank you, um, mister..."

"Grey, Digby Grey," and held out his hand.

Lisbeth accepted it. "Nice to meet you."

Percy caught Lisbeth's eye and winked. "Excuse me a minute. I need to find a friend." She turned and retreated through the crowd.

"I've actually been a fan of yours since I saw you at the Empire earlier this year. You were quite impressive as Dorothy Manners in Richard Carvel."

"Thank you. And what is it that you do, Mr. Grey?"

"Please. Call me Digby."

"Very well, Digby," she paused. "But the question stands."

Digby smiled. "I'm in finance. Wall Street."

"Hmm. And what brings you to Nantucket?"

"Actually, my family has lived on Nantucket for several generations. We were in whaling with a ship known as Gratitude."

"Really? But no more?"

Digby laughed. "No, no more whaling. The last whaling vessel from Nantucket departed over thirty years ago. My grandfather sold the ship and retired. When he passed away, my father nearly squandered the entire family fortune in a series of very poor investment choices. Fortunately, I have been able to rebuild much of that over the last ten years or so in New York."

Lisbeth looked up at him admiringly. "So how often do you make it back to the island?"

"As often as I can," replied Digby. "Especially in the summer. It's my favorite time." He looked down to see her flute was empty. "Can I get you another glass of champagne?"

"That would be delightful."

Digby grabbed a glass from the tray of a passing waiter. "Here you are, Miss Hopper."

"Lisbeth, please," she said laughingly.

"Lisbeth," Digby smiled. "Since we are on a first-name basis, may I perhaps have the honor of inviting you to a picnic party on the beach tomorrow afternoon?"

"A beach picnic?"

"Yes. It's a bit of a tradition with our family. We have it every year and invite dozens of our relatives and friends to join us on Sconset beach for good food and drink. There will be a clambake, of course as well as lobster and nothing but the best wines. It is a wonderful event, I can assure you."

"That sounds lovely," replied Lisbeth.

"Wonderful!" exclaimed Digby. "Can I call on you around six tomorrow afternoon?"

"Of course. I'm staying at the Shanty; it's on Starbuck Lane."

"Perfect," said Digby. "Until then?" He reached for Lisbeth's hand and lightly kissed it.

"Until then," smiled Lisbeth.

Digby turned and walked away. Lisbeth excitedly sought out Percy to share the news.

* * *

Lisbeth woke to the chatter of her cottage mates. She rolled out of bed, careful of the low rafters, put on her robe, and made her way to the kitchen. Percy was sitting at their small table with their other two cottage mates, Sue Spilner and Daphne Waters. They were enjoying their morning coffee. Percy was reading to them from the newspaper in her hand.

"What is all the excitement?" she asked the group.

Percy smiled back at her. "Today's edition of the Inquirer and Mirror has a full review of the opening last night."

"And what does it say?" asked Lisbeth, a little apprehensive.

Percy snapped the paper open and read. "It says, and I quote, 'If anybody had the impression that Siasconset was a dull, sleepy place, devoid of any real pleasures, the illusion must have been dispelled last night when the first notable entertainment in the new Casino building was held. Performers from New York and London, including the esteemed Anne Gilbert, the lovely Percy Barnes, and the simply captivating Lisbeth Hopper, all appeared on the boards and portrayed delightful entertainment.'"

Percy put the paper down, smiling broadly. "Yay, us!"

Lisbeth laughed and smiled. "I'm so happy it was a success."

"And I'm sure you are happy that you met Digby?" said Percy, smiling.

"Yes, he was pleasant enough."

"Are you nervous about the picnic?" asked Daphne.

"No, not really. It's just been a while since I've been on a formal date. I would prefer to go as a group with all of you."

"You'll have a great time," said Percy. "And you know, I warned you that you might meet a rich, handsome man." She laughed at her own cleverness and took a sip of coffee.

* * *

Digby arrived at the Shanty on time. It was another perfect Nantucket day, the air cool and dry, a light breeze blowing from the south.

"Miss Hopper," said Digby at the door.

"So formal, Mr. Grey?"

Digby laughed and said, "Not at all, Lisbeth. Just trying to make a good impression."

"Consider it done. Ready?"

Digby held out his arm. "Absolutely."

Lisbeth inserted her arm through his, and together they strolled down the lane toward the beach.

"How are you finding Nantucket?"

"Oh, it has been a wonderful time. To be honest, I am going to have a hard time leaving in a few weeks."

"I know what you mean. I always hate to leave and return to the city. It is such a special place for me."

They slowly made their way to the beach and walked across the soft sand to the party. True to his promise, there were several dozen people there, all enjoying good food and drink. Before she knew it, the sun had set, and it was beginning to get dark. Fog had moved in, and the air felt chilled and damp. A large bonfire had been lit, and people gathered around it to warm themselves.

"Would you care to go for a walk with me," asked Digby. "The moon is due to rise shortly, and seeing it emerge from the ocean is truly spectacular."

"Of course," said Lisbeth excitedly and took his arm.

They walked down the beach along the waterline and soon were out of sight of the party. A few seagulls complained as they passed by. A slight breeze rustled the beach grass while the waves produced a dull roar. Above them, the sky was purple-black, and the first stars were beginning to emerge. Venus, shining brightly, held the audience in the southern sky.

Digby stopped and turned to Lisbeth. Holding her shoulders, he moved in and lightly kissed her mouth. Startled at his sudden move, Lisbeth stepped back.

"I have only just met you. I'm not that type of girl, regardless of what you might think of actors."

"Oh, c'mon. It's just a little kiss." He stepped closer to Lisbeth and wrapped his arms around her. He tried to kiss her again, this time more forcefully. His hand moved down to cup her breast.

"Digby! No!" She pushed herself back, trying to escape his embrace.

He grabbed her arms and pulled her in closer, his strength overpowering hers. Struggling, she wriggled an arm free and slapped him hard on the face.

He recoiled, his face contorted with anger. "Aah, you want it rough then?"

"No! I don't want it at all!" Scared, Lisbeth turned and desperately scanned around her for help. No one was near.

"You and I are going to have a little fun," said Digby menacingly. "I know you want to. But I appreciate the acting; I really do. Your virtue is safe with me. I promise I won't tell anyone."

"No!" screamed Lisbeth. "Help, help!" she yelled. The gulls looked at her curiously, the only ones to hear her plea.

"Come here! Kiss me the French way."

"No!" Lisbeth started to run, the heavy sand impeding her efforts. She was quickly out of breath and slowed.

Digby tackled her from behind and pinned her face into the sand. "Oh, come on. What's a little fun between friends?"

She wriggled beneath him, trying to get free, but his bulk held her down.

"Now relax. It will be a wonderful experience, I assure you. You will love it." He clumsily pushed her dress up and slipped himself out of his trousers.

A muffled scream came from the sand. Her body twisted and turned, trying to stop his assault. She tried one last time to throw him off her and nearly succeeded. Digby turned and grabbed a rock. With a swift motion, he struck the back of her head, silencing her scream immediately.

"That is so much better," he said. "Let me show you how much I care about you. Let me make you feel good."

Minutes later, finished, Digby stood up. He looked down at Lisbeth, her body quiet and still.

"Wasn't that wonderful?" he said. "I told you you would like it."

Lisbeth offered no response.

"Lisbeth?" He reached down and turned her over. Lisbeth's vacant eyes stared back, devoid of energy or life.

"Lisbeth!" yelled Digby, alarmed.

He shook her body and called her name repeatedly. She was gone.

Panicked, Digby grabbed her ankles and started dragging her toward the water. Her dress rose up to cover her face. Pulling her into the cold water, Digby stumbled and fell flat. Picking himself up, he again grabbed her ankles and worked her to deeper water, past the surf, to where the currents were strong. He felt her body go light and begin to pull away. He released her under the dim light of the newly risen moon. Venus watched as she rode the tide away.

CHAPTER TWELVE

F riday arrived all too slowly. Rob was looking forward to sharing what he had learned about Lisbeth and if he was honest with himself, excited to see Pip again. There was just something about her.

He hadn't washed the Wagoneer since he had arrived on the island, and it was dearly in need of a good cleaning both inside and out. Dead bugs from nine states and over a thousand miles still smeared the grill, hood, and windshield. Inside, scattered empty snack food bags and the detritus of many meals on the road covered the carpets and clung to the cushions. The dust from the shell street left a hazy white coating over the entire car. He had scoured the cottage for supplies and cobbled together a basic arsenal to bring the classic old Jeep into a more presentable position.

He was lost in thought while drying the navy blue paint and didn't notice the sound of footsteps crunching on the shells as they approached.

"Hey, Rob."

Startled, he turned to find Dee standing by the hood of the Wagoneer.

"Hi, Dee. You surprised me there!"

"Oh, sorry. I hope I didn't scare you."

"Not at all - I was just a bit lost in thought." Rob turned to dry some water from the old chrome bumper.

Dee nodded. "Rob?"

Rob stopped drying and looked up. "Yes?"

"About the other night. When you asked me about all the people you had seen around the village."

Rob stood upright and stared intently at Dee without saying a word.

"I'm afraid I wasn't totally honest with you. You see, there are not a lot of off-season residents in Sconset like you, probably just a handful. But there are what I would call more permanent residents that come and go during the winter," said Dee.

"You mean year-rounders?"

"Something like that."

"Oh, okay. Well, thanks for the clarification."

"Sure, Rob. I just didn't feel very neighborly after we talked the other night."

"That's quite alright. I just appreciate having someone else on the block with me. Would feel very lonely if it was just me here," said Rob.

Dee smiled softly back at him but didn't reply. Rob turned his attention to cleaning some stubborn bugs off the headlights.

"Well, I see you are busy. I'll leave you to it."

He looked up. "Sure thing. Enjoy the rest of your day."

"You too," Dee replied. She turned and walked back toward her cottage, her footsteps barely making a sound.

Rob continued cleaning the headlights as she watched her leave.

What was that all about?

He finished cleaning up the outside and turned his attention to the interior. Pulling out the floor mats, he shook them out to clean all of the sand and debris that had accumulated over the past couple of weeks. He quickly wiped down the dash and windows and finally gave a spritz of a lemon-scented cleaner into the carpets. He feared the inside smelled of old bourbon. Satisfied, he headed back into the house to change.

Rob had taken the time to freshen his wardrobe. Since he lost Sarah, he hadn't been able to do more than the occasional load of laundry, and his clothes had started to look worn and dated. Wanting to make a good impression, he went to town and shopped for some new clothes ending up with a pair of Nantucket Red slacks and a blue checked button-down. He finished the outfit with a pair of casual loafers the salesperson claimed was quite popular with the New England set.

He arrived at the Atheneum just as Pip was coming through the main door, her shift over. Rob opened his door, stood beside his car, and waved to her. She waved back and quickly made her way down the bricks and over to him.

"Nice car," she said, her face beaming with enthusiasm as always.

"Thanks," replied Rob. "It's been a good car but it gets really crappy mileage. And gas here is expensive!"

"The price we pay for living on an island thirty miles at sea," replied Pip. "Thanks for picking me up. Are you still game for some coffee?"

"Absolutely," said Rob. "And I have learned a lot about Lisbeth Hopper."

"Really? I'm curious."

Pip hopped into the passenger seat and closed the door. She looked around, admiring the leather seats and the clean interior. She glanced over at Rob and looked down at his pants, and laughed softly. "Are we turning you into an islander?"

"What do you mean?" Rob asked cautiously.

"You're wearing Nantucket Reds."

Rob looked down at his pants and back up to Pip. He was blushing slightly. "I really needed some new clothes, and the salesperson said these were popular here."

Pip laughed out loud, her eyes bright. "Oh, Rob, you are too cute!"

Embarrassed, Rob asked, "What's wrong with them?"

Pip stopped laughing and placed her hand on his shoulder. "Absolutely nothing. I'm sorry. I just find it endearing that you want to be more like us natives." She gently rubbed his shoulder.

"Hmm, okay," said Rob, unassured. "Where to?" he asked with more confidence than he felt.

"Let's go to my favorite coffee shop. It's on Old South Road, close to the airport," she replied.

Rob started the car and pulled out. After a couple of blocks, he turned onto Main Street, and the old Wagoneer began swaying heavily side to side over the cobblestones.

Pip looked around the interior of the old Jeep and glanced behind her. Touching the leather armrest, she said, "This really is a nice car. Are you the original owner?"

Rob laughed, "No, I actually just bought it a few weeks ago, mainly because I knew I was coming here and I wanted four-wheel drive."

"Hmm," said Pip. "Well, you picked a beauty. Oh, turn left here."

Rob turned onto Orange street and accelerated up the shallow hill. He looked over at Pip. "It is nice, but it cost me dearly. I bought it on an online auction site and made the mistake of having a few whiskey's during the last hour of the auction. I got in a bidding war with someone from Florida, and though I won, I did spend way more than I had planned to." Rob rubbed the dashboard. "But she is a nice car. I call her the not-so-cheap Jeep."

Pip laughed. "I love that! What year is it?"

"1982," said Rob. "Actually, just about as old as me."

Pip smiled. "My dad had a '79. It was beige with a brown interior. Talk about bland! But his rusted out badly, and he got rid of it when I was still pretty young. I have pictures of me riding in it, but I really don't remember it. He would love this."

"Well, maybe I can take him for a ride sometime," said Rob.

"Definitely," said Pip.

As they drove, Pip pointed out local landmarks from her youth; where she went for piano lessons, the lumberyard where she worked summers, and her favorite sandwich shop. Before he knew it, they had pulled into the small shell parking lot of the coffee shop. Like just about every other building on the island, it sported faded cedar shake shingles on the walls and roof and was trimmed in white.

"Looks cute," said Rob.

Pip smiled. "It is. And it is owned by some friends of our family. I've been coming here since they opened. And so much better than those national chains."

"I wondered about that, why I hadn't seen any. I would think they would flourish here."

"Well, they probably would if they were allowed."

"Wait. Franchises aren't allowed?" asked Rob.

"Nope," replied Pip. "That's why we don't have any fast food places or any of those other national chains that are cookie-cutter versions of places in California, Florida, or wherever. It's how we keep the island authentic."

"Refreshing," said Rob.

They got out of the car and made their way in. Ordering a couple of lattes, they made their way over to a table by the window overlooking a freshly mown lawn bordering a forest laden with pine trees and scrub oaks.

"So what did you find out about her?" asked Pip.

"Lisbeth?"

"Yes. Was she brutally murdered, or is all of that just a tall tale they told us kids?"

"Well, all signs point to the fact that she was murdered. She was found washed up on the beach down by Tom Nevers and dressed apparently for an elegant afternoon picnic. The stories I read suggested that a wealthy Wall Street banker, some guy named Digby Grey, was likely the killer, but they didn't have enough evidence to pursue the case. Not to mention that he was a very prominent businessman whereas she was just an actress."

"That's certainly no excuse!" exclaimed Pip.

"Of course not," said Rob. "But different times."

Pip's face was set determinedly. "An actress, really?"

"Yes, apparently had a very promising career, but that all ended that August night on the beach. Here, I printed out a picture of her for you." Rob pulled a folder sheet of paper out of his pocket and handed it to Pip.

Pip unfolded the paper and stared deeply into the picture. The picture was taken the night of her performance at the Casino, and she was in costume. "Wow, she was beautiful."

Rob smiled sadly and nodded. "Yes, she was. And apparently very talented as well. She was also very young, and many expected her to go far."

Laying the picture down on the table, Pip said, "So sad. And so pointless. All so some rich guy could get his kicks. And they never caught him?"

"As I said, he was a wealthy banker from New York. Not enough evidence to pursue."

"Wasn't there anyone there to protect her? To pursue justice for her?"

"She was staying with a group of women - and yes, they were staying in the cottage I'm renting no less - and they tried to get the police to arrest Grey, but it proved fruitless. No evidence. There were a dozen or so other actors that supported the arrest, but in the end, they did nothing. When September rolled around, they all packed up and headed back to New York. Everyone here seemed to forget the whole incident."

"That is just so sad," said Pip. She picked up the picture again and stared at it silently. After a few moments, she said, "I wish there was something we could do for her."

"Like what?" asked Rob.

"I don't know. Some kind of memorial to her. Some recognition of her life. It all just seems like such a waste." Pip put the picture back down on the table. "Did you, by chance, see anything about her ghost?"

Rob smiled, happy at the change of topic. "Oh, there was a mention or two about that, but always around Halloween. So I suspect it was just some local pranksters pulling something off."

"Huh," said Pip, hoping for more.

She took a sip of her latte and stared out the window. Slowly she turned and looked at Rob. "So, what do you think of Nantucket so far?"

"It's been nice. Very different from St. Louis, that's for sure."

"In a good way?"

"Yes, definitely. It's been good to get away; try somewhere new."

"Are you here alone?" Pip asked.

Rob looked down at the mug in his hands and spoke without looking up. "Yes. I lost my wife about six months ago. Cancer."

"Oh, Rob. I'm so sorry."

"Thank you," said Rob. "It was the worst thing I ever went through. Coming here has been an escape for me. Everywhere I went in St. Louis reminded me of her."

"How long were you married?"

"Ten years. I met her just after I graduated from college."

"How did you guys meet?" asked Pip.

Rob smiled wanly. "She needed change."

"Change?"

"Yes, for the dryer. I was a year out of college and living in an apartment in St. Louis. I was at a laundromat, and she was short a few quarters to finish her load. So she asked me if I had change for a dollar. We struck up a conversation, and then one thing led to another," his voice trailing off, his eyes getting wet.

Pip reached out and placed her hand on top of his. "I didn't mean to stir up anything painful."

Rob smiled and slowly withdrew his hand. "That's okay. You didn't know. And honestly, being here has really helped me grieve. I still wake up thinking about her, missing her, but every day the pain seems to lessen a little bit."

"What did you do in St. Louis?"

"I ran a handyman company. I'm an engineer by training but found that office life wasn't for me. So I put up my own shingle and started a business. Fortunately, Sarah was very successful - she was an executive with a major St. Louis company - so I didn't need to worry too much about earning a lot at first. But over time, I did okay."

"Kids?"

Rob shook his head slowly. "No. Not even a dog. Not that we didn't want to. But when we started trying, it was too late. That's how they found her cancer."

Pip stared intently at Rob and said, "I can't imagine how hard that must have been on you."

"Thank you. But enough about me. Tell me a little about you."

Pip sighed and sat back in her chair. "Not a whole lot to say, really. I was born and raised here on the island. My dad works for the Steamship Authority, and my mom is a nurse at the hospital. I graduated from Nantucket High - go Whalers! - and then went off island to college."

"Was it tough leaving the island?" asked Rob.

"Not so much tough as it was…different. This is really such a small and unique community. I knew just about all the year-rounders and a bunch of the summer people. And everything is just self-contained here. Over there," she crooked her thumb over her shoulder and continued, "it's big. People don't seem to care as much about each other. I just never really felt comfortable."

She paused and took a sip of her latte.

"When I graduated, I got a job in consulting, one of the 'Big Four'," she held up her arms in air quotes. "But I was miserable. I was traveling non-stop, and I hated the work. So after a few years, I quit and came back here. I started at the Atheneum a few weeks after I got back. It's been almost five years now."

Rob looked at her, an admiring smile on his face. "And you are happy here?"

"Yes, absolutely. I mean, I know I don't make anywhere near the money I did as a consultant, but my life is simpler, fuller, and by far happier. Besides, I get to meet a lot of interesting people. Like you." She smiled.

Rob returned her smile.

Pip glanced at her watch. "Oh, I better get going."

"So soon?"

"Sorry. I volunteer over at the Whaling Museum, and they are having a major event there tomorrow night. A fundraiser." Pip started to stand and stopped. "Actually, do you have any plans for tomorrow night?"

"Me? Um, no. My calendar is pretty open for the next six months," Rob chuckled.

"Then join me."

"At a fundraiser? I'm not sure I would fit in with all of those wealthy Nantucket people."

Pip smacked his shoulder teasingly. "You would fit in just fine. Besides, the Whaling Museum is awesome, and I could give you a tour. I know you are interested in whaling, at least by the books you checked out this week."

Rob smiled, "Very true. Okay, I'm in. Shall I pick you up?"

"Probably better if we meet there. I need to be there early to help with set-up. So why don't you shoot for seven."

"Got it. I will look forward to it."

"And Rob," said Pip. "Please don't wear those pants."

Rob looked down at his pants and then back up at Pip. They both burst out laughing.

CHAPTER THIRTEEN

J ack sat in the library at Gratitude. There was a fire roaring in the hearth and a freshly poured glass of bourbon on the side table. He stared deeply into the fire and thought about making Three disappear. The idea scared yet thrilled him. But he was also very troubled at how quickly this turn had come about. They had been married barely four years. One had lasted over ten years. Two had been closer to eight. Was he really down to four years? This was a trend line that was not going to be sustainable. At this rate, he would be going through a woman every year or two. Managing that and not getting caught would take nothing short of a miracle.

He had barely been successful with One. There had been a lot of raised eyebrows with her death. Two had brought wary sympathy. When Three died, assuming the next year or two, how would he execute that without raising suspicion? It was the sort of puzzle he relished, but the stakes were high. He would not survive prison. The death of Three would have to be clearly not his fault, out of his control.

A solution needed to be found fairly quickly as he was losing control of her. Even though it had only been four years, he was seeing the same warning signs he had seen with Two. She was pushing back. It wasn't much right now. Some passive-aggressive actions, such as serving him weak coffee - he had fixed that with a slap across the face - and some outright defiance, such as disappearing at social functions. He wasn't really worried about that; he knew she couldn't go far. They were on an island, she had very little money and no real friends. And she could complain about him all she wanted, but no one would believe her. He was Jack Reiner, after all, a leading philanthropist and a major pillar of the community. No, her behavior was annoying but not concerning. It was the control issue that really bothered him.

But that puzzle would have to wait. First, he had to get through tonight successfully.

Tonight was very important to him. They were attending a major fundraiser at the Whaling Museum, and he needed to make a great impression with the current board. He had always been very generous with the Museum and had donated millions over the years. But he wanted more. He wanted some control. And it wasn't like a wife he could force to submit to his desires. Now he would need to persuade and charm them to get his way. His donations would help, but he would also be judged on his character. And even though it didn't make sense to him, he would be judged based on his relationship with his wife. Was he loving, caring, thoughtful? Was he a kind man? One who would care for the Museum as he would a wife?

Thinking of that expectation brought a wry smile to his face. Yes, he was the perfect example of a family man and a caring husband. He had killed the first two and was seriously thinking about how to eliminate the third. Doesn't that make him a good candidate? I can bring a lot of value to a family-focused organization such as this. He almost spit out his bourbon on that one.

His mind wandered back to the possibilities with Three. How could he manage her disappearance? The good news was that he had time. Her resistance was still weak, and he could manage her effectively with some force. But he knew from experience that force over time would likely increase her resistance, not weaken it. So the time was coming. He figured he probably had a year, two at the most, before he would have to address the issue head-on.

But how to do it? The First had drowned swimming. The Second had "run away." What was Three going to do? Car accident? Plane crash? Could he somehow make it look like natural causes - cancer or a heart attack? Given his first two, though, there would be some natural suspicions. He could always hire someone to do it for him but abhorred the loss of control. And given his wealth, subsequent blackmail was always a possibility. No, he had to manage it directly.

Ideally, it would happen with plenty of witnesses and alleviate him of any possible guilt. People would likely then just feel sorry for him, a cursed man who had lost three wives. He chuckled at the thought of their pity. He had always enjoyed brain teasers, even from a young age, and this one would keep him busy for a while. He would enjoy putting his imagination to work.

Jack took a final sip of his bourbon and stood up. Time to make sure Emily knows the ground rules for the evening. He walked up the stairs and into their master bedroom. Emily sat in a wingback chair by the window, her eyes staring vacantly out onto the moors below, her auburn hair disheveled and spilling over her face.

"I need you to be on your best behavior tonight," said Jack. "I want to get a board seat at the Museum, and that takes more than money. You need to help convince them that I'm perfect for the position."

Emily turned her head away from the window and slowly locked her eyes on Jack's. Her face was tired, and her eyes red.

"You need to get yourself cleaned up and presentable," Jack said forcefully. "And I'd like you to wear that black gown you wore last year at the MOMA gala."

Emily stared back, her arms crossed.

"And the whale pin with the diamonds. It will send a very subtle but powerful message to the board."

Emily remained silent.

"Finally, no more than two glasses of wine."

She looked up at him and whispered, "And what if I don't?"

Despite his size, Jack was quick, and he closed the distance between them in a heartbeat. Emily recoiled back, her eyes wide in terror. Jack got in her face and said threateningly, "You know, I made my first two wives disappear, and trust me, I can easily do it again. And the way I feel right now, I am about ready to make that happen!"

He scowled at his wife and raised his hand to strike her. Emily sunk back into the chair as far as she could and lifted her hands to defend herself.

Jack slowly lowered his hand, but his face was still red with anger. He slowly pulled back from her. "Now, can I count on you to behave tonight?"

Emily looked back at him like a doe looking down a hunter's rifle. She whispered weakly, "Yes."

Jack cupped a hand to his ear. "What was that? I didn't hear you."

"Yes," said Emily a little louder. "You can count on me."

"Good," said Jack. "Be ready by 6:30. I don't want to be late." He turned and walked out of the room, closing the door behind him.

Emily curled into a ball in the chair and wept.

CHAPTER FOURTEEN

R ob was feeling a bit nervous as he drove to town. Pip had warned him about all of the deer on the island, and the feeble headlights of the forty-year-old Jeep weren't doing a very good job of lighting his way. The last thing he wanted to do was to hit Bambi. He kept his speed down, and his eyes scanned the road ahead vigilantly. Before he knew it, he was at the rotary, and he veered right onto Orange Street. Minutes later, he eased into a parking spot just down from the Whaling Museum.

He got out of the car and slipped his blazer on. He had heeded Pip's advice and had worn some simple khakis and a light blue button-down from his meager wardrobe. Combined with the coat, he hoped he would be presentable enough. He walked the block to the museum and stopped at the main entrance. He was anxious. What would these people think of a midwestern boy? Would they mock his accent or his clothes? He briefly entertained the idea of reversing course and just going back to the cottage. But he thought of Pip, took a deep breath, and opened the door.

A rush of warm air greeted him, along with the sounds of dozens of people talking, laughing, and clearly enjoying themselves. He stopped in the foyer.

"I see you took my advice."

Rob turned to see Pip smiling at him. She was dressed in a modest skirt and blouse. Despite her simple attire, she looked amazing.

"I did. I hope it's okay," Rob said nervously.

"It's perfect, actually. You'll fit right in."

"Thank you. By the way, you look great."

Pip smiled and looked down at her skirt and blouse. "Thanks. I don't worry too much about clothes and just kind of cobbled this outfit together."

"Well, it works. Trust me," Rob said and smiled warmly. "Have you been here long?"

"Just a couple of hours," replied Pip. "We had a bunch of set-up to do. And I needed to help the caterers get organized. But we got it all finished without any problems. I think it is going to be a fun and successful night."

"I've been looking forward to it. So tell me a bit more about the museum."

Pip guided him out of the foyer and walked him into a large hall. A massive whale skeleton hung from the ceiling. Under it were dozens of people sipping cocktails and enjoying hors d'oeuvres.

"Well, the museum has been here for years, since 1930, to be exact. The building much longer. Originally they made candles here - very high-quality ones from the oil inside a sperm whale's head, called spermaceti. Actually, from whales such as this one," and she pointed at the skeleton hanging from the ceiling.

"But with the decline of the whaling industry in the late 1800s, so went the candle factory. The building was used for storage and even an antique shop, but the Historical Association bought it in 1929 for the expressed purpose of starting a museum."

"That is fascinating," said Rob.

"Yes, it is. And the impetus to start the museum came from the donation of a large private collection of whaling-related items from a seasonal resident."

"Really?"

"Yes. And there are all kinds of exhibits. I can show you a few, but you'll really need to come back and go through it properly. It's probably the neatest thing on Nantucket."

"I'll add it to my to-do list."

"Excellent," said Pip, her face beaming. "How about a drink?"

"Absolutely."

Pip slipped her arm in his and walked him over to the temporary bar set up in the corner of the room.

"What'll you have?" asked Pip.

Rob looked at the bartender, "Bourbon and water, please."

Pip smiled and turned to the bartender. "Same."

Rob looked at Pip with surprise. "You like bourbon?"

"Love it. It's really all I drink except maybe an occasional glass of wine."

"Hmm," said Rob. "Not what I expected."

"What, you thought I'd be drinking hard seltzer or a cider?" Pip said teasingly.

Rob blushed. "Sorry. I wasn't really sure what you'd like. But bourbon is a surprise. A pleasant one. Do you have a favorite?"

"Angel's Envy Rye, when I can get it. Otherwise, Knob Creek. You?"

"I'm a Weller's man myself. Preferably the twelve year. But I enjoy Buffalo Trace as well."

"I think I'm going to like you," said Pip smiling broadly.

The bartender handed them their glasses. Rob turned to Pip. "To you. Thanks for being my first friend on the island."

"And to you," said Pip. "Thanks for not wearing those pants." They clinked glasses and took a sip.

"Is it me, or does bourbon just taste better in the fall?" asked Pip.

Rob smiled. "It is definitely best in cooler weather." Rob took another sip and looked above him. "That whale skeleton is really amazing."

Pip's eyes followed his upward. "Yes, it is. And a pretty cool story as well. As I mentioned, it's from a sperm whale. The whale was found washed ashore, dead, on Low Beach, just down from Sconset, back in the late nineties. They petitioned the federal government to keep the skeleton for the museum, and that request was granted a year or so later. It took a few years to clean the bones thoroughly and then reassemble them here. But the end result is nothing short of fantastic! It is one of our most popular attractions."

"I can see why," said Rob.

Looking past Rob, Pip said, "Oh, there is someone I think I should say hello to. He's a very generous donor and looking to get more involved. Join me?"

"Sure."

Pip led them across the room to where Jack and Emily were standing and talking to the museum director.

"Mr. Reiner?" asked Pip.

Jack turned toward Pip, his size almost overwhelming the space between them.

"Oh, hi. Tip is it?" he said condescendingly and held out his hand.

"Uh, Pip, sir. So good to see you." Pip shook his hand.

"Nice to see you as well. Have you met my wife, Emily?"

"I haven't had the pleasure." Pip turned to Emily and shook her hand.

"Let me introduce Rob McGlynn. He is new to the island."

Rob held out his hand. "Nice to meet you, Mr. Reiner." As their hands touched, a feeling of dread washed over him. A vision of a woman's body floating in the surf swirled through his mind.

Oh my god, who is this man?

"Is something wrong?"

Rob, clearly upset, blurted out, "Um no, no…. I'm okay. Sorry. Just… I don't know." He slowly withdrew his hand, but his eyes remained locked on Jack's.

A little rattled, Jack, said, "And this is my wife, Emily Reiner."

"Hello," said Rob, taking her hand. It felt cold and clammy in his as if he was shaking hands with a corpse. "Nice to meet you," he stumbled.

"And you," said Emily robotically, her eyes glazed and vacant.

"Excuse us," said Jack tersely, and grabbing his wife's elbow, walked her briskly away.

Pip quickly turned to look at Rob. "What was all that about?"

"I don't know," replied Rob. "It's just something there is not right. Shaking his hand, I just got the weirdest feeling."

"A feeling like what?"

Rob was quiet for a moment before responding. "Death."

"Death?"

"Yes. The last time I felt that was in the cancer ward with my wife. The day before she died."

Pip was quiet for a moment. "I am sure he is okay. He is a very wealthy contributor whose family has been part of the island fabric for many generations. He lives in a big house off Polpis Road, just past the turn for Wauwinet. He can be a bit gruff sometimes - I've heard a few stories - but I think he's okay."

"And what about her?" asked Rob. "She seemed almost in a daze."

"She's probably just not feeling well."

"I'm not sure. It seems like more than that."

Before she could respond, a voice behind her said, "Hello, Pip."

Broken from the moment, she turned and smiled. "Hello, Mr. Bois! I was hoping I would see you tonight."

"It is nice to see you. All well?"

"Yes, doing great. How about you?"

"No complaints. Is this a friend of yours?"

"Oh, I am so sorry," said Pip, embarrassed. "Peter Bois, I'd like you to meet Rob McGlynn."

"Nice to meet you, Rob," said Peter and extended his hand.

Rob took his hand. His grip was firm, warm, and dry. "Pleasure to meet you, sir," said Rob. "Are you involved in the museum?"

Pip interrupted. "Involved? I'd say! Mr. Bois has given millions to the museum and is one of our most passionate advocates. He's also on the board and is helping to shape our future direction."

"Impressive," said Rob. "What got you interested in the Whaling Museum?"

Peter paused. "It was nothing, really. I found out that I had some family that were whalers back in the 19th century. They sailed on a Nantucket whaler called the Paragon. That kind of sparked my interest, and I wanted to learn more about it."

Pip turned to Rob. "He's being very humble. Mr. Bois knows more about the Paragon and the acts of whaling than anyone I've ever met." She turned to Peter. "It's almost like you were there!"

Peter blushed and stammered out a response. "Well, um, I've just done a lot of reading on the subject. It's become a passion of mine now that I'm retired."

"What did you do before you got into, um, whaling, Mr. Bois?" Rob asked and took a sip of his bourbon.

"Please, call me Peter," he said, smiling. "I ran a plastics company in Connecticut. We sold it a few years ago, and now I spend my time here on the island with my wife and kids."

Pip stepped in. "Please don't sell yourself short." She again turned to Rob. "Mr. Bois's company invented a new type of plastic that breaks down in saltwater. He licensed that technology to other plastics companies and used those funds to start a new foundation on the island called The Jack Tate & Tristam Coffin Foundation."

"Interesting," said Rob, impressed. "Were those your family members?"

Peter took a sip of his drink. "Actually, no. Jack Tate was a dear friend of mine growing up. Unfortunately, he drowned off the south shore back in 1994. Tristam Coffin was a first mate on the Paragon and a direct ancestor of Jack's. So it seemed very fitting to honor both of them."

"I think that's wonderful," said Rob. "What does the foundation focus on?"

"Our work is focused on enhancing the lives of the people on Nantucket. Our primary areas of investment include affordable housing, family services, conservation, and finally, arts & culture, like the Whaling Museum."

An elegant woman with short brown hair and energetic blue eyes appeared at his elbow. "Please don't get him started," she said teasingly. "He could talk about the foundation and Nantucket for hours."

"My wife knows me all too well," said Peter, smiling warmly. He put his arm around her waist. "Rob, this is my wife, Charlotte."

"Nice to meet you, Charlotte," said Rob.

"And you," said Charlotte. "And do I detect a bit of a midwest accent there?"

Rob blushed. "Yes, I am from St. Louis. I've only been on the island for a week or so."

"Are you really?" Charlotte exclaimed. "So am I!"

"You're from St. Louis? How did you end up here?" Rob asked excitedly.

"Peter and I met in college. One thing led to another, and well, here I am," said Charlotte laughing.

Soon Rob and Charlotte were in a heated exchange about all things St. Louis; neighborhoods, favorite restaurants, the Cardinals, and of course, which high school they both went to. Pip and Peter watched them talk and laughed at their shared passion.

"Okay, you two," said Peter, interrupting them. "We need to circulate."

Charlotte reluctantly stepped back. "So fun to meet you, Rob. I hope we get a chance to talk about home again. And I hope you enjoy your time here. It truly is a magical place."

"Thank you. I really enjoyed our discussion and will look forward to more," said Rob smiling. And turning to Peter, "It was a pleasure to meet you, sir. I would love to hear more about your work here on the island."

"I would enjoy that. Please feel free to stop by our offices. We are on Main Street. Pip can show you where," and nodded at Pip.

"I sure can," said Pip. Peter and Charlotte walked away holding hands. Charlotte whispered something into Peter's ear, and he laughed.

Taking Rob's arm, Pip said, "Now let me show you something else. My favorite spot at the museum."

They walked through the large hall to a spiral staircase. Rob followed Pip as they made their way up the narrow, winding steps. At the top of the stairs, they walked through a door and out onto a rooftop deck.

"Welcome to Tucker's Roofwalk!"

Rob was speechless. Spread out in front of him was Nantucket Harbor, lights twinkling on the water accompanied by the slow pulse of red from the Brant Point lighthouse. Above, a black velvet sky was ablaze with stars. The air was chilly and damp, a slight breeze rustling through the trees.

"This is amazing," said Rob breathlessly.

"Yes, it is," replied Pip. "You can see why it's my favorite spot here. And I'll tell you a secret."

"What's that?"

"When I get married, I want to have the ceremony right here."

"That certainly would be amazing. Do you have someone in mind?"

Pip went quiet. Clearly, he had touched a nerve.

"I'm sorry. I didn't mean to pry."

"It's okay. Ancient history." She paused, unsure of how much she really wanted to say. Finally, she turned and looked at Rob. "When I was working as a consultant, I was living in Boston and met this guy through a colleague. I won't say it was love at first sight, but we hit it off, and it turned serious pretty quickly. On our first anniversary of meeting, he asked to marry me."

"Sounds wonderful. What happened?"

"Let's just say it turned out we had different value systems."

"How so?"

She let out a long sigh and looked out over the water. "Embezzlement."

"Embezzlement?"

Pip snorted. "Yep. He was a crook. He was a CPA by training and was working in the accounting department of a large software company. He thought he could supplement his income by making himself a vendor to the firm, creating fake invoices, and then paying them by cutting himself checks from the company."

"Wow."

"Yeah. It was actually very clever. He made it work for almost two years but was discovered through an annual audit. All told, he had made off with nearly a hundred thousand. I learned about it when they came to our apartment to arrest him."

"Oh, Pip. That must have been shocking."

"That's putting it mildly. You think you know someone. You are ready to spend your life with them. And then you find out who they really are. But at least there's a bright side."

"A bright side?" asked Rob, surprised.

"Well, I learned about it before I married him. And it was the catalyst that led me back to Nantucket. So as my grandmother likes to say, it all worked out in the end."

Rob smiled and, anxious to change the topic, said, "I can see why Charlotte called this place magical."

"It certainly is. But unfortunately, I need to get back downstairs. I am supposed to be working the silent bid table and do not want to neglect my duties."

"Oh, okay," said Rob, disappointedly.

"You stay. Enjoy the view. Find me when you can."

Rob smiled. "Will do."

Pip took one last glance over the harbor and then slowly retreated through the door.

Rob watched her leave and then turned back toward the water. Certainly, Missouri had some beautiful scenery but nothing like this. This was spectacular. And he was starting to understand the lure of the water. Being from the landlocked midwest, he had always been a bit skeptical about the stories he had heard about the romance of the sea. But he was starting to get it.

An hour passed quickly, and he reluctantly pulled himself from the view. He headed downstairs, taking his time to look at a few of the exhibits. He found Pip actively engaged in conversation and thought it best to take his leave and let her focus on her duties for the evening.

He slid up behind her and whispered in her ear, "Good night, and thank you."

Pip turned quickly. "Leaving so soon?" she asked, clearly disappointed.

"I am. But I had a wonderful time. Thank you for inviting me. I will definitely be back to enjoy the museum more thoroughly."

"Well, drive safely," said Pip and gave him a quick peck on the cheek. "And look out for deer."

"I will. And I'll see you at the library."

She smiled in return and then turned back to her group.

Rob headed out of the museum and walked the block to his car. It had been a long time since he had enjoyed an evening like this. As he drove home, thoughts of the night replayed in his mind, and he found himself smiling. It was the first time he had felt himself since he had lost Sarah. He felt pangs of guilt that he was having fun without her but reflected on their conversation in the hospital shortly before she died. He knew in his heart that she would want him to be happy and have nights like this.

I think she would like Pip.

He made his way back to the cottage and, grabbing a bourbon, walked down the hall and out onto the patio. He settled into one of the Adirondacks and looked up at the blanket of stars above him. He was no astronomer, but he did recognize many of the common constellations. He could see the big dipper very low on the northern horizon. Following a straight line from the right edge of the cup, he quickly found Polaris and the tail of the small dipper. He turned and angled his head to the south and easily found Orion's Belt. With the clear night, he could even make out Orion's sword.

Rob took a sip of bourbon and thought of the many times they would lay on a blanket and look up at the stars. The light pollution from the city often washed out many of the fainter constellations, but they were almost always guaranteed to see a falling star or a satellite transiting above them as it made its way around the globe. Almost on cue, a meteor streaked across the sky, burning brightly enough to briefly make it feel like daytime.

Was that a sign from Sarah?

The thought made him both happy and sad. Happy to think that maybe indeed, she was able to communicate with him from wherever she was, but sad that he was here, in the chilly evening, alone. Lost in thoughts about her, he stared at the sky for hours and managed to finish off his first bottle of bourbon. He made a mental note that he would need to restock on his next trip to town.

Taking a last glance at the stars, Rob stumbled his way into the house and shuffled into the bedroom. He dropped his clothes on the floor, gathered the sheets on the unmade bed, and slid inside. In seconds, with the help of some of Kentucky's finest, he was fast asleep and blissfully unaware that his time on Nantucket was about to change drastically and alter his life forever.

CHAPTER FIFTEEN

The sun filtered through the window and landed directly in Rob's eyes. Wincing, he sat up quickly and leaned over to the bedside table for his phone, the screen informing him that it was well after ten o'clock. A quick view of the weather app told him to expect a sunny but chilly day with highs only in the fifties. He put the phone down and massaged his forehead where a Kentucky grain-induced hangover had made itself comfortable.

Ugh. I probably could have skipped that last bourbon. Or two.

He slowly swung his legs over the edge of the bed and stood up. He went to the bureau and grabbed some jeans and thick socks. Pulling a sweatshirt over his head, he plodded his way down the hall to the kitchen and fired up the coffee maker. Sarah had always made a habit of preparing the machine the night before, and Rob silently thanked her for instilling in him the same routine. He grabbed a large cup from the cabinet and some cream from the fridge while the maker popped and bubbled away. As soon as the level reached a few inches, Rob grabbed the pot and filled his cup with the strongest brew.

Standing by the sink, his hands wrapped around the warm mug of coffee, he stared out over the hedges and took in one of the bluest skies he had ever seen. His mind wandered to his evening with Pip. Clearly, she must like him, no? She seemed so pleased to see him and had spent a lot of her evening with him. And she had wanted to introduce him around. But after years of being out of the dating scene, he really did not trust his instincts and thought he was probably being too optimistic where she was concerned. She probably just liked him as a friend. Further clouding his thoughts, despite the promise he made to Sarah, he was struggling to even imagine himself with another woman.

A soft knock on the front door snapped him out of his internal debate.

He walked through the main room and, looking through the small window on the door, could see Dee standing there, her long brown hair waving in the breeze. Rob struggled a bit with the old latch before he was able to get the door open. Dee was standing on his doorstep.

"Good morning," said Rob.

"Good morning," replied Dee, smiling faintly. Her cheeks were white despite the cold. "How are you doing this morning?"

"I'm good. Thanks. How are you?"

"I'm well." She paused, the silence a bit awkward.

"Good. Erm, what can I do for you?" Rob asked finally, anxious to break the quiet.

Dee looked up at him expectantly, her brown eyes shining with intensity.

"Is everything alright?"

"Yes, it is. I'm sorry. I was just going to ask if you wanted to take a walk with me."

Startled, Rob blurted out, "Oh, of course. Sure." He started to go back into the house, stopped, and turned back to Dee. "Can you give me just a minute? I need to grab my coat and refill my coffee." He paused. "Actually, would you like to come in? And would you like some coffee?"

Dee looked past him into the cottage. A look of anxiety passed quickly over her face. "Thanks, I'm good. I'll just wait outside. And please take your time. I know this is a bit out of the blue."

Rob went back into the house, returning quickly wearing a light windbreaker and a fresh cup of coffee, now steaming away in a silver travel mug. "Which way would you like to go?"

"Would you mind if we walk towards Ocean Avenue?"

"Not at all," replied Rob. "It's my favorite view on the island," adding with a smile, "maybe even the planet."

Dee smiled knowingly. "It absolutely is."

They walked through the fence, closed the gate with the latch clicking loudly, and turned left on Starbuck Lane. The crunch of shells under his feet was the only sound disturbing the late-morning stillness.

"So, how is the book coming?"

Rob turned to her, frowning. "Unfortunately, it isn't."

"Isn't?"

"Isn't coming. At all."

"I'm sorry."

"It's okay. I mean, honestly, I don't know what I'm expecting or why I thought I could do this."

Dee looked at him. "Well, if it were easy, then everyone would do it."

Rob stopped walking and stared at her, his eyes wide. Just then, Dee started laughing, and Rob quickly followed suit.

"Thank you for that," Rob said after the laughter finally subsided. "I always thought that was the lamest quote ever."

"Me as well," said Dee. "My mom used to say that to me growing up when I was struggling with something - schoolwork, ballet classes, and especially my piano lessons. It always struck me as the most inane and inappropriate thing to say. It was like she wasn't sure how to manage my struggles. Honestly, a simple hug or some words of understanding would have worked much better."

"I couldn't agree more," said Rob. After pausing, he said, "I do think there is a book inside me. I know there is. But I am just struggling to come up with a good storyline."

"Can I hit you with another lame quote?" asked Dee, smiling.

"Sure."

"Write what you know."

Rob chuckled. "Creative writing 101, right?"

Dee paused. "I'm not a writer. But maybe it's a good idea just to get started."

"Well, I have a confession to make. I've been trying that approach since I got here and have yet to produce a solid paragraph."

"I'm sorry. It must be so difficult. But I'm sure it will come to you."

"Thanks. I'm not giving up yet. It's a promise I made to my wife, Sarah, and a goal I've had for years. It will take a lot more than a few weeks of frustration to make me abandon this dream."

Dee looked up and smiled at him. "Good."

They walked for a few minutes in comfortable silence. He took a sip of his coffee.

"So you've been to the Whaling Museum?" asked Dee, more of a statement than a question.

"Yes, last night, in fact. How did you know?" asked Rob, a bit shocked she knew his movements.

"I have my ways," said Dee teasingly.

"Hmm, I guess this island is pretty small, after all." He took another sip before continuing, "There was a fundraiser for the museum. The librarian, Pip, from the Atheneum invited me."

"That sounds fun. I haven't met her, but I'm sure she's nice. Are you two dating?"

Rob almost spit out his coffee. "Oh, no. Just friends."

"Interesting," said Dee. "I'm wondering if maybe you met my ex-husband."

"Really?" said Rob, surprised at the question. "What's his name?"

"Jack Reiner."

Rob stopped in his tracks and stared at Dee. "He was your husband?"

"Yes. Tell me why you seem so shocked."

"Well, it's just…I don't know. You seem so nice. And he seems like…"

"An asshole?" Dee interrupted.

"Yes."

Dee grunted and said. "Let me tell you, if he were only just an asshole, my life would have been so different."

"I'm so sorry. I had no idea you were married to such a man."

"It's funny, you know. When you meet someone, you fall in love, and you think you know them. Sometimes they turn out to be exactly who you think they are, and sometimes, well, sometimes they couldn't be farther from your expectations."

"Is that what happened with you and Jack?"

Dee looked straight ahead as she answered, "At first, he was exactly the man I fell in love with; caring, thoughtful, fun. But as time went by, he changed. By the time we separated, he could not have been more different."

"How so? If you don't mind me asking."

"Not at all," she replied, looking out over the water. The waves glittered under the sun, marred only by a few passing seagulls. "The changes started a few years after we were married. It was so subtle at first that I didn't even realize it was happening. But then it became much more pronounced as he started to try and control everything I did; where I went, who I talked to, what I read and watched even. At first, I tried to laugh it off, trying to convince myself he was just really caring about me. But then he hit me."

"Hit you?" Rob replied, shocked.

"Yes. We had been invited to a party, and I just didn't really want to go. It was the end of the summer, and we had been to one event after another. I was tired and, to be honest, wanted to just stay home and relax. But he wouldn't have it. At first, he asked nicely, but then that quickly turned to demanding when I wouldn't acquiesce. When I still refused, he punched me so hard in my stomach that I collapsed on the floor."

"Oh, Dee, that must have been awful."

"It was. And then only got worse. His violence with me became directly proportional to how much I resisted him. The more I pushed back, the more physical he was."

They continued walking, the beauty of the scenery around them spoiled by the age-old acts of a cruel man on a caring and loving woman.

"Why didn't you leave him?"

"And go where? I had no money, no friends, no family to turn to. And to be honest, I blamed myself. I've never had a lot of self-confidence and thought that maybe it was something I did, something I could manage. I did for a while, but then…"

They had arrived at the bike bridge, negotiated the small concrete pillar at the entrance, and stopped midway.

Dee turned to Rob. "I'm sorry to drop all of this on you. I know we haven't known each other very long, but I feel like I can trust you."

"Of course, you can."

Dee paused, looking out over the water. A seagull cried in the distance, and the wind rustled the leaves of the trees at the entrance to the bridge. Down on the beach, she could just make out a couple walking along the water holding hands. She wanted to cry at everything that she had lost because of Jack Reiner.

She turned back to Rob. "I am really hoping you might be able to help me."

"Of course. I'd be happy to do whatever I can."

Dee hesitated, reluctant to speak.

"What is it?" asked Rob sweetly.

Dee took a deep breath and said, "Have you heard the term winter resident?"

Rob, taken aback, said, "Well, yes, sort of, I guess. I've heard the term but am not totally clear on what it means. Is it someone who has died but comes back to the island as a spirit?"

"That's essentially it, yes," said Dee.

"Why do you ask?"

Dee looked out again over the blue waters of the Atlantic before answering Rob in a clear and calm voice. "Because I am a winter resident of Nantucket."

Rob stared at her in shock and disbelief. "You are what?"

Dee smiled sadly. "Yes, shocking, I know. Unbelievable. Impossible. I'm sure other words are rippling through that creative mind of yours."

"But, but…"

Dee held up her hand. "It's okay, Rob. It's a lot to take in, and I'm sure the last thing you were expecting me to say." She smiled and looked back out on the water. "But I assure you it is true and as real as what you see standing in front of you."

The shadow on the sundial was slowly moving past noon, but for Rob, it felt as if time was standing still.

This cannot be true. How can I be talking to a spirit, a ghost?

"Dee, I'm sorry, but that just seems way too weird for me. Are you trying to give me ideas for the book?" he asked nervously.

"I wish it were just an idea for a novel," she said wistfully. "But it's true, all of it."

"I'm sorry, but I can't…"

Dee put her finger on his lips. They were light to the touch and very cold. "You must believe me, Rob. Because I need your help."

"My help? For what?"

"To bring justice to Jack Reiner."

"Justice?"

"Yes, justice. I want that man to account for what he did for me. I want him exposed for the bastard that he is. And I want to prevent him from killing again."

Rob felt the click of connections coming together. "Emily?"

"Yes! Emily. We need to save her."

Emotions and doubts swirled through Rob's brain. "Oh my god, I don't know. I'm just a midwestern boy who's been on the island for a couple of weeks. What the hell can I do? Who the hell is going to even listen to a thing I have to say?"

"I know. I know that you are new here. But you can also see me."

"See you? What the hell does that mean?"

Dee paused before replying. "The vast majority of people living and visiting the island are clueless to the world around them. The world of the winter residents."

"The world of the winter residents?" asked Rob incredulously.

"Yes, the world of winter residents. My world." She waved her arm around, pointing out houses and cottages all around her. "There are hundreds like me all around us right now. Like everyone you saw on the bluff walk last week. Those are winter residents. Men and women who return to Nantucket during the off-season to remember their lives here and relive their memories. Men and women who you would call dead."

Rob thought back on his brief time here and all of the people he had seen, faces behind curtains and realized what she was saying.

"And this village is especially active as it served countless happy memories and happy moments for so many."

"Oh, my god."

Dee smiled at his understanding. "Yes! You are one of a small percentage of living people that can see us unaided. And after meeting you I knew that you could be the one to help me finally get justice."

Rob turned to Dee and asked warily, "So you are..."

Dee finished the sentence. "Dead. Yes, Rob. I am dead. Murdered by my husband just over six years ago and buried in the dunes on a warm, foggy night out near Great Point."

Rob just stood and stared at her, his face a mixture of shock and confusion.

"Everyone thinks I had some sort of mental breakdown and ran off. But that's just what he told the police to deflect any suspicions from him. You see, I was his second wife. His first wife had," Dee held up her hands flashing air quotes,"'drowned' while swimming."

"And they never suspected him?"

"Oh, of course, they did. Everyone wanted to know why the hell he didn't try to save her. But it did look like an accident, and given his status on the island and his wealth? No one wanted to pursue it."

"So what can I do? They are going to think I'm insane if I start talking about winter residents and helping out a ghost."

"Oh, Rob, I would never ask that of you."

"So what are you asking?"

Dee paused. "I just want you to help the authorities find my body."

"Find your body?"

"Yes. The story that Jack told everyone was that I ran off. But if they find my body here on the island, then that should help tip suspicions against him."

Rob looked at Dee nervously.

"What is it?"

"How did he...um...how did you...?"

"How did he kill me?"

"Yes," said Rob.

"I threatened to leave him. I mean, it really was only a threat, but that's all it took. I guess he thought I was serious and maybe afraid of what people would say. Or what I might tell them. So he hit me hard in the stomach and then he covered my face with a pillow. I couldn't breathe. That's all I remember before things went black." She paused and looked out over the water. "I'm not sure he really meant to do it, at least that night."

"Oh, my god." Rob stared at her in sadness and disbelief.

"I miss being alive. Especially here." She looked wistfully at the ocean. "I miss the smell of the sea and the moors. I miss the cool tingle of the water on my feet and the feel of the sand as it squishes between your toes. I miss the touch of another person."

"I'm so sorry."

She looked at him, her eyes heavy with sadness. "You can't bring me back to life, but you can make me happy. Help me expose him."

Rob watched her, his face mirroring her pain. "How can we help them find your body?"

"Tell them where I am buried."

"You know where you are buried?" asked Rob, shocked.

"I do, Rob. I know exactly where I am buried. I visit my body often, especially on beautiful days like this."

"You visit your body?"

"Yes, Rob, I do," said Dee sadly. "It connects me to the life I once had. The life that he took from me. The life I want Emily to keep."

Rob's mind was reeling. "So what do we do now?"

"Now, I walk home with you. Let you recover and think about what we've talked about. I know it's a lot to take in."

"Um, okay," stammered Rob.

"And tomorrow, we can start fresh," replied Dee confidently.

She motioned with her arm and led him off the bridge toward Starbuck Lane. They walked in silence back to his cottage and parted at the front gate. Rob opened the gate, paused, and watched Dee walk down the street toward her house. She was a beautiful woman, and he found himself oddly attracted to her. He looked up at the sky.

But she's dead? How the hell can I be talking to a ghost?

He looked back down the street. Dee was gone.

CHAPTER SIXTEEN

R ob fumbled with the old latch. The harder he pressed it, the more it resisted his efforts. Frustrated, he stepped back and took a deep breath. He walked back up to the door, put his thumb on the latch, and gently pressed. The door opened. Remembering to duck, he walked into the main room feeling overwhelmed, his mind reeling.

Dead? Is she insane? Am I?

Rob paced agitatedly through the room, thoughts weaving in and out of his mind. How could this be? I just met this woman a few weeks ago, and now she's telling me her life story? Or is it her death story? What was happening to him?

What is her story?

Rob thought for a minute and then walked into his office. He opened his laptop and navigated to the Inquirer and Mirror website. The screen was packed with articles about local news and activities, results from the town's school sports teams, and ads for local businesses. In the upper right corner, a small box contained a magnifying glass and six grayed-out letters: Search.

Clicking on the box, Rob keyed in "Deidre Collins" and hit the enter key. The browser churned for a few seconds, and several links appeared. In the middle of the page was the one that captured his attention:

Deidre Reiner missing. Police concerned about mental state.

Rob clicked the link, and the article appeared on his screen along with a picture of Dee hanging off the arm of Jack at some social function.

By John Smithe. Posted Thursday, September 2, 2010.

Deidre Reiner (Nee Collins), wife of well-known local philanthropist, Jack Reiner, was reported missing by her husband earlier this week. Citing a potential mental breakdown, police are investigating what might have happened to the 41-year-old woman.

Ms. Reiner apparently has a long history of mental illness, according to her husband. The Nantucket Police have confirmed that Mr. Reiner had tried unsuccessfully to get her treatment, but she was uncooperative and refused his efforts. It is not known what, if any, mental health disease she may have been suffering from. Police suspect she may be trying to get back to her home state of California.

Rob looked up from his screen.

California? I thought she said she was from Pennsylvania.

He returned to the story.

At this time, there is no suspicion of foul play and every reason to believe she is alive and most likely off island.

Readers might remember Mr. Reiner's first wife, Margaret Reiner (nee Booth), drowned while swimming off Great Point. Her body was later recovered off the south shore.

Ms. Reiner is described as 5' 7" and 140 lbs. with shoulder-length light brown hair and brown eyes. Her husband reported that she was probably wearing jeans, a gray turtleneck sweater, and white sneakers. She was last seen in Sconset near the area of Milestone Road and New Street Saturday afternoon. If you have any information about her, please contact the Nantucket police on their non-emergency line.

Rob finished the article and stared intently at the picture alongside the text. It was obviously taken at one of the many galas and social events they attended as he was wearing black tie and she a long black gown. She looked elegant and beautiful, but he could see the sadness in her eyes. Her vacant stare reminded him of what he had seen on Emily's face the night before. According to the caption, the picture had been taken just a few weeks before her disappearance.

Her disappearance.

Had she escaped his abuse and made it off island? Had she returned to Nantucket to seek revenge? Was Reiner right in claiming that she was mentally unstable?

I would think claiming to be dead is probably at least one sign of being mentally unstable.

Despite the doubts floating through his mind, something just felt right about everything she had said to him about Jack Reiner. And certainly, the way his wife Emily had acted brought its own mess of suspicions. And honestly, what did he have to lose in believing her story? The only risk was that the few people he knew on the island would think he was crazy. Most of them probably already thought he was a bit different, living in a small cottage on a windswept island, by himself, over the winter.

And then a thought hit him. Pip.

He looked at his watch and realized he had time to get to the Atheneum before it closed. Maybe he could grab Pip for a drink and talk to her about things. Hell, she was the one who told him about the winter residents in the first place. He grabbed the keys to the Wagoneer, fumbled his way out the front door, and made his way to town.

* * *

He arrived a few minutes before five and sat on a bench in the front courtyard to wait for Pip. He didn't have to wait long. She bounced out of the main doors and made her way quickly down the steps. She looked up and, seeing him, stopped in her tracks.

"Hi, Rob. What are you doing here?" she asked, surprised.

"Just thought I'd stop by and say hello. And to thank you for last night. I really had fun."

Pip smiled warmly. "I'm so glad. I really enjoyed it too. I'm just sorry I had to work. So I didn't scare you away with my penchant for felons?"

Rob laughed. "Absolutely not. I don't scare that easy." He paused briefly, looking at the gorgeous Greek Revival facade behind her. Lowering his eyes to hers, he said, "Can I interest you in a bourbon?"

"Oh, I'd love to, but I am supposed to meet a friend to help train her new dog. I wish you would have texted me."

He smiled wryly. "Well, I would have if someone had been kind enough to give me their number."

Pip chuckled. "Oh, right. Hand me your phone, please."

Rob pulled out his phone and handed it to Pip. She keyed in her number, adding a little red heart at the end of her name, and then handed it back to him.

Rob saw the heart and smiled. Maybe she really did like him after all.

"Tell you what. Let me call Macie and let her know I'll be an hour or two. After all, the puppy's just a few months old. What's another couple of hours going to do?" Pip pulled out her phone, typed a message quickly, and hit send. She looked up at Rob. "What did you have in mind?"

"Well, I was hoping you might have an idea. I still don't know my way around here."

"Hmm. Okay. Let's go to the Brotherhood. They have a nice bourbon selection and probably one of the neatest bars around."

"Sounds good. Lead the way," said Rob extending his arm.

Pip smiled. "It's just down a few blocks here," she said, guiding him out onto Federal Street.

They made their way to Broad Street, and Rob found himself standing in front of an old plank door inset into a brick foundation. He looked at Pip skeptically. "Is this it?"

"Yep. And my advice is to watch your head." She grabbed the handle and walked quickly through the door. Rob followed, and heeding her advice, duck walked down a short and narrow entry hall with very low ceilings. At the end, the hostess was at a lectern and looked up expectantly.

"Hi, Jen," said Pip.

"Hey, Pip. How have you been?" replied the hostess.

"I'm good, thanks. Is it okay if we sit at the bar?"

"Sure, it's pretty open. And Michael will be happy to take care of you."

"Thanks."

She led Rob over to a small bar with a dozen padded stools. They found a couple near the end and took their seats. Rob looked around and felt almost as if he were in the hold of an old sailing ship. The ceilings were low, the light dim, and the whole place had an air of history and permanence.

"This place is awesome!"

"I thought you might like it. It's one of my favorites."

"I can see why."

"Hey, Pip," said a gravelly voice.

"Mike! Great to see you." She turned to Rob. "And I'd like to introduce you to Rob McGlynn. He just landed on the island a few weeks ago."

Mike held out his hand. "Nice to meet you. Where are you in from?"

"St. Louis."

"St. Louis, huh? Well, I hope you like our little island."

"I do, thanks."

"So what can I get you two?"

"I think a couple of bourbon and waters, please, Mike."

"Bourbon preference?"

Pip looked and smiled at Rob. She turned to the bartender and said, "Nor'easter, please."

Mike nodded and turned to make their drinks. Rob looked confused.

"Nor'easter?" he asked curiously.

Pip smiled broadly. "It's local. Made here on the island. And it's really good."

"Hmm, okay. I'll give it a try."

Mike returned with their drinks.

Rob took a sip and smiled. "Wow, that is good."

"I thought you'd like it," said Pip. "You know I would never steer you wrong."

Rob held up his glass. "Thank you again for last night… and for not steering me wrong."

Pip raised her glass. "You are welcome." She took a sip and looked at Rob. "So, how are you doing?"

Rob smiled thinly. "I'm doing okay. But to be honest, I had a bit of a weird experience today that has left me a little confused. Freaked out, actually."

"Really," said Pip, concerned. "What is it?"

Rob took another sip of his bourbon. His eyes scanned the room as if looking for spies before settling back on Pip's. He said in a hushed tone, "You remember a few days ago you told me about the winter residents."

Pip laughed and said, "What, you've seen a ghost?"

Rob's face went blank.

Pip looked at him, her eyes widening. "What, really?"

Rob looked down at the counter. "Would you think I'm crazy if I said yes?"

"Well, um, maybe just a little," Pip said teasingly.

"I'm serious."

"Uh, okay. What happened?"

"It started when I met a lady last week on a walk, Deidre Collins. In fact, she's the one that encouraged me to come to the Atheneum, so in a way, she's responsible for introducing us," said Rob smiling softly.

"But she's not real?"

"It turns out she is staying in a cottage down the street from mine, so we've talked a few more times, casually, you know? But this morning, she came by and asked me to go for a walk. It was a beautiful day, so I figured, why not? She seems like a nice lady, and to be honest, it is good to have a friend in Sconset."

"Did something happen on your walk?"

Rob paused to take a sip of his drink. "Yes. She confessed to me that she was a winter resident."

Pip looked startled. "Wait, you mean she told you she was a winter resident? Actually used that term?"

"Yes."

"Wow. Sounds like she may have some issues to deal with," said Pip, swirling her drink. "We do have some good therapists on the island that I'm sure could help her."

Rob looked at Pip, his eyes locked on hers, "Deidre Collins was her maiden name." He paused. "You would know her as Dee Reiner."

"You mean Jack Reiner's wife!"

Rob nodded.

"But she disappeared years ago; it was the talk all around town. Everyone suspected that she had run off, had some sort of mental instability if I remember correctly," said Pip.

"And did they ever find her? Or hear from her?"

Pip thought for a minute. "I don't think so. Or at least, I never heard."

"Well, it turns out she's living three cottages down from me," said Rob. "Although maybe living is too strong a word."

"Wait, are you serious? You're not shitting me?"

"I wish I was, Pip. But that's not the biggest part of it."

"You mean there's more?"

"Yes. She asked for my help."

"Your help? For what?"

Rob looked down at his drink and swirled the cubes in the glass. "To bring her husband to justice."

"Her husband?" said Pip, her mouth agape. "You mean Jack Reiner?"

"Yes."

"Justice? Justice for what?"

Rob hesitantly replied, "Her murder."

Pip nearly choked on her drink. "Her murder?"

"I know, I know. It sounds crazy. Hell, it IS crazy. But she said he killed her in a fit of rage and buried her in the sand. She claims she can take me to her body." Rob looked down and twirled his finger around the edge of his glass. "And as insane as this is going to sound, I think I believe her."

Pip stared at Rob intently. She placed the back of her hand on his forehead. "Are you feeling okay? You don't have a fever," said Pip sarcastically.

"I'm serious! This has scared the bejesus out of me, and I have no idea what to do. Hell, three weeks ago, I was in Missouri. I might have been depressed, but at least I wasn't dealing with all of this shit out on a little island I've never been to before!" Rob finished his drink in a long swallow and set it heavily down on the bar. "And to be honest, I'm about ready to take the next ferry out of this damn place," he said softly, his face buried in his hands.

Pip placed her hand on his arm. "I'm sorry, Rob. I didn't mean to belittle what you've experienced. I just wanted to make you laugh."

Rob rubbed his face, stopped, and looked at Pip. Her eyes sparkled with intensity and concern. He smiled thinly. "It's okay. I'm sorry to get upset. It's just been such a weird few weeks. I thought I was coming here to escape and start a new life, but this isn't exactly what I had in mind."

"I understand; I really do." She sat up and took a deep breath. "Okay, let's just say this is true, that you met Dee Reiner and not someone just trying to play games with you. I guess the first question is whether or not she's really a ghost. Or has she recovered from whatever issues were troubling her, and she has returned here looking to regain her old life back?"

"I had the same thought. But she doesn't strike me as someone out for revenge. And based on what she told me, I don't think she is in any hurry to get that life back."

"What do you mean?"

"She told me at first, he was a loving and caring husband, but that changed slowly over time. He was very controlling and eventually abusive. Mentally and physically. When she threatened to leave him, well, that's when he killed her."

The realization of what they were talking about settled on Pip like a bad meal. "Oh my god, we really are talking about a woman's life. Her pain. Her murder."

"Yes," said Rob sadly. "We are talking about her death. And trying to bring her killer to justice."

Pip looked at Rob warily. "Okay, let's just say that what she has told you is all true. How the hell would you bring justice to him? He is one of the most powerful men on the island."

"I think the only hope we have is to convince the authorities to resume the search for her and hopefully find her body. Maybe an autopsy would show the cause of death and then maybe lead suspicions back to him?"

Pip emptied her glass and signaled to Mike for another round. She looked back at Rob. "Convince the authorities? Based on the confessions of a ghost?"

"I know, I know. They'll walk me out of the building. Or worse, they'll have me committed."

Pip smiled wryly. "Well, the sheriff of Nantucket County is my cousin. We could go talk to him and feel him out."

"The sheriff is your cousin!" Rob exclaimed. "Why didn't you mention that earlier?"

"Well, A, he's a pretty busy guy, and B, what you are claiming is pretty crazy. He might think I'm nuts, too, just because you and I are friends," she said with a twinkle in her eye.

Mike returned with their drinks.

Rob raised his glass. "Thank you for believing me."

Pip lifted hers. "I knew when I met you that it would be interesting getting to know you, but really, you have delivered way beyond those expectations," she smiled and clinked his glass.

Rob took a long sip and placed his glass down on the bar. "So, when can we go see your cousin?"

Pip thought for a moment. "Well, I'm heading off-island tomorrow for a librarian conference in Boston. I should be back Thursday afternoon."

"Seriously, a librarian conference? What do librarians do at a conference?" asked Rob, smiling and happy to break the tension.

Pip became defensive. "A lot, really. It's a three-day conference with the National Librarians Association. We engage with authors, participate in discussions on programming and marketing, explore new ways to serve our customers, learn about new technologies, and a lot more."

"Oh, Pip, I'm sorry," said Rob laughing. "I didn't mean to demean you or your profession. I just really didn't know that there was actually such a thing."

She looked at Rob sternly, her arms crossed. "Did you ever go to a handyman conference?"

Rob smiled broadly. "Well, they didn't call them that, but yes, I did go. And I get it now. I'm sorry. Please forgive me?"

Pip's face slowly relaxed and then lit up. "I got you didn't I?"

Rob laughed. "Oh, you little shit."

Pip smiled, her eyes dancing. "Seriously, I'll be back Thursday, so let's plan on seeing Fred - my cousin - on Friday."

Rob grinned. "Friday it is. And thank you."

"You are welcome. Now, can we talk about something else?"

CHAPTER SEVENTEEN

R ob had been dreaming about Sarah. In it, they were back on the rooftop where they had celebrated their tenth anniversary. In typical dreamlike fashion, the familiar place had taken on a perverse feel, the sleeping brain adding all sorts of weird features and odd decoration. But Sarah was Sarah, and she was pleading for him to help Dee and save Emily. In his dream, she was hugging him, and he was relishing every moment. He opened his eyes, and the remembrance she was gone was like a punch to the gut.

He lay in the bed and stared at the ceiling, thinking of the dream of Sarah and what could have been. His mind wandered to his discussion with Pip. Did she think he was a complete and total idiot? Or, at best, just some guy from Missouri with a very strange and unusual story. Whichever she thought, it didn't reflect well on him. He felt a pang of guilt thinking of her so soon after his dream of Sarah.

Rob walked to the kitchen, hit the power button on the coffee maker, and thought about his day. The weather was cloudy and cool, perfect for writing. But that had been going so poorly that his office was beginning to make him feel anxious, as if he were headed to the dentist for a root canal. He had hoped writing would be an escape, a balm for his soul. But in reality, the opposite was happening.

Hearing footsteps on the shells, he looked out the window to see Will and Boomer walking by the cottage. He wondered if Will had met Dee yet. Or could even see her and the other winter residents. Hell, was Will a resident? And Boomer?

The coffee pot filled rapidly, and Rob pulled it out, poured himself a cup, and retreated to the living room. Saturday morning, the third week of October, and the college football season was well underway. He had thirty minutes until his favorite pre-game show started, so he turned on the Boston news hoping to catch the latest weather. A talking head was giving details about a murder that had occurred earlier in the week and an arrest of the suspect who just happened to be the victim's husband. The video cut to an office where a local therapist was talking about the incident. The caption on the screen informed him that she was an expert in domestic battery and abuse cases. Ron turned up the volume, his interest piqued.

"Domestic violence is a pattern of behaviors used to gain or maintain power and control between an abuser and their victim. Often, as in this case, that occurs within intimate partners such as a husband and wife. The abusive partner will use a variety of tactics to keep their victims within their control. Sadly, when fearing a loss of control of the victim, or losing control of their own anger, these cases can end in homicide, or more properly, in this case, uxoricide, the killing of one's wife."

Rob muted the volume and let the words sink in. They could have been talking about Dee. And with a start, Rob realized that Emily's life really was in danger. A second thought sent a chill through his heart. He and Pip were the only people that had the necessary information to save her life.

He grabbed his phone and knocked out a quick text to Pip to wish her a good morning and thank her for the discussion. He also hoped she had a successful conference in Boston and would look forward to seeing her Friday. He hit send and put the phone on the coffee table face down.

The meteorologist was now on the screen showing a map of New England with symbols of rain in the bottom half and snowflakes on the upper half. Nantucket, a little blot on the map out in the ocean, had a sun peeking through clouds. Rob unmuted the sound. "So much of New England will see some form of precipitation over the next day or so, but then some clearing should occur early in the week. But as we said at the top of the newscast, we are keeping a close eye on our long-range forecasting models as they are suggesting a weather system will form off the Carolina coastline, strengthen rapidly, and move quickly up the coast potentially becoming our first Nor'easter of the season. Stay tuned for more updates. And you can always download the WCVB weather app to receive instant updates, notifications, and warnings."

Rob muted the volume again, his thoughts returning to the situation with Pip and how they could possibly convince her cousin to reopen the case. And if he were honest, he was feeling a little bit sorry for himself for being thrust into this situation. All he had wanted was to escape and ease the pain of Sarah's loss, not be thrust into some supernatural quest.

His phone dinged with a message from Pip. He smiled as he read it. Her texting style reflected her personality - optimistic, bright, and energetic with the use of lots of emojis to make her points. She thanked him for the message, claimed she was good, and thanked him for trusting her enough to open up about his experiences with Dee. He thought it might have said a few other things as well but wasn't exactly sure what the latest meanings were for some of the emojis she used. Despite only being in his 30's, it made him feel a bit old.

The morning passed quickly, and Rob enjoyed watching a replay of the prior weekend's football with his beloved Mizzou Tigers taking on their SEC rival Arkansas. Even though he knew the score, he still found it a thrilling game that went down to the wire as the Tigers kicked a last-second field goal for the win. That excitement waned quickly as Rob recalled his conversation with Pip and the realization of his situation and his upcoming meeting with the sheriff. He decided to find Dee and update her on his progress.

He fumbled his way through the front door - that old latch was most certainly not his friend - and made his way down the street toward Dee's. He was feeling nervous as the reality of who - or what - she was had become evident to him. Arriving at her cottage, he stepped on the porch and, with butterflies in his stomach, knocked on the door. He listened for sounds of movement, but all was quiet inside. He walked over and peered in one of the large windows only to see a dark room with old-fashioned furniture, some of the pieces covered in protective sheets. There was no sign of life.

Would there be signs of life even if she were home?

Somewhat relieved, he turned to head back to his cottage. He had only gotten a few dozen feet past her front gate when he heard a voice call out to him.

"Rob?"

He pivoted around, his feet crunching in the shells. "Oh, hi, Dee."

"Were you coming to see me? I hope this means our talk yesterday hasn't scared you away."

Rob hesitated, not sure how to respond. He wanted to say: Actually, you scared the crap out of me, and there is nothing more I want to do right now than to run screaming all the way back to St. Louis and never see you or this island again. Instead, he just smiled tightly.

Dee continued, "I know what we talked about yesterday is a lot to take in. And I want you to know how much I appreciate you giving me the benefit of the doubt. And for trying to help me."

Her graceful elegance and pleasant tone quickly warmed him back to her plight. "Sure. I just hope I can help."

She motioned to the door with her hand. "Please, come in."

Rob ducked through the low doorway and entered what looked to be the living room. As he had seen through the windows, the room was filled with older furniture, and with very little natural light making its way through the curtains, it was dark and gloomy. The space emitted a very weird, almost otherworldly vibe. It was almost as if he had stepped back in time. There were no conveyances of modern life - no televisions, computers, or even a telephone.

"This is, um, quaint," said Rob nervously.

Dee smiled knowingly. "It's okay. I know it might seem a touch dreary and uninviting, but given what I am?" she sighed. "It's really all I need."

The realization that she was truly dead hit him with a wave of sadness. In his short time on the island, he had become fond of Dee. Besides being strikingly beautiful, she had been kind and thoughtful to him. And she was living - if you could call it that - in a really depressing old cottage. He felt sorry for her.

"Please. Sit."

Rob sat on one end of a couch facing the window. Dee took position in a wingback chair facing him across a cocktail table. The cushion did not deform under her body.

"I wanted to tell you that I shared your story with my friend Pip, the librarian from the Atheneum."

Dee leaned forward in her chair, anxious to hear the news.

"It took a bit of convincing - and to be honest, I'm not sure she really believes me or is just being friendly - but she has offered to introduce me to her cousin, the sheriff of Nantucket County."

"That is a great start," she said excitedly.

"Well, a start is all it is. Honestly, I'm afraid the man will look at me like some nut job and throw me out of the place. Maybe he'll deport me off the island?" he added jokingly.

Dee smiled at him assuredly. "Rob, you are one of the most honest and genuine people I have ever met. I've no doubt the sheriff will be skeptical, but I know you can win him over."

"Tell me how," he said earnestly. "What evidence do I have that a crime has been committed? Is there anything more you can tell me to help convince the man to take action?"

Dee lowered her gaze. "Sadly, no. Jack was very careful while I was alive. He was beating me, yes, but the bruises were hidden. He would never do more than slap me in the face or a punch in the gut - not wanting to leave a mark - so no one would ever have seen any outward evidence of his brutality. As I shared with you, I had no friends or family to lean on, no witnesses or confidants. Hell, for the last year or so, the bastard had taken away my phone and my access to the internet. I really had no way of connecting with the outside world. I was trapped in Gratitude."

"Gratitude?" asked Rob.

"Yes, that is the name of his house, his mansion out on Polpis Road. It was built in the 19th century by his ancestors."

"A bit ironic, isn't it?"

"What's that?"

"That such a brutal man would live in a house named Gratitude."

Dee snorted. "Oh, the name has absolutely nothing to do with his family feeling any sort of appreciation or gratefulness for their position in life. It was named after an ancestor's whaling vessel who made the family fortune by hunting and butchering whales."

"Oh," said Rob knowingly. "I've actually been doing some reading on whaling. An absolutely brutal business. Cruel to both man and mammal."

There was a moment of silence between them as they each reflected on the savagery of another time.

Finally, Rob spoke. "I have a question."

"Yes?"

"I read an article about your disappearance in the local newspaper, The Inquirer and Mirror. In the piece, it states that Jack thought you might be heading back to your home state of California."

"California?" said Dee, confused. "I'm from Pittsburgh. Why would he say that?"

"I don't know. Could he just have made a mistake? Maybe stressed under the situation."

"A mistake about where your wife grew up? Don't you think most people would remember that?"

Rob reflected on one of his early dates with Sarah. They had gone to a new restaurant in St. Louis's fashionable Central West End. Over a meal of good pasta and wine, she had shared her childhood growing up. She had talked about her high school days, her summer jobs, her neighborhood friends, and her parents. He could never forget those details; they were burned in his memory as if he had lived them himself. How could Jack Reiner forget such a thing about a woman he loved?

"Rob?"

"What? Oh, sorry, I was lost in thought there."

"I was saying that I think I might know what happened. Why he said I was from California."

"And?"

"He's confused me with his first wife, Margaret. She was from central California."

"Really?" asked Rob, surprised.

"Yes. Jack purged the house of all of her things not long after she drowned, but I found an old notebook book of hers that he had missed. In it, she wrote about her hometown, a small city called Watsonville. I looked it up on a map, and it is about fifty miles south of San Jose. That is what he must have been thinking about when he talked to the police about my disappearance."

Rob thought for a minute. "But, would he make such a fundamental error? The man seems too smart for that."

"Actually, given how he treated me - and I assume Margaret - it makes total sense. He really didn't view us as individuals with our own histories, passions, and dreams. He saw us simply as objects for him to control. He didn't care about us or our past. All he cared about was managing us to satisfy him."

"Hmm," said Rob.

"What? What are you thinking?"

"Maybe we can use that against him. With the sheriff, I mean. Don't you think that might get their attention?" asked Rob.

Dee smiled knowingly. "Yes, perhaps, but you'll need proof. You have a computer, right?"

"I do. And a printer. It was delivered last week."

"Good. Look up my school. I went to Cranberry Township high school outside Pittsburgh. I bet you can find a photo of me - maybe my class picture - and show that to the sheriff."

"It's worth a shot," said Rob. "Anything else you can think of?"

"What else did the article say about me?"

"Not much, really. Mainly that they feared you were unstable."

"Do you think I'm unstable, Rob?" asked Dee anxiously.

Rob paused for a moment. Hesitating, he said, "Well, you've told me you are dead and claim to have been murdered by your husband. I don't think you could blame me if I were inclined to believe their theory."

"Hmm," said Dee. "Let me show you something."

She stood and walked to the center of the room. She closed her eyes, and a look of intense concentration came over her. Rob watched as her body began to shimmer and then fade away. Soon

Rob could see right through her, her gaseous body floating like a light fog in the middle of the room.

"Oh my god!" Rob exclaimed, clutching the arm of the couch.

And then, just as suddenly, she reformed in front of him, her long brown hair and shapely figure filling the space.

Shocked, Rob asked, "What was that?"

"I'm sorry if I scared you. But I wanted to prove to you that I am indeed dead."

"What were you doing?"

"Transiting."

"Transiting? What the hell is that?"

She paused. "It's how I move through time and time's layers. Some people call it the other side. Others might call it the afterlife. It's essentially another plane of existence in the spacetime continuum."

"What?" said Rob, his eyes wide.

Dee sat back down in the chair and looked at Rob comfortingly. "It's not something for you to think about. Or worry about. It can't hurt you. You'll experience it for yourself when your time comes."

Rob sat on the couch, dazed by what he had seen. And confused by its implications for Dee. But then his mood suddenly brightened. Does that mean that he could see Sarah again? He looked at Dee expectantly. "Can anyone come back from the other side?"

"I'm afraid it's not that simple."

"What do you mean?" Rob asked, disappointed.

"There are rules," said Dee. "And there are costs," she added softly.

"Costs?" asked Rob confused.

"I've already said too much. My intent was just to convince you that I am dead. That I wasn't unstable when I disappeared. I disappeared because I was murdered by my husband." She started to cry.

Rob didn't know what to do. "Is it possible for me to hug you?"

"Oh, Rob," she laughed, her cheeks wet with tears. "You are too sweet. But I'm not sure that would be the best idea. I may appear real enough to you, but I promise you I won't feel real. And I fear I may carry the scent of the grave about me. But I do appreciate your kindness."

Rob, gaining his composure, nodded. "I'm just sorry."

"Me too."

Rob glanced at his watch. The kick-off for the Alabama game was just minutes away.

"You need to go?"

Embarrassed, Rob said, "There is just something I want to see. A football game on TV."

"I understand."

He rose from the couch. "If you can think of anything more that might help me with the sheriff, please let me know." He paused and smiled knowingly. "You know where to find me."

"I will."

Rob nodded and started to leave.

"Rob?"

He turned. "Yes, Dee?"

"Thank you."

Rob smiled thinly and walked out of the cottage. It was only a few hundred feet to his front door, but it felt like a mile stretching out in front of him. The greatest mystery of life had possibly just been answered directly in front of his eyes. There is life after death. Or some form of existence after death. His mind reeled at the possibilities and the implications. He had so many questions now, and he hoped that Dee might be able to answer some of them. Could she perhaps answer the biggest question of all - would he see Sarah again?

He smiled at the thought.

CHAPTER EIGHTEEN

R ob spent the rest of the week immersing himself in his modest book collection from the Atheneum. It had been a very welcome distraction after his experience at Dee's. And it had given him a lot of time to think. He needed no further proof that she was indeed dead; the transiting thing that she had done in front of him had put the nail in that coffin, so to speak. But it had also opened up a whole slew of possibilities which gave him an entirely new perspective on life.

His phone pinged late Thursday afternoon with a text from Pip. She was back on the island and looking forward to seeing Rob on Friday. She suggested meeting for lunch before heading to see the sheriff. Rob confirmed, and they agreed to meet at a restaurant in town close to the sheriff's office shortly after noon.

Rob tossed and turned the entire night, unable to settle his mind, his thoughts dancing between possibly seeing Sarah and learning more about the other side. Could she somehow come to visit him? Would he see her again? Eventually, he gave up trying to sleep and lay awake staring at the ceiling, waiting for dawn.

Friday morning broke foggy, a nearly solid wall of gray greeting him as he looked out his bedroom window. For the second time in a few days, butterflies were flying around his gut, thinking about the unknown ahead of him. Would the sheriff think he's crazy? Would he rally to his side and help his cousin? Or would he just dismiss him out of hand?

Those thoughts swirled through his head as he drove to town. He made his way to Main Street, parked the old Wagoneer on the cobbles, and walked down Water Street to the restaurant, The Rose & Crown. Pip was standing at the front entrance waiting for him, wearing an old-style yellow slicker, her hair damp from the fog. After a brief and slightly uncomfortable hug, they went in and took their seats.

"How was your trip?" asked Rob.

"It was good. Interesting."

"How so?"

Pip said seriously, "You know, what a lot of people don't realize is that running a library is a lot like running a business. We have all the same opportunities and challenges. We need to serve our customers and manage our financial health. This weekend I saw some new technologies I think would really help us engage with our customers."

"Like what?" asked Rob.

"One that really excites me is augmented reality."

"Augmented reality? Really? I'm only slightly familiar with the subject, but how could that help the Atheneum?"

"Well, for example, let's say you came in looking for books on whaling. With augmented reality, you could hold up your phone, and on the screen, you would see an image of a whale swimming through the book racks. By following the whale, it would lead you to the section on whaling."

"Huh. That sounds kind of cool."

"Cool, yes. But also kind of expensive. Anyway, enough about me. How was your week?"

Rob briefly thought about sharing his experience with Dee's transiting but decided against it. "I think I might have something that will help persuade your cousin."

"What's that?"

Rob pulled out a folded sheet of paper and handed it to Pip.

"What's this?" she asked.

"It's the high school yearbook photo of Deidre Collins, class of 1987."

Pip unfolded the paper and stared at the image of the woman she knew as Dee Reiner. "She was beautiful, wasn't she?"

Rob replied, "Yes, she was. And I think this could help us convince your cousin."

"How is a picture going to help us?" asked Pip skeptically.

Rob pulled out another piece of paper and handed it to Pip. "This is the article that ran in The Inquirer and Mirror the day after Dee disappeared."

Pip scanned the document. "Okay."

"Reiner claimed she was possibly heading back to where she grew up. California."

"Okay, so?"

"She wasn't from California. She was born and raised outside Pittsburgh. That yearbook photo?" he said, pointing at her picture, "that is from Cranberry Township, a suburb of Pittsburgh."

Pip's eyes widened in realization. "He didn't know where his own wife grew up?"

Rob said, "Exactly! How could a man forget such a core detail of one's wife?"

"Well, he could have been stressed by the situation. But I get what you mean. It's worth a try."

Pip handed him back the paper. Rob folded it and put it in his pocket. He looked at Pip. "Tell me about your cousin."

Before she could answer, the server appeared at the table. "Hi, I'm June, and I'll be taking care of you today. What can we get you two?" she asked brightly.

Rob looked up and smiled. "I'll have the chowder, please. And an iced tea."

"I'm sorry, sir, we don't have iced tea. We only make that during the summer."

"Really?" asked Rob quizzically. "Okay. Just water, then."

She wrote on her pad and turned to Pip. "And you, miss?"

"I'll just have the small caesar."

"Any protein?"

"Um, yes, how about some shrimp. And a water too, please."

She finished writing on her pad. "Got it, thanks. I'll get that right out." She turned and headed to the kitchen.

Pip looked at Rob. "Where were we? Oh, right, Fred."

"Fred?"

"Fredrick Boston, my cousin, the sheriff. "Pip put her elbows on the table and cradled her chin. "Good guy. Lived on the island all his life. He knows just about everyone and is very well respected. Has to put up with a lot of the local political crap, but you get that anywhere, don't you?"

"Do you think I have a chance of convincing him?"

"Honestly?" Pip sat back in her chair. The server appeared with their lunch and placed the dishes on the table. Pip picked up a fork and tucked into her salad. She took a few bites before continuing. "I'd be surprised. He's a pragmatic guy. Plus, what, it's been six years? But worth a try. How's your chowder?" It came out chowda.

"Delicious." As Rob thought about presenting his case to the sheriff, the butterflies joined the chowder in his belly.

They finished lunch and walked across the street to the sheriff's office. Like many of the buildings in downtown Nantucket, it was constructed of red brick with white trim. The three-story structure featured an entry door surrounded by pediment and pilasters and five white sash windows. At the peak of the gable, an oculus window was framed in a square inset of brick. Rob surveyed the building and was impressed with its symmetry and simple elegance.

Pip walked confidently up to the door and pulled it open. Rob followed, and they made their way into a small lobby. Pip gave her name to the receptionist, and they sat down. Rob heard the receptionist on the phone, and shortly after, he heard steps approaching from down the hall. A tall, fit African-American man entered the room. He wore a black button-down over gray combat pants with a wide leather belt holding a holstered gun. Pinned on his left breast was a shiny gold six-pointed star. His face brightened, and his mouth opened into a broad smile when he saw Pip.

"Hi, Pip!" he said energetically. "So good to see you." He leaned down to hug her.

Pip smiled and pulled away. "Hi, Fred. Thank you so much for seeing us." She turned and motioned to Rob. "Let me introduce you to my friend. Fredrick Boston, this is Rob McGlynn."

"Hi, Rob," said Fred, extending his hand.

"Mr. Boston," said Rob, taking his hand. His grip was firm and dry.

"Please call me Fred. Are you new to the island?" he asked, his voice a rich baritone.

"Yes, I arrived a few weeks ago."

"Where from?"

"St. Louis."

"Ah, the Cardinals. My grandfather was a huge baseball fan and loved the Cardinals. He always dreamt of going there to see a game but never made it."

"I'm sorry to hear that."

Fred smiled sadly. "We don't always get to realize our dreams do we?"

Rob nodded his head.

"Anyway, I reserved a conference room for us. Why don't you two come on in." The sheriff led them down the hall and into a small conference room. A brown laminate table had seating for ten, but they all took seats at the end closest to the door.

"Can I get you two some coffee? Water?"

Pip responded, "Thanks, Fred. But we are good."

Fred leaned back in his chair, his hands clasped in his lap. "So, what is it you guys wanted to see me about?"

Pip looked at Rob, and he took his cue. He scooted forward on his seat. "Sir, I believe we have evidence that a crime was committed. A murder, in fact."

"A murder?" said Fred, intrigued. "We don't normally get many of those on our small island."

"Yes, sir. A murder. We believe it happened about six or seven years ago."

"Okay. And you believe it happened here, on Nantucket?" he asked, his finger pointing down to the ground.

"Yes, sir."

"And who was the victim?"

Rob paused. "It was Dee Reiner."

"Dee Reiner? Jack Reiner's wife? She wasn't murdered. She ran away. Had some mental issues. I led that investigation myself, and every bit of evidence suggested that she ran away, back to California."

"Evidence?" asked Rob nervously.

"Yes, evidence," said the sheriff. He leaned forward in his chair and placed his arms on the table. "There was a clear electronic record that essentially documented every step along her journey. We have a ferry ticket, credit card receipts, and cell phone tower pings from her phone from Hyannis all the way to Los Angeles with multiple stops along the way."

"Multiple stops?" Pip asked

Fred turned his eyes to her. "Yes. We have receipts from her credit card for hotels and restaurants in New York, Chicago, Kansas City, Vegas, and several others."

Rob asked, "How was she traveling?"

Fred let out a sigh. "Now, that's a bit of a mystery, I will admit. We couldn't find any documentation for her transportation, at least with her credit cards. There was no rental car, bus receipts, airfare. Nothing. We suspect she must have been met in Hyannis by a friend, and then they likely drove west together."

"And you couldn't locate this friend?" asked Rob.

"No. But the electronic trail did support Mr. Reiner's claim that she was heading home. Unfortunately, the trail stops there. We have a few receipts from LA, but all activity stopped a day or so later. Even her cell phone appeared to have been turned off."

Pip asked, "Isn't that unusual? That she would get to California and disappear? At least electronically?"

Fred responded, "Well, we assumed that she was back with family or just decided to start fresh. We made inquiries with local authorities, but they were unable to locate her." Fred paused and looked at Pip, then Rob. "Look. This wasn't a missing person case, just a woman who, for whatever reason, had left her husband. If it wasn't for Mr. Reiner's position on the island, we probably wouldn't have done much of anything. As it is, we invested as many resources as we could to try and locate her, but in the end, it was fruitless. Figured if she wanted to be found, she'd get in touch with her husband."

Rob sighed and said hesitantly, "But Dee Reiner wasn't from California."

Fred's eyebrow raised, and he leaned forward in the seat. "What do you mean, wasn't from California?"

Rob handed him the yearbook picture. "This is her yearbook photo, 1987."

Fred stared at the picture. "That looks like her. A bit younger, perhaps."

"Yes, taken at Cranberry Township high school, just outside of Pittsburgh, where she was born and raised."

Fred held the picture and massaged his chin. "Hmm, that is interesting."

Rob took a deep breath and said earnestly, "I know this sounds crazy, but I think that Dee Reiner was murdered by her husband."

Fred's eyes widened. "Based on this?" he said incredulously, pointing at the picture.

"How does a man forget where his wife is from?" said Rob.

The sheriff paused, looking at the picture. He turned to Rob. "Look, I get it. But forgetting where your wife came from is not a crime. And it is certainly not enough for us to reopen the investigation."

"But sheriff," said Rob.

Fred held up his hand. "I really appreciate your interest here, and I know you are trying to do the right thing." He glanced at Pip. "But there is no way I am going to put my reputation and career on the line on a hunch. Or on the memory loss of a grieving man." He put the paper down on the table. "Besides, we kept Mr. Reiner apprised of the investigation for months following her disappearance. And the few times I talked to him, I did sense that, in some ways, he was relieved that we hadn't found her. Between us, I don't think it was a very happy marriage."

"Of course, it wasn't," said Rob. "He beat her!"

Fred looked at Rob intently. "Mr. McGlynn, how long have you been living on this island?"

Rob looked down at his hands. "Three weeks," he said.

"Three weeks. And you know that she was beaten how? You have evidence of this?"

Rob thought for a minute and glanced at Pip. She subtly shook her head.

"What about his first wife?" asked Rob.

"His first wife? She died in a swimming accident."

"Doesn't that seem coincidental to you that the man has lost two wives?"

Fred shifted in his chair impatiently. "Sad, yes. I can't imagine the pain he must have gone through losing two wives. But that's all it is. A coincidence. Bad luck."

Rob looked crestfallen. He looked at Pip. She inclined her head to the door. Time to leave.

"Now, if that's all you have, I'm afraid I must conclude the discussion. I've got a court date this afternoon that I must prepare for." Fred stood. Pip and Rob followed suit.

Rob extended his hand. "Thank you, sheriff. I appreciate your time. And your consideration."

Pip gave him a quick hug. "Thanks, Fred."

They exited the conference room, walked down the hall, and out of the building. Standing on the sidewalk, Rob looked up to see some patches of blue sky. The fog was finally breaking up.

"Boy, that went well," said Pip sarcastically.

Rob looked down at his feet. "The man must think I'm crazy. Three weeks here, and I'm accusing a prominent local of murder with no evidence except a thirty-year-old yearbook photo? What was I thinking?" he said, exasperated. He looked up at Pip. "And I'm sorry to drag you into this. I hope it doesn't hurt your relationship with him."

"Fred?" said Pip, chuckling. "He's family. Next time I see him, he'll probably tease me about it and my taste in friends." She smiled at him.

"How the hell did I get into this mess?" asked Rob looking up at the sky.

Pip looked at him sympathetically. "Do you think that maybe…"

"Maybe what?" asked Rob cautiously.

"That you should move on."

"Move on?"

"From this, trying to bring justice….," said Pip, her voice trailing off.

Rob looked up at Pip. And then he thought of Dee. And of his dream of Sarah. "I can't, Pip. I wish I could, but I can't. Something is telling me that I need to see this through."

"So what's our next move then?"

"OUR next move?"

"Yeah, silly. In for a dime, in for a dollar, as my mom likes to say. So what's our next move? Surely we can find something that might be able to convince Fred."

Rob thought for a moment and then looked at Pip, his eyes bright with energy. "I know what we need to do."

"What's that?" asked Pip.

"Find her body."

Pip's eyes widened in shock. "Find her body? How are you going to do that?"

Rob looked at Pip calmly. "I'm going to ask her."

CHAPTER NINETEEN

Rob drove back to Sconset. Despite only being late afternoon, the light had already taken on the feel of dusk. This far east and north saw the sun set fairly early in October. Rob glanced at his watch and saw he only had an hour of light left. Not enough time to find Dee and start looking for her body. That would have to wait until morning.

He pulled the Wagoneer up the cottage, got out, and slammed the door.

"How did it go?" Dee was standing in the street, looking at him intently.

Rob jumped. He had just driven right over the spot where she was standing. Could she appear that quickly? He gathered his composure and said, "Not too good."

"He didn't believe you?"

"That's putting it nicely. He essentially repeated the same story. That you ran away. And they apparently have evidence of you going all the way to California."

"Evidence? What evidence? I never went to California."

"The sheriff claims to have credit card receipts from hotels and restaurants all the way from Hyannis to Los Angeles. They also had cell phone records documenting the exact route you took."

"The route I took? I didn't go to California. Hell, I didn't have any credit cards or a cell phone. Jack took those away from me," she said angrily. "I wonder how the bastard pulled that off?"

"I don't know, Dee."

"And what about my yearbook picture. That my husband forgot where I was from?"

"He dismissed it as memory loss from a grieving man."

"A grieving man?" said Dee, snorting. "I'm sure Jack was laughing the whole time at how easy it was to mislead the police."

Dee started pacing, her head down, her long brown hair flowing in the breeze. She stopped and looked at Rob, her brown eyes blazing. "So that's it? The bastard is going to win? Can you think of anything else?"

Rob looked intently at her. "Yes. I think our only option is for you to take me to your body."

Dee looked at him, surprised. "Rob, I can't ask that of you. All I wanted to do was for you to get the sheriff to relook into things. That is too much."

"If we are going to bring justice to Jack, then this is what we need to do," said Rob, with more confidence than he felt. "The question is will we be able to find it?"

"As I told you, Rob. I know exactly where I am buried. I can lead you there." She looked at the old Jeep. "That has four-wheel drive, right?"

"It does. Why?"

"Because we will have to drive about five miles over the sand to get to the location." She looked at Rob closely. "Can you do that?"

"I've never driven on the beach before," said Rob nervously. "But I'm sure I can figure it out. Would you be able to ride in the car with me?"

Dee paused. "Do you remember I told you there were rules? And costs with my, um, situation?"

"I do."

"The short answer is yes, I believe I can. But I'm not exactly sure what might happen along the way."

Jack smiled. "Okay, well, I guess we can just manage those things as we go."

"Are you sure about this?"

"I am. It's too late to go today, though; the sun will be setting in under an hour. Should we plan on leaving in the morning?"

Dee nodded. "Yes, please."

"Okay. What time?"

She looked at him steadily. "When you are ready, I'll be here. Good night, Rob." She turned and walked toward her cottage.

Rob watched her make her way down to her house and through her front gate. He turned and headed into his cottage.

The butterflies were flying. He needed a drink.

* * *

An azure blue sky greeted Rob when he woke. He had slept with the windows open, and the air in the bedroom was chilly and carried the fresh scent of fallen leaves. He shivered as he got out of bed and quickly dressed. Closing the windows, he turned on the little oil-filled radiator in the corner and prayed it would help warm the room while he was gone.

I'm going to find a body today.

Rob took his coffee into the office and opened his laptop. He pulled up a map of Nantucket and tried to get his bearings. His cottage was on the eastern edge of the island, and if he remembered correctly, Dee had told him she was buried near Great Point. Rob traced his hand on the map, starting on Starbuck Lane, and followed the lines through the village and then northward up the eastern edge of the island. If he was reading it correctly, they would have to turn on Wauwinet Road, pass through the little village of Wauwinet, and then on to the sand. He took a sip of coffee. If his estimate was correct, it should only take an hour, maybe two, to get to the location. But then what?

He printed out the map for reference, closed his laptop, and headed to the kitchen for a refill. Taking a sip of coffee, Rob stared out at the blue sky and wondered how he would handle the day. Could he do this? What would the body look like? Would it smell? Would he get sick? The butterflies stirred.

Pulling a travel mug from the cabinet, Rob poured in the remains of his cup and then topped it off with fresh coffee from the maker. He grabbed a coat, the keys and headed out the back door. He made his way to the small shed behind the patio and explored the tools at his disposal. He had never tried to dig up a body before and wasn't exactly sure what he might need in terms of equipment or resources. The selection was meager. He grabbed the only shovel he could find and carried it to the car.

He was loading it into the back of the Wagoneer when a voice behind him made him jump.

"Good morning, Rob."

"Ah!" Rob said and turned quickly, his face white. "You have to stop doing that."

"What?" asked Dee.

"Sneaking up on me. Can't you make some noise like footsteps to at least give me a little notice before you, um, appear?"

Dee smiled softly. "Sorry. I'm not sure I can, but I'll try."

Rob looked at Dee, and his heart went out to her. Seeing her, it was easy to forget she was dead and didn't have the same natural abilities as the living.

She looked at him intently. "Are you sure you are up for this?"

"I'd be lying if I didn't admit I was nervous. But yes, I am ready."

"Okay then." Dee went to the passenger side and tried to open the door but couldn't get the latch to move. When she tried to apply strength, her fingers simply flowed through the metal like water pouring through a sieve. She looked over at Rob.

He saw her eyes and ran around the car to help her. "Here, let me get that," said Rob, and he opened the door for her.

Dee got in and sat in the passenger seat. Rob noticed that the seat cushion didn't deform under her weight. Her body was also partially transparent, as if she were using energy to sit in the car versus staying opaque. Rob closed the door carefully, walked around the front of the car, got in the driver's seat, and started the engine.

"Great Point, right?" asked Rob, his voice trembling.

"It's near there, yes."

He put the transmission in drive and pulled away from the cottage. They made their way out of Sconset and onto Polpis Road. Despite the chill, Rob had opened the sunroof to enjoy the blue sky in an attempt to help calm his nerves. He had also cracked his window to get some fresh air.

"I can't tell you how much I appreciate this. I'm sure it can't be easy for you."

Rob looked at her quickly and smiled. "Let's just say that this sort of thing is not in my wheelhouse."

She smiled in return. "And what are your plans once we find me?"

"Well, I've seen enough crime shows to know that we probably want to disturb the grav..., I mean, site, as little as possible."

"It's okay. Call it what it is. My grave."

Rob shifted on the seat uncomfortably. "Okay. We will want to protect any possible evidence if we can. So maybe we just take a picture of you to show the sheriff?"

"I would think that would get more attention with him than a yearbook photo," said Dee.

Rob chuckled nervously. "Let's hope."

"Oh, turn here," said Dee, pointing.

Rob slowed the Wagoneer quickly and turned right onto Wauwinet Road, the old Jeep leaning heavily.

"If we had gone straight, it's just a mile or so to Gratitude, Jack's house. You can't see it from the street, though; it's down a long driveway," said Dee.

"Knowing what happened there - and what is still happening - I don't think I ever want to see it."

Dee nodded and turned to look out the window at the passing beauty of the landscape. There were very few houses - just scrub pines and the occasional green pasture. They entered the small village of Wauwinet. Rob had slowed the Jeep to barely a crawl.

"Keep going straight," said Dee. "The road turns to dirt up here and then to sand."

A sign warned him that only four-wheel drive vehicles were allowed past this point. Rob stopped the Jeep and put it in park.

"What are you doing?" asked Dee.

"I need to lock the front hubs," said Rob. "I have to be honest; I have never used four-wheel drive before, so I had to read the owner's manual to make sure I knew what I was doing." He got out of the car, leaving the door open. He quickly locked both front hubs and hopped back in. He slid a lever on the side of the transmission tunnel toward him, and a light on the dash came on. Rob looked at the light closely. "Good!" said Rob. "We are now in four-wheel drive."

Dee was not impressed with this accomplishment. "Just keep going and follow the tracks. I'll show you where to turn."

"Okay," said Rob. He accelerated slowly, and soon the dirt turned into heavy sand. The Jeep began to labor heavily and lurched its way along the path. Rob started to get nervous and worried the old Jeep might not be up to the task. A few times, he thought they might actually be getting stuck as it seemed the tires were digging into the sand. The scent of hot oil wafted into the passenger compartment.

"I'm sorry, Dee. I don't know what's wrong. It shouldn't have to work this hard." Fearing the engine might overheat, Rob stopped the car and put it in park.

"What's wrong?" asked Dee, concerned.

"I don't know. It says four-wheel drive is engaged, but the car is really struggling."

As they were talking, a green pickup was coming the other way. It pulled abreast of the Wagoneer and stopped. The window rolled down, and a man leaned out. "Everything okay?"

Rob looked over at him. "Hi. Not really. The car is having a really tough time with the sand.

"What do you have your tires down to?"

"What do you mean?"

Smiling knowingly, the man got out of the pickup and made his way through the sand and over to Rob's window. He was dressed in olive-colored slacks with a matching button-down shirt. A patch on his breast pocket read Park Ranger. He looked at Rob. "Did you let the air out of your tires?"

"The air out of my tires?" replied Rob, confused.

"Yes, sir. Is this your first time driving on the beach?"

"Um, yes."

"Well, you can't do that unless you take some air out of your tires. That way, instead of the tires trying to drive through the sand, they will float up on top of it. It's a lot easier on the vehicle."

"Oh, okay. I didn't know that."

The ranger smiled. "Here, let me help you." He pulled out a silver tire pressure gauge from his shirt pocket and kneeled down by the front wheel. Seconds later, the sound of air hissing from the tire followed.

Rob jumped out of the car. "Thank you for your help. Is there anything I can do?"

"Yes," replied the ranger, handing him a second gauge. "Go drop the pressures on the passenger side to 14 PSI."

"14? Seems kind of low."

"Trust me. Your Jeep will thank you."

Soon all four tires were down to the prescribed pressure. Rob walked over to the ranger and handed him back the gauge. "Thank you again for your help."

"That's what I'm here for." The ranger looked around the vehicle. "So what are you doing out here all on your own?"

"On my own?" Rob stole a glance over his shoulder at Dee in the passenger seat. She was sitting upright and looking intently back at him. He looked back at the ranger. "Um, I'm new to the island and was out just doing a little exploring."

The ranger smiled. "I hope you enjoy yourself. Just remember to fill your tires back up when you head home. There is a compressor for that purpose on the right side of the road a few hundred feet after it turns back to pavement."

"Great. Will do. Thanks again."

The ranger smiled, walked back to his truck, and got in. Rob watched him drive off, then turned and got in the Jeep. He looked at Dee. "He couldn't see you could he?"

"No. As I told you, very few people can."

"Does that mean if I were to take a picture of you, nothing would appear?"

Dee nodded. "The lens isn't sensitive enough."

"Hmm, okay. Ready to try again?"

Dee smiled and nodded.

Rob dropped the transmission into drive and hit the gas. The Jeep gathered speed quickly and was soon floating smoothly through the tracks. He smiled. Much better.

They came to a fork in the trail. An arrow pointed to the right and said Beach Access. Another arrow pointed left and said Inner Trail.

"Which way?" Rob asked.

Dee pointed to the left. "Follow the inner trail."

Rob turned the wheel and accelerated towards the inner trail. The path flowed through patches of beach grass punctuated by low scrub and stunted pines. After twenty minutes of driving, they came to another fork. Rob stopped the car and looked at Dee.

"Go left here."

He turned the vehicle and quickly found himself on a very narrow track, the edges bordered by stunted bushes on both sides. He cringed as he heard the sounds of branches screeching down the flanks of the Wagoneer. He looked over at Dee and saw she was getting tense. "Are we close?"

"Yes. See that rise in the trail down there?" "she replied, pointing straight ahead.

"Is that the spot?"

"Just a hundred or so feet past it. There will be a lone pine tree on the right and an old fence line along the left."

Rob followed her guidance. He noted the tree and the fence line and stopped the vehicle. The butterflies had taken flight once more.

Dee looked at him. "I can't go with you."

"What do you mean?"

"Remember I said there were rules?"

"But I thought you said you visited this site all the time."

"I do, Rob," she said, her eyes pleading. "But I, um, get here a different way."

Thinking of her transiting in front of him, Rob nodded that he understood. "So, where do I look?"

Dee pointed. "That last fence post? I'm about three feet past it and slightly to the left, right next to the big clump of beach grass."

He got out of the car, retrieved his shovel from the back, and walked past the car to the spot Dee had identified. He turned to Dee. She smiled and nodded her head.

Rob got to the spot, looked down, and realized that the shovel was overkill. He briefly had an image of plunging the shovel into the sand only to drive it well into Dee's body. No, there was a better way. He dropped to his knees and used his hands to start digging into the sand. It was slow as the sides continued to collapse back to the bottom, but after a few minutes, a hole had started to form. Despite the cool air, he had started to sweat, as much from nerves as exertion. He was beginning to think that Dee had the spot wrong when his fingers hit something solid at the bottom of his excavation.

Slowing his digging, he tried to clear away the sand to see what he had found. At first, he thought it was just a buried piece of driftwood. It was brown, wrinkled, and misshapen. But as he peered down, he realized it was not a piece of wood. It was a hand. He had found her. The realization hit him like a hammer blow. Everything she had said to him was true. She had been murdered and buried out here alone without even a sheet or shroud around her for comfort. What sort of animal would do this?

He looked over at the car and gave a thumbs up.

He excavated carefully around the hand and then cleared enough to see her wrist. What he could see reminded him of ancient Egyptian mummies, dried and desiccated. Satisfied he had cleared enough away, he stood up, pulled his phone from his pocket, and took several pictures. He then kneeled down and took some close-ups of the wrist, her fingers, and her wedding band. Satisfied, he refilled the hole and smoothed the sand. Looking around, he found a plate size stone and placed it on top. He took one final picture capturing both the stone and the fence post for future reference. He put his phone away, brushed his hands together to clean off the sand, and walked back to the car. He opened the door. The car was empty.

Rob looked around him. "Dee?"

She was gone.

Rob got into the car, started the engine, and backed up slowly until he reached the turn-off at the main trail. He moved the shifter to drive, pulled into the track, and headed back toward Wauwinet.

A wry smile appeared on his face.

I'm coming for you, Jack.

CHAPTER TWENTY

Returning from Great Point, Rob felt satisfied and somewhat vindicated. Everything Dee had told him had proven true. And he believed he now had solid proof for the sheriff that Jack Reiner had indeed murdered and buried his wife. He parked the car next to the cottage, returned the shovel to the shed, and headed inside.

Glancing at his watch, he realized that his adventure had taken the greater part of the day and that those butterflies had morphed into hunger pains. He made himself a sandwich, grabbed a seltzer from the refrigerator, and sat down at the table, anxious to strategize just how he was going to approach the sheriff with this newfound evidence.

Chewing slowly, he thought through how the sheriff might receive this. Surely he would want to exhume the grave and confirm the body was Dee's. Certainly, he would order an autopsy to determine the cause of death. But would there be enough evidence to point the finger at Reiner? He took another bite of his sandwich. At a minimum, it should confirm that she was killed. But would it cast light on who had killed her? Would there be enough evidence to prosecute? Rob took a sip of his seltzer and stared out the window. It certainly was a lot more than a yearbook photo.

His phone dinged with a text from Pip asking how his day was going. Rob smiled and quickly texted back: Not bad. Not bad at all. Any chance we could see Fred again on Monday? He stared at his phone anxiously and could see the bubbles of her response pulsing. Then they stopped. Rob jumped when his phone rang. It was Pip.

"Hello?" said Rob nervously.

Pip's voice on the other end was bright and energetic, as always. "Well, I was going to text you back but then thought it would be better to say this in person."

"Say what?" asked Rob.

"Are you friggin' crazy!" said Pip excitedly. "What makes you think my cousin would even give you the time of day right now after that dumpster fire of a meeting with him yesterday!"

Rob had to smile at her choice of words. She really was a unique character.

"Seriously, what has changed in the last twenty-four hours?"

Rob paused, unsure of how best to tell her about his trip to Great Point. He thought about telling her the whole story, from when Dee snuck up on him to describing the exact location of where she had led him to.

"Rob? Are you there?" asked Pip.

"Sorry, Pip. I was just thinking about how to tell you this."

"Tell me what?"

Rob took a breath. "I found her."

"Found who?"

"Dee." Rob paused. "That is, her body."

The line went quiet.

"Pip? Are you still there?"

"I am." Her voice had lost its usual cheery tone. "Sorry. Just trying to process this. You say you found her body?"

"I did," replied Rob.

"How the hell did you find her body?"

Rob coughed uncomfortably. "She showed me."

"She showed you? Who did?"

Rob stood up and walked to the window. He looked out at the hedge as a bright yellow goldfinch landed on the top and fluffed its feathers. His attention turned back to Pip. "Dee did Pip. She guided me directly to the spot where she was buried."

"Dee did…" said Pip, her voice trailing off.

"I know it sounds crazy, but it's true. And I have pictures."

"Pictures?" asked Pip, her voice shaking.

"Yes. Pictures. Of her hand and arm. It is all I was able to physically uncover."

She again fell quiet, letting this news sink in.

"Pip?"

"Rob," she replied, her voice serious. "How are you going to explain this to Fred?"

"Explain what?"

"How you found her body. Are you just going to say a ghost led you directly to the burial site?"

He paused. "Do you think it matters? Wouldn't he be satisfied just knowing the location?"

"He might think that you had something to do with it."

"Me?" said Rob, shocked. "How the hell could I have something to do with her death?"

"Well," said Pip, "you claim you've only been on the island a few weeks. But how do any of us know that's true? How do we know you weren't here six years ago, had a fling with her, and then killed her? I mean, think about it. Only the killer would know where she's buried."

Pip's words hit Rob like a hammer blow. "What? Me? Oh my god, no!" said Rob incredulously. "Six years ago, I was happily married and living in St. Louis. Call any of my friends, and they'll tell you. And I never stepped foot on this island until October. I swear!"

"Relax, Rob. I believe you. I think," said Pip. "It's just that Fred is going to wonder how you knew about a grave site go, and I'm not sure telling him it was a ghost will satisfy him."

Rob paced around the kitchen, the phone clutched to his ear. "Does it really matter at this point," he said softly. "Isn't the important thing that we now have a body in the case of a missing woman. The wife of a prominent local? A case he led the investigation on?"

"You're right, of course. Let me text him and see if he has time to meet us again."

Rob smiled weakly. "Thanks, Pip."

"Of course. I'll text you the details if and when I hear back from him."

"Okay. I hope to see you Monday."

"Me too," Pip replied. "And Rob?"

"Yes?"

"Maybe stay home for the rest of the weekend and enjoy some football? I don't want you finding any more bodies."

"Will do." He smiled, dropped his phone, and ended the call.

Pip had texted him in the middle of the second quarter. Meet me Monday at Fred's at 10, followed by a thumbs up and heart emoji. He replied with confirmation and wondered once again how the hell he had gotten himself into this mess.

* * *

Rob arrived in Town early and parked the Jeep on Main Street in front of the local bookstore. He had a little time to kill, so he ambled down the sidewalk and took in the sights. Most of the stores were closed, the hours limited to the weekends. There were shops of all kinds, from clothing to jewelry to art. As he stood in front of one of the galleries, a small brass plaque caught his attention: The Jack Tate & Tristam Coffin Foundation. He thought back to the night at the Whaling Museum and the couple he had met. He was clearly successful, and she from St. Louis.

I'd like to see them again.

He turned and made his way down Main Street, crossed the cobblestones, and walked down Water Street to the sheriff's office. Pip was waiting for him in front of the door, her face clearly showing concern. They hugged briefly.

"Are you okay?" asked Rob.

Pip smiled thinly. "No, not really. I am a bit concerned about how Fred is going to react to all of this."

Rob nodded. "I know. If I were him, I would certainly wonder as well. I'm just hoping his instincts will kick in, and he'll want to retrieve the body and confirm who it is and what happened to her."

"I hope you're right," said Pip. She looked up at him, her eyes bright. "Ready?"

"As I'll ever be," replied Rob. He grabbed the handle of the door and swung it open. "After you."

They made their way back to the conference room where they had met the week before. They didn't have to wait long. Fred strode into the room, his presence intimidating. He sat down heavily in the chair across from them. "I wasn't expecting to see you two here again so quickly," he said. "I thought we had pretty much cleared things up on Friday."

Pip leaned against the table. "I know, Fred. And we really appreciate you taking the time to meet with us again, especially on such short notice. But Rob here," she turned to him, "has something he'd like to show you."

Fred grunted. "Another yearbook picture? Maybe from her varsity soccer team?" he said sarcastically.

Rob opened his phone and pulled up one of the pictures, and slid his phone over to the sheriff.

Fred pulled it over and glanced at the picture. His face hardened. "What am I looking at?"

Rob cleared his throat. "That, sir, is the grave of who I believe is Deidre Reiner."

The sheriff slowly pulled his eyes from the phone and raised them to meet Rob's. "When was this picture taken?"

"Late yesterday morning. The date and time stamp will confirm it."

The sheriff grunted again. "And where was it taken?"

Rob paused. "I'm not sure of the exact name of the area, but it was a few miles south of Great Point, on a track a couple of hundred yards from the water." Rob leaned over and pointed at the phone. "If you swipe to the right, you'll see I have several more photos of the site."

The sheriff perused the remaining pictures in silence. He settled back on the first picture he was shown and appeared to be thinking intently. Finally, he looked back up, first at Pip and then to Rob. "How in the hell did you find this?"

Rob shifted uncomfortably in his seat. "It's complicated."

"It's complicated?" asked the sheriff incredulously.

"Yessir. I know how this must look to you. But I promise it's on the up and up."

The sheriff leaned back in his chair and folded his hands in his lap. His eyes stared intensely into Rob's. "You were here yesterday with a story about Deidre Reiner's disappearance and crazy accusations against her husband. And all you had for evidence was a high school yearbook picture." Fred leaned forward, his arms resting on the table and his voice forceful. "And today, you show up with pictures of her alleged grave? What the hell am I to believe other than you are playing me with some sort of prank."

"Oh, sir, not at all," Rob stammered. "I truly believe this is her grave, and she was buried there by the person, the man, that killed her. All I'm asking is that you go investigate for yourself."

Fred stared at Rob and then turned to the phone on the conference table. He punched in a number, and a voice came on the line. "This is Sheila."

"Hi, Sheila, it's Fred. What do I have on my calendar this afternoon?"

"Oh, hi, Fred. Hang on, let me check." The line went dead for a minute, and then Sheila came back on the line. "You just have a couple of meetings. The first is the budget meeting with the Town, that's at two. And then you are scheduled to talk about the summer staffing plan with HR at four."

"Okay. Could you reschedule both of those for me, maybe push them to tomorrow or Wednesday?"

"Sure, Fred. Happy to."

"Thanks, Sheila." He terminated the call and turned to Rob. "My afternoon is now suddenly available. I'd like you to take me to where you took those pictures," he said, pointing at Rob's phone.

Rob's face lit up in surprise. "Of course, of course. I'd be happy to show you." He turned and smiled at Pip. He turned back to the sheriff. "When would you like to go?"

The sheriff glanced at his watch. "To be honest, I don't work well on an empty stomach. Meet me back in here at one, and we will head out then."

"Perfect," said Rob, standing up. He reached his hand over the table. Fred stood and accepted it. "Thank you, sheriff. Thank you for taking the time. I promise you will not regret it."

"I hope not," said Fred. Turning to Pip, he said, "and if this ends up as some wild ass goose chase, I'll be holding you accountable." A faint smile was on his lips.

"Thanks, Fred."

"See you at one, then," he said to Rob, turned, and walked out of the room, his footsteps echoing down the hall.

Rob hugged Pip. "Thank you, Pip. Thank you for making this meeting happen."

Pip looked at him with concern in her eyes. "I just hope this works out how you want it to." She paused and then chuckled. "And to be honest, I really don't want him pissed at me."

Rob smiled back. "This will all work out. I promise."

* * *

Pip headed back to work while Rob grabbed a lunch of clam chowder at the Rose & Crown. He was back at the sheriff's office at one. Fred was waiting for him outside by his cruiser, a Ford Explorer. "Are you ready for this?" he asked Rob.

"Yes, sir. Would you like me to drive?"

"Just get in," said Fred, motioning to the passenger door.

Rob quickly obeyed and climbed into the car. He fastened his seat belt and looked over at Fred. "We need to head to Great Point, over the sand. I can then show you the trail that will take us to the site."

"Okay," said the sheriff doubtfully. He put the car in drive and pulled out onto Water Street. They made their way through town with a minimum of conversation. Navigating through the Milestone Road rotary, briefly onto Milestone Road, and then turning left onto Polpis Road, the sheriff turned to Rob and said, "So tell me about yourself."

"What do you want to know?"

"How about just telling me how you ended up here on Nantucket, for starters."

"Oh, okay," said Rob. He took a minute to gather his thoughts and then let the story flow, starting with his life in St. Louis, his marriage to Sarah, her untimely death, and how he ended up coming to Nantucket solely through finding a brochure that his late wife had saved.

"So you came here because your wife had wanted to come here with you when she was alive?" the sheriff asked.

"Yes, pretty much. I just really needed to get away. Too many memories. I needed a fresh start, somewhere new."

"Well, I'm sorry for your loss. All this notwithstanding, I hope you can find what you are looking for here."

Rob looked at the sheriff. "Thank you," he said softly.

They turned onto Wauwinet Road, and shortly they had passed through the little village and were making their way into the heavy sand.

"Don't you need to let air out of your tires?" asked Rob knowingly.

The sheriff smiled. "I'm impressed you would know about that. But no, I keep my tires deflated all the time."

"Isn't that dangerous?"

"Maybe if we were on the mainland. But I rarely travel over forty here, and in case of emergency, I don't want to have to take the time and stop if I need to get on the beach quickly."

Rob nodded. "Makes sense, I guess." He glanced out the windshield. "Okay, follow the inner trail here," he said, pointing at the upcoming fork.

The sheriff steered his SUV to the left. He turned to Rob. "Now what?"

"It's about a mile or so on this trail. Then we will go by a pond, and a few hundred feet past that, we will need to make a left."

The sheriff grunted and looked out the windshield. The SUV moved easily through the tracks, its travel only disrupted by the occasional bumps in the sand. Nearly twenty minutes passed before the turn appeared.

"Right there!" said Rob, pointing excitedly. "Turn left just past that dead pine."

The sheriff did as he was told.

"We are getting close."

"Hmm," said the sheriff.

The truck traversed the narrow path slowly, the branches occasionally scraping the side of the vehicle. They emerged into a clearing, and just ahead, a lone pine tree stood along an old fence line.

"That's it!" said Rob. "It's right there next to the fence line. See that slight rise in the sand?"

"Okay," said the sheriff. He stopped the car and slid the transmission into park. He unclipped his seat belt and exited the car. Rob did the same. The sand was heavy here and made it difficult to walk. Rob led the sheriff to the spot he had visited the day before and stopped in front of the rock he had placed on the grave.

"This is it," he said, pointing at the rock.

"Are you sure?"

"Positive. Let me show you." Rob knelt down, set the rock aside, and began to clear away the sand. Like yesterday, he found the digging difficult as the sand continuously collapsed back into the hole. Sweating, he finally cleared enough of the sand to reveal a desiccated arm. He stood up and looked at the sheriff. "There."

Fred gazed intently down at the hole. He looked at Rob and then kneeled down. He brushed some sand away and felt the skin. "Oh my god," he said slowly. He looked up at Rob, his eyes burning. "And who do you think this is?"

"Deidre Reiner."

The sheriff stood and pulled his phone out of his pocket. "No offense, but I hope you are wrong." He tapped the screen and held the phone to his ear. "Sheila? This is Fred. I need you to notify the coroner and Nantucket PD and have them meet me here immediately." Rob could just make out a voice on the other end of the call. "Where am I? Hang on." The sheriff quickly pulled up a mapping app on his phone and forwarded his location. "Okay, I just texted you the coordinates. Tell them this is urgent, and I need them here ASAP."

Rob walked over and looked down at the grave. Satisfied that he may be bringing Dee's murder to light, he was still struggling to reconcile her beautiful image with this withered piece of flesh buried in the sand. It made his heart hurt.

His thoughts were interrupted by the sheriff's baritone voice. "We also need a crime scene unit here. Get on the phone to Hyannis and make sure they are on the next ferry over." The sheriff looked down at the grave and back up at Rob. "And Sheila? Call

Detective Fisch and let her know we have a possible homicide on our hands."

Fred ended the call and turned to Rob, his face serious. "You and I are going to have a little talk. Get in the car."

CHAPTER TWENTY-ONE

T he drive back to town was quiet. Rob attempted to start a conversation several times but was met with stony silence from the sheriff. He thought he had been doing a good thing by finding Dee's body and hopefully bringing her murder - and murderer - to light. But that confidence was quickly waning as he realized the fragile ground he was standing on. For the first time, he could really see the situation from the sheriff's perspective, and the butterflies returned. Not from nervousness but from fear. The cold rock at the bottom of your stomach fear.

I think he believes I killed her.

He turned his gaze outward and tried to relax by taking in the scenery around him. Despite the view, he couldn't keep his mind away from the position he had put himself in. Here he was, barely a few weeks on the island and knee deep in a pile of shit, as his father used to say.

Fifteen minutes later, the sheriff pulled his Explorer into his reserved spot and keyed the ignition. He turned to Rob. "Come with me." The sheriff got out of the car and slammed his door, leaving Rob alone in the quiet of the car. He watched the sheriff cross in front, pause, and look back at him, his eyes burning. Impatient, the sheriff waved his arm to Rob to get out of the car.

Rob secretly wished he could open the door and run away. Jump in his Jeep, tear back to the cottage, pack up his meager belongings, and grab the first ferry off this rock. Forget Dee,

Reiner, and this whole mess. Go back to the midwest where he felt safe. And then he thought of his first meeting with Dee on the bicycle bridge. How kind she was to him and making him feel welcome. And then he thought of Pip. Her eyes bright, her musical laugh, and how she had made him feel.

There is no going back now.

Rob undid his belt and slowly opened the door. He stepped out of the SUV and followed the sheriff through the door, as a condemned man would follow the executioner.

Once inside, the sheriff directed him to the same conference room where they had already met twice, both within the space of twenty-four hours. "Take a seat and get comfortable," the sheriff said sternly. And then, with a touch of compassion, added, "Can we get you anything? Coffee, water?"

"No, sir. But thank you."

The sheriff nodded. "Very well. I'll be right back." He turned, walked out of the room, and closed the door.

The room fell quiet, the only sounds being the sheriff's footsteps receding down the hall and the ticking of an old clock on the wall. The red hand ticking off each second while the minute hand made slow progress around the dial. It was very similar to the clock Rob remembered from grade school, and suddenly he was back in Miss Reardon's fifth-grade class at Glendale Elementary, nervously watching the clock count down to morning recess. The butterflies in his stomach were churning. He was about to get beat up.

It had started the day before with a simple dispute at the swings. He had been enjoying pumping himself higher and higher, trying to break his personal record. Could he get higher than the bar? Could he maybe even go all the way around? He pumped harder and harder, slowly gaining height with each push. It was exhilarating.

"Hey, you. Get off the swing."

Rob was lost in his pursuit.

"You. Butthead. Get off."

He felt a hand slap at his foot, sending him twisting and disrupting his cadence. He looked down and saw Booger Williams, the meanest kid in the school. Booger also had six inches and at least forty pounds on him. Rob looked up and saw he had nearly broken his record. He regained his equilibrium and pumped harder.

"I told you to get off."

Rob ignored the voice, pulled his legs under him, leaned forward, and prepared to push with all his might when he reached the top of his backward arc. The swing paused at the top; Rob leaned back, extended his legs, and thrust his body forward. As he began his upward swing, he briefly thought he was going to do it when he felt a hand grab his ankle hard and pull him to the side. The swing twisted crazily, and for a moment, Rob thought he could hold on. But the hand pulled harder, and Rob lost his balance and fell off, hitting the ground hard, butt first.

Tears welled in his eyes, as much from the pain as the frustration. He stood up slowly and looked at Booger. "Why did you do that?" His voice pleading and weak.

"Because I told you to get off, dumbshit." Booger grabbed the still-moving swing and steadied it, preparing to get on.

Anger sparked in Rob, and he pushed Booger hard, sending him face-first into the dirt.

Booger scrambled to his feet and quickly brought himself face to face with Rob. "You little piece of crap. I am going to kill you." Rob prepared himself for a blow just as the recess bell rang. Kids quickly made a beeline for the doors, and Rob was all too happy to follow suit.

A voice shouted from behind him. "Tomorrow morning, butthead. Morning recess. You die."

A car horn sounded outside his window and snapped him out of his reverie. He smiled sadly to himself. Here he was, twenty-plus years later, and still feeling that cold hand of dread that he had felt so long ago.

Footsteps in the hall were approaching but definitely not those of the sheriff. They were quicker and higher pitched. Sounded like heels.

The handle turned, and the door opened. In stepped an attractive, fortyish woman with curly, shoulder-length, brown hair. She was dressed in navy slacks with a white blouse. A tan tufted vest completed her outfit. She had a gun strapped to her belt and carried a small black leather notebook that looked as if it had seen many years of use.

She approached the table. "You must be Robert McGlynn."

Rob nervously stood up. "I am." His voice was weak. The butterflies were swarming.

"I'm Detective Tina Fisch." She extended her hand.

Rob took it.

"Please have a seat," she said and motioned to the chair. He did as he was told.

She put her notebook on the table and opened it to a fresh page. She slid her hand under her vest and came out with a pen. She clicked it and made a notation at the top of the page. Rob could see she had written his name, the date, and the time.

"So, Rob. May I call you Rob?"

"Of course."

"Sheriff Boston has asked me to speak to you. Apparently, you helped him locate a body?"

Rob cleared his throat. "Well, um, yes. I did."

"And Sheriff Boston suggested you know who the deceased might be?"

"Um, yes. I think the body belongs to Deirdre Reiner."

The detective wrote in her notebook and looked up at Rob. "And you know it's her because...?"

Rob shifted in his chair. "It's, um, complicated."

"Complicated?" replied the detective sarcastically. "Please, Rob. Tell me how it's complicated."

Rob took a moment to gather his thoughts. He let out a deep breath and decided to just be honest. "When I arrived here a few weeks ago, I met a lady on a walk. I'm in a rented cottage in Sconset, and as you probably know, it's pretty quiet out there this time of year. And since I was new to Nantucket, it was nice to meet someone."

The detective took notes and spoke without looking up. "And who was this lady?"

"She said her name was Dee. And over the next couple of weeks, we became friends."

Detective Fisch raised her head from her notes and looked at Rob questioningly.

"Oh no, not like that," said Rob nervously. "I mean, she's an attractive lady, but it was much more of a platonic relationship."

The detective turned back to her notebook. "Please, continue."

"Well, about a week ago, we were out on a walk and talking about things. I'm trying to write my first novel and was kind of venting to her about things and the struggles I'm having." Rob shifted in his chair again. "We got on to the topic of her husband and how he had treated her badly. Quite badly, in fact."

"Was she more specific than that?"

"Yes, She told me that, initially, it had been a wonderful marriage, but over time he became very controlling. And then he became physical."

"Physical? How?"

"She said he had started to hit her. At first, a punch to the stomach but over time became more and more violent. He also took away her phone, her money, essentially anything that would have connected her to the outside world."

The detective looked up, her eyes locked in on Rob's. "And did she try to get help?"

Rob shook his head. "No, there was just no way. She mentioned she had no family, no friends. She was trapped."

The detective shook her head faintly. "Okay, then, how did you meet and befriend her? How did she finally get out of the house?"

"Well, um, that's where it gets complicated."

"How she was able to escape her husband? Get out of the house, you mean?"

"Um, no. She never got out of the house."

"Never got out of the house..." the detective asked, her voice trailing off.

Rob paused. Took a breath and blurted out. "That's when she told me she was a winter resident."

Detective Fisch put her pen down and slowly looked up at Rob. "A winter resident?" she asked dubiously.

"Yes. Are you familiar with the term?"

"Well, yes. I heard all the stories around the campfire growing up. And that's what they are. Stories."

Rob tried to sound more confident than he felt. "What if I told you that they really do exist?"

"Winter residents?"

"Yes."

"Then I think my next move with you would be to order a psych eval."

"Detective Fisch. I promise you. This is what she told me. Why would I lie?"

"Oh, I don't know. Maybe you killed this person, buried them out at Great Point, and now want to look like the hero."

The fear stabbed in Rob's gut. "Oh, no. No, no, no. I had absolutely nothing to do with that." Rob stood up and started to pace around the room, trying to burn off the nervous energy he was feeling. Detective Fisch's eyes followed him as he crossed from wall to wall. "Hell, I never even stepped foot on this island until the beginning of October!"

"Let's talk about that."

"Talk about what," said Rob exasperatedly.

"Why you are here. On Nantucket."

Rob stopped, turned to the detective, and said, "I'm here because my wife died."

"Your wife died?" asked the detective accusingly.

Rob narrowed his eyes and glared at her. "I lost her to cancer. Ovarian. We discovered it when we were trying to have a baby. She was thirty-two." His body slumped as he spoke, the tension fleeing as memories of Sarah flooded back. He fought back tears.

Taken aback, Detective Fisch spoke quietly. "Oh, I'm sorry to hear that. I really am." She paused to let Rob recover and then continued. "So why Nantucket?"

Rob put his hands in his pocket and blew out a deep breath. "Because she had wanted to come here for our anniversary. And I needed to get away from St. Louis. Away from the memories. So, I thought this might just be the place to escape. And thought maybe I could finally write."

The pen worked furiously and then stopped. "So, you have never stepped foot on this island before early October of this year?"

Rob moved back to the table, sat down in his chair, and spoke plainly. "I have not. And I can give you the names of friends, customers, and family who can all attest to that."

"Okay, Rob. Let's just say, for argument's sake, that what you are telling me is true." Rob started to speak, and she held up a hand. "Hang on. You still haven't told me how you knew where to take Sheriff Boston to find the body."

Rob leaned back in his chair. "It was her. Dee. She led me to her body."

"Led you to her body," the detective repeated skeptically.

"I know what it sounds like, but that is exactly what happened." Rob proceeded to recite their trip to Great Point from the minute they left Sconset to when he took the pictures of her body.

"So if I can track down the ranger who helped you, he can confirm that she was with you?"

Rob shifted in his chair. "Um, no."

"No?" asked the detective cynically.

"Not everyone can see her."

The detective put her pen down and looked up at him. "Not everyone can see her. Well, that's convenient, isn't it?"

Rob was tired. It had been a long day. And the last hour or so with Detective Fisch had drained him physically and emotionally. "I know how it sounds. But it is the truth. From what Dee told me, very few people can actually see them, the winter residents. And I guess I'm one of the lucky ones," he finished sarcastically.

There was a knock on the door, and the sheriff entered. "Detective Fisch. May I speak to you for a minute?"

The detective nodded and turned to Rob. "Stay there. I'll be right back." She stood up and left the room. Rob could just make out snippets of their conversations in the hall.

"...crime scene team should be here in the morning..."

"...no, he hasn't said yet how he knew about the body..."

"... don't think we can hold him yet..."

"...autopsy results could take weeks..."

Fisch entered and stood by the open door. "Okay, Rob. You are free to go for now. But please don't get any ideas about leaving. We will be talking again in the next day or so."

Rob stood, walked toward the door, and paused in front of the detective. He spoke firmly. "Everything I have told you is true. I was just trying to do the right thing."

Detective Fisch nodded. Rob passed by her and walked down the hall.

Footsteps approached behind her. "What do you think?" asked the sheriff.

She turned and faced him. "You know, Fred, I've been doing this a long time. I know I don't have the experience of a big city homicide cop, but I know when I can trust my gut."

"And what is your gut saying?"

"I think he's telling the truth, as crazy as that sounds."

The sheriff grunted. "Let's just see what the coroner comes back with. We should know a lot more about the body in the next day or two."

Detective Fisch nodded. "In the meantime, I'm going to make some calls to St. Louis. I'd like to just confirm at least that part of his story."

CHAPTER TWENTY-TWO

D o you know this detective? Tina Fisch?" asked Rob. He was sitting in the garden outside the Athenaeum with Pip. It had been a couple of days since his interview with the detective and really his first chance to talk to Pip about it. They were in a corner on an old teak bench. It was a cool, foggy morning, and the few remaining leaves on the trees were capturing the mist and occasionally raining it down on the two as they talked.

"Oh, you mean Tuna?"

"Tuna?"

Pip smiled. "With the last name of Fisch and the first name of Tina? It didn't take the kids long to come up with a nickname for her. Tuna really seemed to fit."

"So you do know her?"

"No, not really. I'm sure my dad knows her; I think they were at Nantucket High together," said Pip. Her eyes wandered around the garden before landing back on Rob's. "So she really thinks you may have killed Dee?"

Rob sighed. "I don't know how she could, honestly. But she was questioning me pretty hard yesterday. And I certainly don't think she believes the whole thing about winter residents."

"Can you blame her? I mean, come on, you have to admit it takes some serious suspension of belief to allow yourself to engage in what she probably thinks is a fantasy." Pip paused. "And to be honest, I'm not sure I even believe in them."

"What?" Rob looked at Pip intently. "You're the one that told me about them in the first place! So now you don't believe me?"

She paused and looked down at her hands in her lap. "I just don't know, Rob. I'm sorry. It's just a lot easier to manage when it's hypothetical. Now that you are telling me it's actually real?" Pip shook her head. "I am just struggling to get my head around it."

The two sat quietly, each pondering their own perspective on this new situation. The garden was hushed save the soft patter of dew falling from the trees.

Pip turned suddenly and placed her hands on Rob's. "I know! Take me to meet her!"

"Detective Fisch? I thought you said you knew her, at least through your dad."

"No. I meant Dee. Your ghost. I want to meet her!"

Rob looked at her intently. "You want to meet Dee?" he asked quietly. "I'm not sure what good that will do."

"Well, first of all, it will convince me you're not crazy," said Pip laughing nervously. "And second, it might just help to have an ally standing next to you when you meet with Tuna and Fred."

Rob smiled. "Well, I guess it couldn't hurt anything, and maybe, just maybe, it might help convince you of what I'm dealing with."

"That's great!" Pip exclaimed and then leaned back, suddenly weary. "But do you think I'll be able to see her? You've said not everyone can."

"There's only one way to find out. Is now good?"

Pip was taken aback. "Don't you need to, I don't know, connect with her somehow? Let her know I'm coming?"

Rob laughed softly. "Dee has pretty much appeared to me whenever I expected her to," he paused. "And sometimes when I didn't."

"Hmm. Well, okay, I guess. Where are you parked?"

Rob stood. "I'm just right over there," and pointed down South Water street.

Pip stood and looked at Rob, her face determined. "Let's go before I realize what I'm doing and chicken out."

Rob smiled at her, quietly thanking those that be for her friendship. He helped her up from the bench and led her back to the Jeep.

* * *

As Rob and Pip made their way back to Sconset, Sheriff Fred Boston was meeting with Detective Fisch at his office in the Nantucket county building. It was a generous room with large double-hung windows which looked out across Broad Street to the Whaling Museum. Framed pictures hung on the wall showing Sheriff Boston meeting with various dignitaries, from the current governor to a former president. On the large desk behind him, a framed picture held a place of honor.

"How are Sylvia and the kids?" asked the detective, nodding at the picture.

Fred turned around, glanced at the picture, and smiled. "They are great," he said. "Desmond is playing Whaler football this year and loving it. Sylvia doesn't like it, but she's allowing it for now. And Dana is just starting to look at colleges. They just grow up too quickly." The sheriff sighed. "And how is Ellen?"

Tuna smiled. "She's still adjusting to living on the island."

"Still adjusting," said the sheriff and chuckled. "What's it been now, fifteen years?"

"Seventeen if you can believe it. But as you know, she was born and raised in New York, so it was a big change for her."

"I'm sure it was," the sheriff said. He paused and then said more seriously, "What's the latest?"

"My friend with CSU said it was probably the easiest exhumation they have ever had to do. The body was in a fairly shallow grave, and they had the scene processed in a few hours."

"What kind of shape was it in? From what I saw, it looked almost mummified."

"Actually, it was fairly well preserved, especially considering it was buried without any protection whatsoever. It was significantly dried out, probably because of the drought we've been dealing with here for the past few years. And fortunately, the creatures never found it. We were lucky."

"Physical evidence?"

"Nothing beyond the clothing on the body. She was wearing her wedding band but no other jewelry. No visible tattoos or other unique markings. And there was nothing buried with it."

"Do we have confirmation on the identity?"

"Not yet. I should be getting the preliminary coroner's report later today," said the detective, stealing a glance at her watch. "Maybe by early afternoon."

"So we don't know any more than we did two days ago?" said the sheriff, with a little frustration.

The detective looked up from her notebook. "Officially, no. Her body is on the way to Boston for the autopsy, and we should have results in a few days. But off the record, I can confirm that the body is that of a caucasian female, between 30 and 50 years of age."

"So she does match the description of Deidre Reiner?" he asked hopefully.

"Well, yes, and a few million other women."

"Noted. Cause of death?"

"Again, pending the report, there is not much to share. The techs said her body appeared to be free of any obvious indications of the cause of death."

"Really?" asked the sheriff, leaning forward.

Tuna held up her hand. "Very preliminary. And that was just their cursory look over the body. We'll know more once the autopsy is completed. Given the state of the body, it is quite likely they would miss the more subtle methods of death."

"True. Very well," said the sheriff, standing. "Is there anything I can do?"

"Actually, there is. The Medical Examiner's office is backed up as usual, and they are saying it could be several weeks before we get results. Could you maybe make a phone call for me?"

Fred smiled. "Of course. Happy to. Just please keep me in the loop."

"Of course," said the detective. She stood and made her way to the door before turning back. "You'll be the first to know."

* * *

Rob navigated the old Wagoneer down Milestone Road. Pip was shifting uncomfortably in the passenger seat. Rob looked over at her. "Nervous?"

Pip smiled awkwardly. "Well, yes, a bit. Plus, I haven't been to Sconset in years."

"Really?"

"There isn't any reason for me to be out here, to be honest. My friends, family. They all live in town. Sconset is where all the rich summer people live."

Rob smiled. "Well, I'm certainly not rich."

Pip looked at him intently. "And you are also not here in the summer." She glanced out the window at the passing moors. "Your cottage might be a deal now in the off-season. But in July or August? It would cost you at least ten times as much. Probably even more."

"Ten times?" asked Rob anxiously.

"At least."

"Wow. I had no idea. I mean, I had heard it was expensive, but nothing like that."

"Well, now you know," said Pip forcefully.

The old blue Wagoneer made its way up the hill at the end of Milestone Road and turned down Morey Lane.

"I had forgotten how small it is," said Pip. "And quiet."

"Yes on both counts." He put on his left blinker, slowed, and made the turn onto Starbuck Lane. "And here I am." He parked the Jeep in front of the Shanty and turned off the engine. He placed his hands on the wheel and turned to Pip. "Are you ready for this?"

"As ready as I'll ever be. Do you think we'll see her?"

"I don't know. But before that may I give you a tour of my winter estate?" asked Rob, smiling.

Pip returned the smile. "I would love to see your estate, sir," she said, mockingly snobbish.

"Excellent." Rob hopped out, and Pip met him at the gate.

"After you," said Rob and opened the white picket gate for her. She stepped through and crossed the short brick path to the front door. Rob followed quickly behind her, fumbling for the key in his pocket. The two were suddenly confined in the small space in front of the door. Rob nudged Pip accidentally. "I'm sorry."

Pip looked up at him and smiled warmly. "It's okay," she said softly.

Rob dropped the keys. "Damn it!" he said nervously.

Pip laughed brightly.

Rob stooped and retrieved the keys. He slid the key into the lock and turned it counter-clockwise while gripping the latch. Surprisingly he was able to get it on the first try. The hinges creaked as he swung the door open for her. "Welcome to my humble abode."

She stepped in. "Oh, Rob, this is charming! What a neat little cottage." Her eyes wandered around the room, taking in the unique roof lines, small sashed windows, and the antique prints on the wall. She stopped at the large flat screen on the wall and turned to Rob, raising an eyebrow.

"I never said it was totally historic," he said, chuckling. "Plus, that has been a lifesaver for me with the college football season."

"I bet," she replied.

He led her on a quick tour, very aware that he hadn't been expecting company and wasn't always good at cleaning up after himself. He looked at her sheepishly in the bedroom as he picked up clothes off the floor and again in the office where the wastebasket overflowed with crumpled-up paper.

"So this is where you write?"

"This is where I try to write. And fail miserably." He cast his head down, and Pip saw clearly what a disappointment this had been for him.

"I'm sorry, Rob. I wish I could help you in some way."

Rob looked up and smiled softly. "You have helped." She stepped toward him, and he quickly changed the subject. "Can I get you anything?" He brushed by her and walked out of the small room. She hesitated, then followed.

She found Rob in the kitchen, where he was placing dirty dishes in the sink and empty cans in the recycling container. Rob looked up. "I've got coffee, tea, water." He opened a cabinet, grabbed a glass, and turned to her. "It's probably a little early for bourbon," he said with a wry smile.

"I'm okay." She paused. "Do you think we should, um, try and go find her?"

He looked at the glass and then placed it next to the sink. He looked at her and said, "Only if you are ready."

Pip took a deep breath. "I'm ready."

He nodded. "Okay. Let's go." Rob led her out of the kitchen and back through the front door. He closed the gate behind them with a click, and then the two made their way down Starbuck Lane, their feet crunching on the shells.

"She lives there," said Rob pointing to a small house with a wide front porch. "And I use the term lives loosely."

Pip followed his direction, and her eyes fell on what she thought was a sad-looking old cottage. The porch was uneven. The lawn was overgrown and full of weeds. The privets flanking the entry were in desperate need of pruning. The shingles covering the walls and roof were silver and starting to curl. And the once-white trim was chalky and flaking. The condition of the house did little to calm her nerves.

Rob and Pip walked through the gate and stepped onto the porch. The wood creaked under their weight. Pip made her way to the edge of the porch and looked inside. Rob approached the door and glanced through the sidelight. The living room was dark and quiet. He knocked softly. There was no response.

"Is she here?" asked Pip expectantly.

"It can be hard to tell," said Rob. He knocked again, a little louder this time.

"Hi, Rob," said a voice from behind them. "And is that Pip?"

Rob jumped and turned suddenly. Dee was standing on the street.

"Oh, hi," Rob stammered. "I'm sorry, I didn't hear you." He glanced at Pip. She was looking at him questioningly. Rob stepped off the porch and walked toward the street.

"Yes, I brought her here hoping to meet you."

Dee nodded and kept her eyes locked on Rob's. "What did the sheriff say when you showed him the pictures of my body?"

Rob regained his composure. "Let's just say it was interesting."

"Who are you talking to?" asked Pip.

Rob turned to her. "You can't see her?" And then to Dee, "She can't see you?"

"I told you, Rob, very few people can."

Rob turned to Pip. "You really can't see her?" He motioned his arm to the street where Dee was standing.

Pip followed his hand and then looked back at him, shaking her head slowly, her eyes wide. "You are the only person here, Rob."

He sighed heavily, exasperated, and turned to Dee. "Is there any way you can make yourself visible to her?"

Dee replied, "There's not much I can do, Rob. It's really up to her. And whether or not she is willing and able to accept me and my kind."

"Willing and able?"

"It really comes down to belief and her ability to see beyond the physical world," said Dee. "Only then will she be able to see me."

Rob turned to Pip and grabbed her by the shoulders. He spoke more forcefully than he intended to. "Pip, you need to allow yourself to believe. You are the one that told me about the winter residents. She's standing right there, Pip! Please, open your mind; allow yourself to see her."

"But Rob," said Pip doubtfully.

"Just try! She is right there."

Pip turned and stared at the street. She closed her eyes, and Rob saw her body relax. After a few minutes, she slowly opened her eyes. And gasped. "Oh my god!"

"What is it?" asked Rob expectantly.

"I can see her!" exclaimed Pip.

Dee approached Pip and smiled warmly. "Thank you, Pip. Thank you for letting me into your world." She turned to Rob. "So what did the sheriff say?"

Pip was standing, staring at Dee, her eyes wide and mouth open. Rob looked at her, smiled knowingly, and then turned to Dee. "The good news is I took him to your body. So he most certainly believes a crime likely occurred. He requested a crime scene unit to exhume you, but I don't know much after that."

"Well, that's a start," said Dee.

"They also think I'm the killer."

"What?" exclaimed Dee, her usually soft voice rising.

"Think of it from their perspective. I show up out of the blue and lead the man directly to your body buried in the sand, miles from the nearest house. How could I know those details?"

"Did you tell him about me?"

Pip watched the conversation intently. She slowly brought out her phone, opened the camera, and took a picture of Rob and Dee talking. Looking at the screen, Rob's image was clear but next to him was nothing but a slight haze in the air, as if there was a smudge on the lens. Pip looked back at Dee as she turned and smiled knowingly at her.

Rob continued, "I tried, but it didn't go over well. The homicide detective, a lieutenant Fisch, questioned me pretty intensely."

"Tuna?" asked Dee, smiling.

"What, you know her?" exclaimed Rob. "Er, knew her?" he corrected.

"I met her at one of my husband's events. She was working security, and we struck up a conversation. Such a distinct name, it's hard to forget." Dee paused and looked down the street. She turned to Rob and continued, "It was right after he had hit me the first time. I thought about telling Tuna and asking her for help. But then I thought, I guess hoped, that it was a one-time thing with him." She looked down at the ground, her foot playing with a shell on the street. "But I guess it wasn't, was it?"

"Wasn't what?" asked Pip.

Dee looked up at Pip. "It wasn't a one-time thing. He got more and more physical. And then he killed me."

Pip's eyes went wide as it all came together for her. What this poor woman had been through. What Rob had been dealing with. She told herself then and there that she would do everything she could to bring justice for this woman.

Rob's phone rang, breaking the silence. He pulled it out of his pocket and looked at the number. "It's local." He tapped the screen and lifted the phone to his ear. "Hello?"

"Hi, Rob, it's Detective Fisch." Rob glanced at Pip and Dee and mouthed, "Tuna."

"Oh, hi, detective. How are you?"

"I'm fine, Rob. I just wanted to let you know that the preliminary autopsy report came back, and you were correct."

"Correct?" asked Rob.

"Yes. The body you led us to is indeed that of Deidre Reiner. We had to turn to her dental records for confirmation. We'll also run DNA when we have a comparative sample, but that's a formality at this point. The coroner is confident on the ID."

"That's great," said Rob. "Was there anything else?" His eyes danced between Dee's and Pip's.

"I'll be making the family notification tomorrow morning. And you and I still have some talking to do. I'd like you to meet me tomorrow afternoon. Shall we say two o'clock?"

"Two o'clock," Rob confirmed. "I'll be there."

"Good," said Tuna, and the line went dead.

"What is it?" asked Dee.

Rob turned to her and said sadly. "I'm sorry, Dee. They confirmed that it was your body. I guess they'll be notifying Jack tomorrow."

Dee smiled, "That's great! Do you think they'll arrest him?"

Rob looked at Pip and back to Dee. He shook his head. "I have no idea. But I'm meeting with Tuna tomorrow afternoon. Maybe we will know more after that."

"Thank you. I can't tell you how much this means to me."

Rob smiled. "I'm just glad I could help."

"And it was nice to meet you," said Dee, her eyes on Pip. "Thank you as well."

Pip smiled and turned toward Rob. "It's really Rob that deserves all the credit." She turned back to Dee. "Wait, where did she go?" she asked excitedly.

Rob turned and saw the street was empty. "Welcome to my world," he said with a chuckle. He turned back to Pip and said, "How about that bourbon now?"

CHAPTER TWENTY-THREE

T he driveway leading to the house was long, winding, and paved with shells. Lush grass, freshly trimmed, bordered each side while every hundred feet, a matching pair of maple trees straddled the road. Past the grass and the trees, dense scrub created a nearly impenetrable wall cutting off any hope of escape. Through this natural tunnel, Sheriff Fred Boston slowly navigated in his Ford Explorer with Detective Fisch riding shotgun.

"You know, I could have done this on my own," said Tuna. "It's only a notification."

Sheriff Boston glanced at her. "Actually, it is more than that. It is our only chance to gauge his reaction to the news. To see how he handles it."

"True. So you think he did it?"

"Are you asking me if I believe the story of a crazy man from the midwest who sees ghosts?" asked the sheriff.

"C'mon, Fred. Seriously."

The sheriff navigated a bend in the driveway. Up ahead, it looked like they were getting close as flashes of pale yellow appeared through the dense bushes. "I met with Reiner a number of times during the investigation of his second wife's disappearance," said the sheriff. "And there was always something just off about him. I could never put my finger on it. But it just didn't add up."

Tuna was about to speak when the car emerged from the scrub into a broad expanse of green. A luxuriant lawn, its grass neatly striped from a recent mowing, led to a large, two-story home. It was a house worthy of a successful whaling captain. Built in the Greek revival style popular in the mid-19th century, four fluted columns supported a large gable with a single, half-moon window centered under the peak. Double-hung windows, trimmed in white, contrasted with the clapboard body painted a subtle yellow. The front door, a deep red, was topped with an elaborate pediment supported by two pilasters. The design, meant to impress, was doing its job.

Sheriff Boston pulled his SUV up in front of the door, slid the handle into park, and turned off the car. "I'm going to let you do most of the talking, Tuna. I'm just going to watch."

"Okay, Fred."

They got out of the truck and walked to the front door. An oversize brass knocker in the shape of a whale fluke greeted them. Tuna reached out, lifted the fluke, and hammered it down on the strike, the sound loudly reverberating through the still air. Footsteps, at first faint, grew more loudly as they approached the door. A lock inside slid home with authority, and the doorknob, shaped like a pineapple, turned. The door swung open. Jack Reiner stood in the opening, his large frame filling the space. He was dressed in neatly pressed khakis, a navy blue cable knit sweater, and tan loafers. From inside came the distinct smell of a wood fire.

"Ah, Sheriff Boston. I wasn't expecting you." He reached out and shook his hand. Turning to the detective. "And you are?"

"Tina Fisch," said the detective. "Detective Tina Fisch."

"Nice to meet you, detective," said Jack confidently. He glanced slowly between the two. "What can I do for you?"

"Mr. Reiner, we are here about your wife."

"Emily? Oh, she's out at the moment, but I can certainly have her contact you." And then cautiously. "What do you need to talk with her about?"

"No sir, we are not here for Emily. We are here about Deidre."

A pulse of adrenalin flowed through Jack's body, but his eyes and body posture revealed nothing. "Deidre? What about her? Did you find her?" He did his best imitation of sounding excited about the possibility.

The sheriff stood rigidly next to the detective, his brown eyes staring intently.

"Can we come in?" asked Tuna.

"Oh, of course. I'm sorry, where are my manners?" said Jack. He stepped back from the entry and waved them in. "Please, let's go into the kitchen. It's right through there," he said, pointing.

Jack led them through an expansive living room. A massive brick fireplace with an elaborate mantle was the focal point. Setting perpendicular to the fireplace, a pair of large navy sofas faced each other over an elaborate cocktail table. Across from the fireplace, a large glass-fronted cabinet displayed an impressive collection of antique Canton blue and white porcelain. On the far wall, an elegant curved staircase, its balusters white with a polished walnut handrail, descended, ending in front of the framed opening into the kitchen. Hung around the room were a series of framed oil portraiture of men dressed in their finery. The backgrounds of the paintings and the varied clothing suggested that they were done many years apart.

"This is a beautiful home," said Tuna. She paused and looked from painting to painting. "Are these your relatives?" she asked.

Jack stopped and turned. "Thank you. And actually, yes, they are." He pointed to a portrait over the fireplace. "That is Hezekiah Able. He was a whaling captain and actually built this house," he said proudly. He motioned to a smaller painting hanging on a side wall. "That is my grandfather, John Reiner." And pointing to a third at the base of the stairs, said, "And this is my great, great, grandfather, Digby Grey. He transitioned the family business from whaling to finance in the late 19th century."

The detective was not stirred with Reiner's genealogical display but feigned interest. "Impressive."

Jack smiled arrogantly. "Thank you." He started walking and led them into a huge, modern kitchen filled with the morning sunshine. Large windows framed the wall with expansive views of Nantucket harbor, the blue water twinkling. In the distance, the morning ferry was just rounding Brant Point and heading to Hyannis.

"Can I get you anything? Coffee, tea, water?"

"No, sir. Thank you."

Jack took a seat on a Windsor-backed stool, one foot on the floor, the other hooked to the bottom stretcher. He leaned an elbow on the marble counter and looked confidently at Fisch and Boston, who both remained standing. "So, please, tell me. You found Deidre? Where is she?"

Tuna decided to take the blunt and forceful approach. "She's dead, sir."

"Dead?" said Jack, acting surprised.

The detective paused, assessing his reaction.

"Dead?" Jack repeated more forcefully. "I don't understand."

Sheriff Boston took a step forward and said, "We found her body buried in a shallow grave near Coskata Pond out on Great Point."

"Her body? Grave? What are you saying?" said Jack, his voice rising. Despite his calm exterior, the adrenalin was charging through his body.

How the hell had they found her!

"We believe she was murdered, sir," said Tuna. "We believe she was killed and then buried to hide the crime."

"Killed? When?"

"We are still waiting on the final coroner's report, sir, but we believe it happened shortly after your wife disappeared six years ago."

"But she ran away," said Jack and turned to the sheriff. "You showed me the evidence. The credit card receipts, phone records. You thought maybe she had gone home to California." He turned back to Tuna. "And you are telling me she is dead."

"I'm very sorry, sir."

Jack stood and walked to the window. He looked out over the lawn as a rabbit with strange white fur nibbled the grass. His mind was racing. The rabbit, startled by an enemy unseen, bounded under a privet.

Sheriff Boston stepped towards him. "She was from Pittsburgh, sir." Detective Fisch looked at the sheriff questioningly.

"What?' said Jack, confused, turning to face him.

"Your wife was from the Pittsburgh area. Not California."

"I know that!" said Jack, irritated. "What the hell does that have to do with this situation?"

"We are just trying to determine what happened to her," said the sheriff. "I know it's been years, but is there anything you recall that could help us? Anything maybe you didn't know or share with us at the time?"

Reiner looked steadily at the two law enforcement officials.

Think Jack. Think!

Seconds passed, and then Jack walked over and sat down heavily in an upholstered chair. He lowered his face into his hands and sighed. Rubbing his cheeks, he looked up at the sheriff.

"I'm afraid I might not have been one hundred percent honest with you back then."

"Okay," said Sheriff Boston. "What did you hold back?"

Jack paused and then said nervously, "She was having an affair."

"Deidre was?" asked Tuna.

Jack looked at her. "Yes."

"And you decided not to tell us this?" said the sheriff angrily. "Why?"

Jack pretended to fight back tears. He looked at the sheriff and said, "Because I was embarrassed. And I have a certain level of, um, stature in the community. I didn't want people to know she made a fool of me."

Boston looked at the detective and raised an eyebrow. Tuna nodded imperceptibly and turned to Jack. "Can you tell me more about this affair? Do you know who she was seeing?"

Jack dropped his hands into his lap and started rubbing his thighs. "I don't know who it was. Damn, I wish I did!" he exclaimed and stood up. He walked over to the window and gazed out on his kingdom. The strangely furred rabbit was back. He looked back at the detective. "But I was going to find out. I had made some inquiries, quietly, for a good private investigator who I could hire to find out. But trust me, that is harder than it sounds on this little island."

"You didn't discover who she was seeing?"

Jack crossed his arms. "No. I didn't. I just woke up one morning and realized she was gone. That's when I called you lot."

"So I'm guessing you suspected that she had run away with this person, whoever it was?" asked Tuna.

Jack nodded in confirmation.

"Did you know she was unhappy with you?" asked Tuna.

Jack's eyes blazed with anger briefly before he recovered his composure. "No. I thought she was very happy. I gave her everything she ever wanted and treated her like a queen."

Tuna nodded. "Could we perhaps look through her things? Maybe there might be a clue as to who she was seeing."

Jack grunted. "I cleaned out all her things a year or so after she disappeared. I donated them to the Thrift Shop at the hospital."

"Everything?"

Jack went back to the window. "Yes. Everything." He turned to face the detective. "It might sound a bit callous, but based on what this man here told me," he motioned his arm toward the sheriff, "I figured she was gone and never coming back." A strange smile came over his face. "And in the end, I guess I was right."

Detective Fisch looked at Sheriff Boston and then back to Jack Reiner. He stood defensively, his arms crossed, daring her to say more.

"Very well, sir. We will leave you to your grief. If you have any questions for us, please don't hesitate to reach out to either Sheriff Boston or myself." She turned and started walking to the front door, the sheriff by her side while Jack followed, anxious for them to leave his house. She stopped in the living room, her eyes dancing from portrait to portrait. She turned to Jack while pointing at a portrait on the side wall. "And who is that again?"

Jack glanced at the portrait. "That is Digby Grey."

"Hmmm," said the detective, staring intently at the picture. "Interesting." She paused and then said, "Thank you again, Mr. Reiner. We will be in touch."

They exited the door just before it closed firmly behind them, the bolt sliding home with authority. Climbing into the SUV, Tuna turned and said, "What do you think?"

The sheriff started the car and put it in gear. "That man is guilty as hell."

"So you sensed it too?" said Tuna.

"Absolutely. That whole story about the affair? What a crock of shit. That man killed her, and now he's trying to cover his tracks.

Convenient that all of her belongings were disposed of, don't you think?"

Tuna looked out at the passing scrub. "Very convenient. Let's just hope there is some evidence from the body that might help point the finger in his direction. If all we have is a six-year-old corpse, I'm not sure how we are going to be able to go after him."

The SUV disappeared down the drive as a pair of intense hazel eyes watched it leave from a slightly parted curtain in an upstairs window. A tear was tracing slowly down a bruised cheekbone.

"What was that all about with the portrait?" asked the sheriff. They had reached the end of the drive and turned on Polpis Road.

"Digby Grey?" responded Tuna. "It didn't hit me until we were leaving, but I knew I recognized that name."

"Recognized it in what way?"

Tuna was quiet, absorbed in the view out of the SUV's window. It was a beautiful fall day, the sky a brilliant blue, and touches of reds and oranges were scattered through the moors. She tried to lose herself in the beauty that was the exact opposite of the evil she had just left. Finally, she turned to Fred. "Digby Grey was a person of interest in the death of a young New York actress who was visiting here on Nantucket."

"Really?" said the sheriff, surprised. "He was a POI?"

"Yes, although he was never formally charged. He claimed that she had left him at a beach picnic he had invited her to. And whatever had happened to her occurred after she left him."

"How do you know all of this?" asked the sheriff.

Tuna chuckled. "It's kind of a quirky interest I have. When I'm eating lunch at my desk, I go through the online archives of the

Inquirer and Mirror, looking for mysterious deaths and murders on the island."

The sheriff made the turn onto Milestone Road. "And you read about this Digby Grey?"

"Yes. Just last week. As I said, never formally charged, but from what I read, he was probably guilty as hell."

The sheriff smiled sadly. "I guess the apple doesn't fall too far from the tree."

She turned and stared back out the window. "His ancestor probably got away with murder. Let's not let history repeat itself."

CHAPTER TWENTY-FOUR

Emily Reiner sat huddled in her chair by the window, looking out at the taillights of the SUV. Had she been able to get out of her room, she would have run down the stairs and thrown herself into the arms of the sheriff and begged him to rescue her from this monster. But Jack had been locking her in her bedroom for the past few months. His control over her had become absolute.

The last straw for her had been the fundraiser at the Whaling Museum. First, he had commanded her on what to wear and how to behave, and then he threatened to hit her when she pushed back the littlest bit. But typical Jack, he was back in her room minutes later apologizing for his behavior, claiming he was stressed about the evening and brought her a glass of Sauvignon Blanc as a peace offering. She had grudgingly accepted his apologies and the glass of wine, hoping it would relax her and make the evening with him a bit more bearable. It was only when they were on the way to the event that she realized he had slipped something into the alcohol. Her thoughts were foggy, her balance was off, and she was struggling to concentrate. She knew she looked great - she had seen his eyes light up when she came down the stairs - but knew she was nothing more than a trophy wife hanging off his arm. He might as well have taken a mannequin to the event.

Looking back on the evening, she felt pangs of embarrassment at how she must have been perceived. She had barely been able to form two words when she had met the librarian from the Atheneum and her friend and then had almost lost her balance only to be saved from falling on the floor by that wealthy patron, Peter Bois. Jack had been quick to place fault on a broken heel on her shoe, and Peter seemed to accept that. But she had seen the look in his wife's eyes, Charlotte, and felt the shame. She had looked at her with pity thinking she was intoxicated or high and embarrassing her husband. If only she knew the truth.

Emily had retreated to her bedroom, really more of a prison cell, and had decided then and there that it was time to finally take control of her situation. She had spent years faulting herself for the way that men treated her. It had started at a young age when her father had consistently broken promises and forgotten major milestones in her life. She had been alone at her junior high graduation. Mom was home in bed nursing a major vodka hangover while he was traveling on business, which she felt was code for I'm with my other family and much happier with them, thank you very much.

And things didn't get better from there. Mom had made the high school graduation - hooray - but fell asleep shortly after she sat down in the auditorium and then proceeded to vomit into the lap of the man sitting next to her, coincidentally the father of one of her few friends. And calling her a friend was really being generous. She was one of the few peers at the school who would even acknowledge her presence.

She had last talked to her father at her mother's funeral. Following the service, she had returned to school, finished up the semester, graduated with no family or friends in attendance, and then moved to New York. If there was one thing that she could trust in her life, it was her looks. She had the ability to turn heads and attract men. Sadly though, she always seemed to attract the wrong ones, the ones like her own father who were unreliable, intolerant, and unaffectionate. They had wanted just one thing from her.

After a series of one-night stands with more men than she cared to remember, she had met Seth. He was a successful broker on Wall Street and seemed to fall head over heels for her. They had only dated for a few months when he proposed. The ceremony had taken place at his family home in upstate New York, and then they had a wonderful honeymoon in California wine country. It was the happiest time of her life.

That lasted a few years before she sensed his feelings for her were changing. And the changes were subtle; not quite as talkative or loving, sex became more strained and infrequent, and he spent more and more evenings at work. She had suspected an affair but was truly shocked when she caught him with their maid, an attractive young Latina girl. He had been on his knees to her begging forgiveness, and despite her misgivings, she had granted it to both him and the girl. She caught them again a week later.

She was done with men treating her like crap. She might have lacked a strong sense of self-esteem, but she knew she was a decent person and deserved better. Enough was enough. The challenge now was how to break Jack's hold on her. He controlled everything. She had no computer, no phone, no access to the outside world except when he needed her to attend an event with him. And she had few responsibilities in the house besides preparing meals and making sure his laundry was clean.

So how to break his grip?

The first thing she did was to stop drinking. Jack didn't know this, of course, as she didn't want to tip her hand. But all alcohol and any drugs slipped into them were poured into a plant or the sink when he wasn't looking. But she made sure to act like she was drinking and became quite adept at feigning drunkenness. Of course, she had had a great role model in her mother and knew how to be very convincing.

Her opportunities to escape would be few and far between. On the one hand, she could slip away from him at one of the events they attended - Jack would think she'd be too drunk to get far away. But he rarely let her out of sight anymore and would even accompany her to the bathroom. He would, of course, pretend that he was being nothing more than a gentleman, but in reality, it was just his way to ensure her obedience.

The other option would be to slip out of the house. This presented its own unique set of challenges. Assuming she could even get out of her room - the door was usually locked from the outside - and slip out of the house unnoticed, she would still be several hundred yards from the nearest road and miles from Town. She might be able to walk or hitchhike to the hospital or the sheriff's office, but that would mean she would need at least an hour, likely more, before Jack noticed her absence. That was unlikely.

In either case, where would she go? She had no family, friends, or even trusted acquaintances that she could count on to harbor her. She had no money, no resources, and no proof of the way he had treated her. He was careful to focus his energies on softer parts of flesh that would only bruise and heal quickly. Yes, he had slapped her many times but rarely put his full force into it. It was intended to be more of shock value than pain.

Wherever she ran, he would be close behind and ready with a story for the authorities. Yes, she's been battling with depression for the last year or two. Yes, she's been drinking more. No, she's struggled to adapt to island life and feeling very isolated and estranged from her friends and family on the mainland. I've been trying to get her help, but she can be quite obstinate. And now she's gotten it into her head that I'm some sort of monster, a control freak, that just wants to keep her locked up at home. Honestly, officer, I'm not sure what more I can do to help her if she doesn't want to be helped.

Of course, Jack had the invisible protective cloak of wealth, privilege, and position. He was highly respected in the community for his philanthropic efforts, and despite the disappearance of his first two wives, few on the island would be suspicious of his behavior. Quite the opposite was more likely. The poor man had suffered the loss of two wives, and now his third wife was showing signs of instability and paranoia. Oh, where would it ever end for this poor man?

The thought of how people viewed him made her want to vomit.

She flirted with the idea of killing him. Or just wounding him, at least severely enough to give her an escape window. But in either case, she would have to go toe to toe against him, and he had all the advantage. He was over a half foot taller and had over a hundred pounds on her. He was also on guard and ever watchful, cautious that she might make such an attempt. It would not end well. She feared that she would end up like his prior two wives as she had every confidence that he was responsible for both of their deaths.

No. A direct assault on Jack would not work. She would have to match his wits and be more clever than he.

After much internal deliberation, and she had plenty of time for deliberation, she narrowed it down to two options. Escape his arm while at an event or slip out of the house when his attention was elsewhere. Neither would be easy, and both would require good timing and luck. And in both cases, it would require finding someone to run to that could protect her from him. It took her a while to solve that puzzle, but in the end, it kept coming down to one name. Charlotte Bois.

Despite how she looked at her at the fundraiser, she was confident that Charlotte would help her. She, too, was married to a powerful man, and surely her husband, Peter, wasn't perfect. She had heard a few stories about him, and it sounded like Charlotte was a strong woman capable of defending herself against strong men. She also knew Charlotte's house was only a few miles from Gratitude. She could be there in an hour on foot, even faster by bike or car.

But that would only work if she found herself at another fundraiser with the Bois'. She could excuse herself to the ladies' room and ask Charlotte to join her. Jack wouldn't dare to try and accompany them both. Once alone, she could confess her situation and throw herself on Charlotte to save her. That might work. But the fundraiser at the Whaling Museum had been the last major philanthropic event of the season. The next one would be in April during the Daffodil Festival. She couldn't wait that long.

That left one option; escape from Gratitude. She had to laugh to herself at the irony of it.

The two luxuries that Jack had allowed her were books and a television. She read incessantly, more as an escape than of interest, and the TV just provided background noise, so she didn't feel quite as alone as she was. One evening with her head buried in a Grisham novel, voices on the TV captured her attention. It was two men on a history program talking about how grand, old houses frequently had hidden spaces designed into the structures. As the owners were almost always wealthy, these secret spaces gave them ample opportunity to hide valuables or even sneak out of their own homes undiscovered. It got her thinking. Could Gratitude have a similar concealed escape?

She started going over her bedroom in fine detail, exploring every bookcase, every piece of molding, every picture and painting. She dug into her closet and felt every inch of the wood floor. It took her nearly a week of intensive search before she finally found it.

It had been at the end of her closet. The space wasn't any bigger than a few feet wide, and a bit deeper, and her first exploration hadn't revealed anything of interest. But late one afternoon, she had been looking again, and the sun had shown through the closet opening and cast its light on the far wall. There she could just make out the outline of a small door. A jib door.

Emily had found the door but hadn't yet discovered how to open it. That took several more days of intense exploration until she discovered a small latch concealed in the upper corner of the bookcase. When she had first seen the latch, she had assumed that it was just a structural piece of the bookshelf. But now she realized it was more. Lifting the latch triggered a pulley system that unlocked the jib door. A spring propelled the door open a few inches, where she could then get a purchase.

She swung the door open and peered inside. There she found a narrow set of spiral stairs, no more than a couple of feet wide, that descended down to what looked like the first floor and beyond. Smiling and satisfied, she gently closed the jib door and returned back to her armchair. Curled into a ball, she thought through her next steps. She needed to be careful here as she would probably only have one chance. If Jack discovered this hidden staircase, then it was over. He would have it sealed, and that would be that.

But she needed to know if and where it led anywhere. Could it be an escape, or was it another dead end in her life? And she was reluctant to explore it unless she knew exactly where Jack was and what he was doing. The only time that usually happened was after they had a fight, and he slept in the guest room. It would mean pain for her, but it would be worth it.

Jack had come to her bed that night with bourbon on his breath and a bulge in his pants. She had thought briefly about rejecting his advances but was concerned that with his state of inebriation, he might cause her more harm than he intended. No, it would have to wait a day.

The following afternoon when she had been let out of the room to make dinner, she had told Jack she had wanted a divorce. She knew it was a futile ask, but it would spark his anger and initiate a confrontation. And spark it did. Jack railed against her, viciously calling her an ungrateful bitch and better off as crab food like his first two wives. He had slapped her hard twice, and she had retreated crying to the bedroom. As with prior fights in the past, when it was time for bed, she heard Jack on the stairs, heard the key in her door, the lock sliding firmly, and then his footsteps down to his room.

She waited for two hours to ensure he had fallen into a deep sleep before she slipped out of the covers. She grabbed the emergency flashlight kept in the drawer of the nightstand and tip-toed over to the bookcase. She slowly lifted the latch and then winced when she heard the release of the jib door. It sounded like a bullet going off. She stood, breathing heavily, waiting to hear the heavy fall of his footsteps in the hall. But they didn't come.

Satisfied that she was safe, she slowly swung the door open, its rusty old hinges softly protesting. She eased her way into the space and delicately placed her foot on the first step. It creaked slightly. She waited. Then took another step. Another soft creak. Again she waited. The stairs spiraled down, and she slowly made her way to the first landing, stopping in front of a short, smooth wall. The stairs looked to continue downward to what she assumed would be the basement. On the wall was a small latch. She slowly lifted it and pushed. A small section of the wall swung open into the main living room. She ducked and stepped through and walked several feet into the room. Turning around, she saw that the opening was part of the wainscoting under the portrait of one of Jack's ancestors. How had she never noticed this before? She examined the door and saw that the molding had been cleverly designed to fully hide the opening. And she also saw that there was no way to release the door from this end. This escape path was one way only.

Satisfied, she ducked back in under the portrait of slowly and softly closed the small opening. She felt the door latch, and then she turned and made her way further down the stairs being as quiet and cautious as she could. The staircase ended in front of a small wooden door that featured the same style latch as the first floor. She lifted and pushed. The door would not budge. She pushed harder and managed to get the door open a few inches, enough for her to peek her head out and see where she was.

The space was damp and dank. It smelled musty, and her flashlight highlighted rusty pipes hung from the ceiling and swaths of spider webs covering nearly every surface visible to her. She had never seen this room but had to think it was part of the basement. She pushed again, harder, and was able to open the door enough for her to slip through. She turned around and saw a pile of old boxes stacked up against the door.

On one end of the room was another wooden door which she assumed led to the main part of the basement. On the opposite side was a long tunnel. She followed that, noting that the floor was covered in dirt and dust. She was leaving footprints. But she doubted anyone, especially Jack, had been down here for years. Emily continued for several hundred feet and was ready to turn around when she came to another small wooden door. This one was clearly old and showed signs of rot around its edges. The hinges were rusted solid, and despite her efforts, she could not get the door to budge. She looked around for something to help her pry the door open, but all she found was an old metal pipe a foot long. Way too short of giving any sort of leverage. And she felt she was on borrowed time.

Hanging onto the pipe, she made her way back to the staircase, where she moved the boxes out of the way, doing her best to smooth the dirt on the floor to hide the evidence of the door opening. She closed the door behind her and made her back up the stairs as slowly and deliberately as before. Reaching the second floor, she propped the pipe up against the wall, made her way through the jib door into her closet, and closed the door. She felt the door catch and heard the latch click in the bookcase.

Nearly two hours after she had started her adventure, she returned back to her bed and crawled under the sheets, a huge smile on her face. For the first time in years, she felt she had some level of control in her life. Emily had regained some small command of her situation, and she was going to use it to gain her freedom.

Now all she had to do was to lay low and wait for the right moment. It would probably be soon. She could feel it.

CHAPTER TWENTY-FIVE

J ack paced back and forth through the kitchen, his mind racing. How the hell had they found her? He had been very particular in selecting the site, knowing that it was well off the path used by fishermen and others visiting Great Point. True, he hadn't buried her too deeply but thought he really hadn't need to worry about it.

"Damnit!" he screamed. He curled his fists into a ball and pounded on the kitchen island.

Slowly he calmed, began to gather his thoughts, and took inventory of his position. What did they really have beyond a six-year-old decomposing corpse? He knew there were no witnesses to the burial. And certainly, there were no witnesses when he smothered her with the overstuffed pillow from the sofa. Granted, he had to put his knees on her shoulders to hold her down, but he doubted those marks would be visible after all these years in the sand. He did have some scrapes from her fingernails on his face, but those had healed quickly, and the one time he had had to go out, he had used some of her makeup to hide the wounds. And all of her clothing and personal effects had been donated years before. No, there was no evidence or witnesses that could point the finger at him.

That left the body.

Jack didn't watch much television, but he did know some of the basics around police procedures. Since they had ruled the death suspicious, then a detailed autopsy would be completed along with whatever analysis they could complete given the state of the body and the grave; DNA, tox screen, trace, latents. He was confident they wouldn't find much of value in any of the analyses they completed. Her tox report would show nothing as he closely had controlled her food and drink in the final months. It would come back as normal. Likewise, any trace evidence could easily be addressed.

Yes, officer, of course, she has fibers from our house; she lived there. And yes, there were fibers from one of my sweaters on her. She enjoyed wearing them. Said it made her feel closer to me.

He chuckled softly at the thought.

What about the autopsy?

He had been very careful when he had corrected her to make sure he did not cause any fractures or breaks in her skeletal system. All his corrections had been targeted at the soft flesh so as not to leave any lasting evidence of his work. What he didn't know was whether or not any of the more recent bruises would still be visible after being buried for six years. He'd need to think about how to address that if and when that question ever came up. It's not like he let her do much physically, especially in the last year or so of her life. And it couldn't be something pat like a fall down the stairs. He would need to think that through a little more, but he knew he would enjoy the challenge.

He didn't know if smothering someone would leave any evidence, although he suspected not. He was smart enough to know that strangulation left all sorts of physical evidence.

It was not how he had planned it. In fact, her death had not been planned at all, and he thought that was probably where he went astray. With the First, he had carefully thought through exactly when and what would happen. And with the exception of a few suspicious stares from friends and townspeople, it had pretty much gone off exactly as he had expected. The authorities bought the drowning story - because she had indeed drowned - and also accepted his story that he had realized too late she was in trouble, and she was too far out in the water for him to reach at least without endangering himself. The autopsy of the First had confirmed the drowning, while the tox report had shown significant amounts of alcohol and tranquilizers. *Yes, officer, she had been drinking too much. And she often took prescription pills for her anxiety. I tried to get her help, but she wouldn't listen. I was so worried about her. Her death was devastating. I should have been able to do something.*

He smiled at the thought of how easily the police had bought his story. But that smile vanished as he thought about Second and what had happened in his study those six years ago.

She had ambushed him. He had been enjoying a drink by the fire in his study while reading the Wall Street Journal. He had heard her footsteps descending the stairs but had assumed she was probably headed toward the kitchen. Instead, she had entered his study and declared she was leaving him. He had tried to calm her and assure her he could change, but she had none of it. His tone changed from assuring to threatening, and claimed she would die before she walked out that door. She had smiled, turned, and started to walk toward the front door. Startled by her unusual level of disobedience, he had scrambled to quickly restrain her. She had fought back hard, scratching his face and biting his hand. Then she had kicked him in the groin. Bent over in pain and feeling rage flowing through his body, he had slammed her to the floor and grabbed the pillow from the couch. His anger did the rest of the work. She was dead within minutes of kicking him.

It had taken him a while to regain his breath, his composure and for the pain in his groin to ease. Then he took action. He dragged her still body into the garage and stuffed her in the freezer. He hadn't bothered to change her clothes, but he did remove her jacket. He figured the less he messed with the body, the better. Later that day, he had called the police and told them she had disappeared. That had brought its own set of challenges, but he had managed them easily enough. He, of course, had been devastated, and the police had done everything they could to try and locate her. But he was confident, and wrongly so, it turned out, that she would never be found.

He had waited a few weeks for just the right weather and moon to present itself. The forecasted nor'easter had provided the perfect incentive to get the job done. The disposal itself had taken just a few hours, and he was confident that no one had seen anything out of the ordinary. Anyway, he had just gone fishing that night, hoping to catch the right tide for stripers and blues. And maybe a bonito.

He walked back over to the windows and looked out. It was his favorite view in the house, and it never failed to help calm him. He tried to put himself in the position of the detective and see what she really had against him.

No physical evidence. At least none that couldn't be explained away. Clean tox report.

Worst case, he thought, would be they would come and search his home looking for a possible weapon and any other potential evidence. That would be a useless waste of their time. He had replaced the floors in his study, recycled the freezer, and had even sold the old Land Rover. There was absolutely nothing here.

But that left the community reaction and the potential impact on his life on the island. The police hadn't made any mention of publicizing the discovery but he had to assume that people were going to find out one way or the other. And that meant trouble. Throwing out his suspicion that she had been having an affair had been a knee jerk reaction. He hadn't fully thought through the implications of that statement but now saw it as the most effective narrative for plausible deniability. It was certainly a tenuous explanation. It wouldn't be the only episode of infidelity on the island - winters can be long and boring - but none of them ended with a body buried in the sand. It was his best hope of deflecting the expected accusations but it would require a high level of performance on his part. He must be seen as being deeply betrayed and crushed at the realization that she had been murdered by this mysterious lover. He must be devastated.

He smiled at the thought. It might actually be kind of fun.

Of course, there were those that would never believe that story. Fuck them. They might not believe him but you can be damn sure they would be the first with their hands out looking for a donation to their pet charity or cause. Wealth was his magic cloak of protection. Money covered a lot of sins. It always did and he intended to use it to its maximum effect.

That left Emily. He would need to do something about that problem. Having her locked up in her room would raise some eyebrows and .he couldn't risk her throwing herself on the police begging to be saved. But the right drugs at the right time would ensure she was sleeping peacefully in her room. *I'm sorry, officer, my dear wife has been dealing with severe allergies, and she is resting in her room. But I'd be happy to have her call you if you think that's necessary.*

He smiled arrogantly and looked back out the window. He was confident everything would be okay. He just needed to keep Three under control and delay his next steps for her for a while. But not too long. He was starting to get that itch. Soon it would be time for Three to go, but he would be patient. He had to be patient. And given everything he had learned with the first two, her disappearance was going to be perfect. What was that expression? Third time's a charm.

He chuckled out loud. No. Everything was going to be okay.

* * *

"So, tell me about your family," said Rob. He and Pip were having a coffee and sitting on a bench along Main Street.

Pip eyed him curiously. "I was waiting for that question."

"What? What do you mean?" asked Rob, surprised.

"Ever since we met my cousin, the sheriff, I figured you were trying to figure out my whole family situation."

"Oh, Pip, I'm not like that. I just want to get to know you a little better. You've pretty much heard my story. Just curious about yours."

Pip wrapped her hands around the paper cup and blew across the top. Steam wafted up from the hot coffee. She took a tentative sip and then sighed. "I'm sorry, Rob. It's just in this day and age, you never really know how someone is going to react."

Rob gently placed his hand on her wrist. "I just want to know about you."

Pip smiled warmly at him. "Well, like many others, my ancestors came to Nantucket to make a living in whaling. In the early 1800s, for an uneducated man, it could be highly lucrative. Or fatal as many, many men died aboard whaleships." Pip laughed sadly. "But for my ancestor, Absalom Boston, he was quite successful. He was born here, his dad was a former slave, and his mom was a Wampanoag. They were the indigenous people on the island. Absalom married and had eight children, most of whom remained on the island."

"Wow," said Rob. "I think it's amazing that you know your heritage that far back. I barely know much of mine past my grandparents."

Pip smiled. "What's amazing," she said, "is the challenges they faced and the life they created. They truly were exceptional people."

"I bet," said Rob.

"And there are still quite a few of us on the island. We have a family reunion every five years or so, and at the last one, we had over three hundred people attend."

"Three hundred!"

Pip laughed. "I know. The Boston family tree has gotten quite large." She paused and took another sip of coffee. "But only about thirty of them still call Nantucket home, like me. The others are spread all over the country and the world."

Rob looked at her admiringly. "That is so cool."

"I guess. To be honest, I don't know any differently. Family has always been a huge part of my life."

"Honestly, it makes me a little jealous. I mean, I have cousins, aunts, uncles, and all that, but we are very spread out and never really see each other beyond the occasional post on social media. You? You have a community of family."

"I guess I'm lucky in that way."

Rob stole a glance at his watch.

"Do you need to go?" asked Pip.

"Yeah, in a few minutes. I have my follow-up discussion with Tuna."

"I hope she doesn't arrest you," Pip teased.

Rob's face fell. "Do you think she will?"

Pip burst out laughing. "Oh, Rob, you are too funny. No, of course not. She's not going to arrest you. She probably just wants to talk through things one more time and confirm your story."

"And doubt me again. About Dee, that is."

Pip placed her hand on his arm. "Does it really matter if she believes you or not? You've done your job. You found Dee, and now the police know she didn't run away. Hopefully, they can get Reiner for her murder."

"I hope you're right. I guess I just don't have a lot of confidence that they are going to get him."

"Let's cross that bridge if and when we come to it. But for now, go talk to Tuna and get things settled with her."

"Will you back me up?" Rob asked nervously.

"Back you up?"

"About Dee. I mean, you saw her. Heard her. You could substantiate my claim that she is the one who told us about her death."

Pip hesitated. "I guess, Rob. But to be honest, I'm really not sure what I saw."

"You saw Dee!"

Pip nodded slowly. "You're right. I did. And I will. Back you up, that is. I guess I'm still trying to understand things."

Rob smiled knowingly. "Join the club!" and laughed softly. "But thank you for believing in me. And in Dee."

"Of course. Now, you better go."

Rob stood up. "Okay, wish me luck."

Pip got up and gave him a peck on the cheek. "Good luck. And let me know how it goes."

"Will do."

He walked down Main Street and made the turn on Water Street. Entering the county building, Detective Fisch was waiting for him in the lobby, a large blue binder under her arm. She extended her hand. "Thanks for coming, Rob. And thanks for being on time."

Rob took her hand. "I always want to stay on the good side of the police," he said half-jokingly.

"Let's go back to the conference room."

For the fourth time in almost as many days, Rob found himself in the conference room talking about a murder. Butterflies filled his stomach.

They settled in chairs across from each other. The fake wood laminated table spanned the gap between them.

"Again, thanks for coming in," said Tuna. "I really just wanted to follow up with you on a couple of things about the death of Deidre Reiner." She laid the binder on the table and opened her notebook.

"Of course. I'd be happy to help in any way I can."

"Let's just start from the beginning, shall we?" said Tuna. "Refresh my memory on how you ended up on Nantucket and how you managed to find Deidre Reiner's body."

Rob paused a minute to gather his thoughts and realized he should just tell her the entire story. He then opened up to Tuna, starting with his wife's cancer diagnosis, her death, the discovery of the travel brochure in the basement, and even his purchase while drunk of the old Wagoneer. He talked about landing on the island a few weeks ago, finding his way to the cottage he was renting, and to when he first met Dee on the Sconset bike bridge. He talked about his ambitions - and failures - to write a novel and to the advice Dee had given him on their walks. And the stories she had shared about the abuse she had suffered under Jack Reiner. He talked about meeting Pip and how she had been the one to encourage him to talk with the sheriff. Nearly an hour later, his mouth dry and emotionally spent, he finished with the story of how Dee had taken him to find her body, how she had vanished shortly after he had found it, and how he had ended up in this very room talking to the sheriff about how a ghost had told him she had been murdered and where he could find her remains.

Throughout his disclosure, Detective Fisch took notes, occasionally stealing a glance at Rob to assess his emotions and state of mind. Only once did she interrupt him, and that to confirm the date of his ferry ride over. When he finished, she wrote a few more notes, put her pen down, and looked across the table.

"That is quite the story, Rob."

"Do you not believe me?" asked Rob anxiously.

Tuna smiled. "Relax, Rob. While I find some of your story, uh, shall we say, illogical, I do believe you are telling me the truth. At least what you believe to be the truth. And I did follow up with the contacts you gave me in St. Louis. They not only confirmed your timeline but also assured me of your character."

Rob relaxed, the tension draining from his body. "So, do you believe that Jack Reiner killed her?"

"I'm afraid I can't really share details of an ongoing criminal investigation. But what I can say is that Sheriff Boston and I are going to make every effort to understand what happened to Deidre Reiner and bring her justice."

Rob smiled tiredly. "Good. Is there anything more I can do to help with that?"

"No, Rob. I believe you have done more than enough. Please leave the rest of this investigation to us. And we will certainly be in touch if we have any further questions." Tuna stood, pushed back her chair, and extended her hand. "Again, thank you for coming in."

Rob stood and shook her hand. "My pleasure. And no need to show me out; I know the way." He smiled and walked out of the conference room.

Tuna sat back down, stretched out her legs, stared at the ceiling, and blew out a long sigh. At this point in their investigation, they really didn't understand what had happened to Deidre Reiner beyond the fact that she was dead. Had she been murdered? Or had she died of natural causes, and someone wanted a natural burial for her? It wasn't unheard of. And surprisingly, Massachusetts law allowed for it - just not on public lands. And not without a permit. So was she after a killer? Or just someone who had committed a couple of misdemeanors?

She wasn't very confident in her promise that they would bring justice to her. Quite the opposite, in fact. Her fear was that the killer would never be caught. And if Deidre Reiner really was a ghost, as crazy as that sounds, what would she or could she do next?

She stood, grabbed her notebook and binder, and went to find Fred to update him on the meeting.

CHAPTER TWENTY-SIX

R ob left the county offices and walked to his car. It was nearing four. Sunset was a little over an hour away, and the light had taken on the warm hue of what photographers call the golden hour. The buildings of downtown Nantucket looked almost magical, framed against the blue sky.

He texted Pip a quick note about his meeting with Tuna and then pulled out of his parking spot and headed to Sconset. He had only driven a few blocks when he realized he was completely and utterly exhausted. The discussion with Tuna had consumed what little energy he had left, and found himself driving as if in a trance, his mind and body on cruise control.

Is it any surprise I am totally wiped out?

In the weeks since he had arrived on the island, he couldn't remember one evening where he felt like he had gotten a good night's sleep. The first few were fitful, being in a strange old cottage as he struggled to settle into a place so different from the midwest. The bird song was different, the nightly insect chorus was different. Even the way the wind blew through the trees carried a unique tone and timbre from what he was accustomed to. And aside from adjusting to a new setting, he was still struggling significantly living a life without Sarah. The hole she had left was not easily filled.

The Wagoneer made its way around the rotary and headed down Milestone Road towards Siasconset.

His planned writing had so far been a failure and had consumed a tremendous amount of his mental capacity, his physical energy and nibbled away at his self-confidence. The pressure he had felt to start his novel, all of it self-imposed, had stressed him on a daily basis. His move to Nantucket had so far been nothing more than a disappointment. He had neither escaped his grief nor delivered one page of his dream.

And then he had met Dee. Reflecting back, it had started to take on a dreamlike quality, more that he had imagined her than actually talking with her, walking with her, and hearing her story. The anxiety and tension had started with her confession to him that she was a winter resident and a victim of her husband's cruelty. And had only escalated when he found himself in the sheriff's office talking with a homicide detective about how he had discovered a buried body on a spit of land he had never stepped foot on. Yes, the relationship with Dee had been mind-numbingly exhausting.

The one bright spot was Pip. She had proven to be a good friend and had helped keep him centered with all of the craziness that he had been through. Even better, she was the only other person who had seen Dee assuring him that he was not imagining her after all. Thinking of her, that quirky smile, her wry sense of humor, and her sheer beauty brought a smile to his face.

Ahead, in the fading light, Rob could see a gray wall crossing the land and bisecting the road. Within seconds he found himself in a dense fog bank and struggling to see the lines on the pavement. He slowed to a crawl, turned on his lights, and kept the left side of the vehicle tight to the center line. His exhausted mind started to see various shapes and images in the fog. What appeared to be an old train chugging parallel to the road pulling a couple of passenger cars teeming with people. A rider on a horse flew by him in the opposite direction, frantically whipping his mount for more speed. A farmer in a field raking hay. Two people on bicycles pedaling casually, riding side by side. He shook his head and tried to clear the images. The Wagoneer slowly veered into the oncoming lane.

A horn blared.

A pickup truck appeared out of the fog directly in front of Rob. Startled, he steered hard to the right causing the old Jeep to lean heavily to the left, its tires screeching. Rob watched in horror as the huge chrome grill of the truck seemed to pass just under his window, and then the whole vehicle vanished into the fog as quickly as it had appeared.

Shaking, Rob pulled over onto the grass on the edge of the road and stretched his arms over the steering wheel. His body was trembling, his heart was racing, and he could feel his pulse pounding in his ears. The near miss had shaken him to the core. Thankfully he had been going slowly because of the fog and had been able to avoid the truck, barely, with his quick swerve back into his lane.

Did I just almost become a winter resident?

He forced himself to smile at the thought and, with it, was slowly able to get himself settled. He peered through the windshield and side windows through the dense fog and continued to see movements in the mist, but his tired brain could no longer identify them. He just wanted to be home, in bed, and asleep.

Carefully he brought the Wagoneer back onto the road and, driving slowly, made every effort to keep the Jeep centered in the right lane. The fog was relentless and seemed to get denser the closer he got to Sconset. Fortunately, he could make out enough of the road in front of him to keep going. The light was fading quickly, and his headlights did little more than light up the fog in front of his car into a dazzling halo. The movements in the mist continued, but Rob was too focused on driving to see them.

He felt as much as he saw his turn onto Morey Lane and made the corner at walking speed. Three deer flashed in front of his headlights, just inches from the hood ornament proclaiming the make of his old SUV. Rob went for the brakes but realized the deer were already gone. Had they even been there? Were they just a figment of his tired brain? His nerves frayed, and on edge from his nearly hour-long trip from town, he shouted and punched the air when he finally saw Starbuck Lane emerge from the fog. His tires crunched on the shells as he made his way the hundred or so feet to his cottage. He pulled up, turned off the lights, keyed the ignition, and let out a long sigh. Home.

Opening the door and stepping out, he stole a glance down the street toward Dee's house. The fog lay like a dense blanket over the village and smothered all available light. But through the fog, Rob thought he could hear snippets of conversations. And laughter. The sounds reminded him of a cocktail party. He fumbled his way to the door and was successful in unlocking it quickly and entering the cottage without slamming his head on the low frame.

After a bite of leftovers and a tall glass of water, he made his way to the bedroom, dropped his clothes on the floor, and slipped between the sheets. He was asleep in seconds and, for the first time in weeks, didn't dream of Sarah.

* * *

Detective Fisch was at her desk going through her blue binder and trying to piece together the feeble evidence they had on the case of Deirdre Reiner. Nantucket was not exactly the type of place where a homicide detective would gain experience and build a career. Based on her lunchtime research of the Inquirer and Mirror archives, she estimated that there were fewer than a hundred murders on the island in the last two hundred years. Many of those deaths actually didn't take place on the island but on ships that called Nantucket home. Fights on whaleships, scallopers, and fishing boats that led to death seemed to be far more common than killings that took place on the island.

But this wasn't her first case and likely would not be her last.

The autopsy had been completed in record time thanks to the sheriff. Being a small municipality, Nantucket did not have the resources or the need to support a full-time medical examiner and instead relied on the service provided by the state of Massachusetts. Fortunately, Fred had friends in high places, like the governor's office, and had pulled in a favor to get the case pushed through quickly. Tuna had printed out the final report and was going through the findings, none of which were remarkable or brought any new avenues of inquiry to her investigation.

It confirmed that the body was that of one Deidre Reiner (nee Collins), who was in her early forties at the time of death. The external examination showed no obvious indications as to her cause of death. The only discoveries of note were bruising to the left shoulder, right breast, and lower torso. It also noted the tattoo of a small sperm whale just above her right ankle bone.

The internal examination revealed two findings of interest. The first is that she had woolen fibers lodged in the back of her mouth and in her throat. Analysis using gas chromatography revealed the fibers were cashmere and could have come from clothing or bedding materials. The other finding that caught Tuna's eye was the x-ray results which identified a slight fracture to the left clavicle. The x-ray also found an older fracture to her left arm that had mended years earlier, likely pre-adolescent.

The toxicology report came back negative for alcohol and drug use, with the exception of trace amounts of ibuprofen. Time and the elements had made fingernail scrapings useless.

Tuna flipped the pages to the summary section and noted that the cause of death was deemed inconclusive.

"Damn!" she exclaimed. She threw the report down on her desk and pushed her chair back. She extended her legs, stared up at the ceiling, and let out a long sigh. She was hoping for something, anything, that would point the finger at Reiner, but this report was tenuous at best at proving any level of his guilt in the death of Deidre Reiner.

She sat back up and pulled her chair into the desk. She grabbed her phone and quickly sent a text. Before she could even put the phone back on the desk, it pinged. She glanced at the screen. The text was short. Call me.

Tuna tapped on the phone icon at the top of the screen and was shortly rewarded with the sound of a telephone ringing in her ear. After a few rings, she heard a click, and a familiar voice came on the line. "Tuna?"

"Man, that was quick."

She heard a soft laugh on the other end of the line. "I'm here to serve, especially for you," and laughed again.

Tuna smiled warmly. "Hey, Mel. It is so good to hear your voice. How have you been?"

Melanie Thompson was a lieutenant in the Massachusetts State Police and had worked several years in homicide covering Suffolk county. She was also a longtime friend of Tuna's, having been a classmate at Nantucket High School, a teammate on the girls' field hockey team, and an occasional lover. She had made the move to Boston shortly after graduation and had rarely stepped foot on the island since. But she and Tuna had stayed in touch and on good terms.

"I'm good. You?"

"Doing okay. But dealing with a pretty frustrating case. I could use a fresh set of eyes and ears."

"Sure. What can you tell me about it?"

"Do you remember the Reiner family? Those wealthy assholes that walked around Nantucket liked they own the place?"

"I do, sort of. To be honest, I've tried to forget that part of Nantucket."

"I get that. Well, the case involves the second wife of Jack Reiner. He reported her missing six years ago, claiming that she was suffering from some sort of mental breakdown and had run away."

"And I'm guessing that you found her?" asked Mel.

"In a shallow grave by Coskata pond, out by Great Point."

"Hmm, so it looks like she didn't run away," said Mel sarcastically.

"No. But there was evidence she did. Sheriff Boston and his team documented an electronic trail from Nantucket all the way to California, where it vanished abruptly."

"No doubt that was carefully planned. The killer probably gave her phone and credit cards to a traveler or an acquaintance with instructions. It certainly shows some level of premeditation. The bigger question is who made the arrangements. Was it by the husband or an unknown third party?"

"My vote would be the husband, Reiner."

"Why do you say that?"

"His first wife died in a drowning accident. Tox reports showed significant levels of alcohol and tranquilizers in her system. Clearly, she should not have been swimming in that condition. That level of incapacity combined with the rip currents? She didn't have a chance."

"What was the husband's involvement?"

"He was with her. He claimed that she was too far out before he realized it and couldn't get to her."

"Do you believe that story?"

"Shit, no. He was probably the one that loaded her up with the booze and drugs and pushed her in."

There was silence on the phone.

"Mel?"

"Sorry, just thinking. Do you have anything on the husband?"

"Pretty much nothing. But my gut is telling me this man is guilty as hell."

"What's Reiner like?" asked Mel. "I never met the man and really only know the family by reputation."

"Do you remember those summer kids we would call the Chads? Those rich, asshole college boys that would descend on the island in July and August and act like they owned the place?"

Mel laughed knowingly. "I remember them. How do you forget such arrogance and entitlement?"

"Okay. Well, imagine them grown up, and you'll start to get the picture of Jack Reiner. Only, he isn't a summer visitor; he lives on the island year-round. And as you probably remember, he's rich as hell and highly regarded in the community for his philanthropy." Tuna delivered the last sentence with disdain.

"I'm assuming you've interviewed him?" asked Mel.

"Yes. Fred and I notified him Monday about the discovery of the body. I could tell that he was shocked that we found her but hid it well. And he was just as arrogant and condescending as those boys who thought island girls were an easy lay."

Mel chortled knowingly.

Tuna continued, "When we pushed him on it, he claimed that she was having an affair, but he did not know who. He stated that he was afraid to share that during the initial investigation of her disappearance because he was embarrassed and concerned about what people in the community might think."

"More concerned about his image than finding his wife?" asked Mel caustically.

"That pretty much says everything you need to know about him."

"Any kids or other family?"

"No. Although he has since remarried. We don't know much about her," said Tuna. She flipped through the pages in the blue binder until she found what she was looking for and read it to Mel. "Emily Reiner, nee Mitchell, thirty-six years old. Originally from New York City. Only child. Reiner is her second husband. Mother dead from alcoholism and alienated from her father."

"Sounds perfect," said Mel.

"Perfect? What do you mean?" asked Tuna, surprised at her friend's comment.

"He sounds like a habitual abuser. This wife, his third, has an almost perfect background for him. No family, likely no close friends. Easy for him to control her. And when he gets tired of her? She'll disappear just like the first two."

"Do you think Emily is in danger?"

"Absolutely. But he won't dare try anything right now. There's way too much focus on him. But give him a few months, maybe a year? He'll be making her disappear just like the first two."

"Then we need to get to her. Warn her," said Tuna.

"If he is what we think he is, that is going to be tough. I'm sure he will try and keep her under lock and key. What else can you tell me?"

"The autopsy was inconclusive in the cause of death. I was hoping you might take a look at it and see if anything jumps out at you. You certainly have a lot more experience in this arena than I do."

"Sure, T. I'd be happy to. I'm a bit slammed right now, but email it to me, and I'll review it tonight and get back to you tomorrow. That work?"

"That would be great," said Tuna. "I really appreciate it." She pulled up the email from the ME's office and forwarded the report.

"Sure. Like I said, I'm at your service."

"You're the best. I just sent it to you. Look forward to hearing your thoughts on it."

"Until tomorrow," said Mel and ended the call.

CHAPTER TWENTY-SEVEN

A shaft of sunlight pierced the blinds on the east side windows of the bedroom and landed directly on Rob's face. He stirred, turned over, and rolled to his side. The bedside clock claimed it was nearly half past seven. Some not-so-quick mental math confirmed he had slept over fourteen hours. He sat up in bed and grabbed his phone. There were a couple of texts from Pip wondering what he was doing and another from Detective Fisch thanking him for his time.

He swung his legs out of bed, put on yesterday's clothes from a pile on the floor, and trundled down to the kitchen.

The dense fog had vanished overnight, leaving another beautiful day in its wake. The sky was a vivid blue, and a slight wind gently brushed the last stragglers of leaves in the trees. Rob made coffee, splashed some creamer in his mug, and made his way out onto the patio. For the first time since his arrival on Nantucket, he felt relaxed and refreshed.

He settled into one of the Adirondacks and sipped his coffee. The air was crisp and chilly and carried the scent of fallen leaves. In the distance, he could just hear the soft roar of the waves crashing onto Sconset beach. A Carolina Wren sang its familiar song from a tree at the end of the patio. Teakettle, teakettle, teakettle. Rob had to smile. Sarah had found birds fascinating and had often educated him about various species they would see in their yard. One Sunday evening, shortly before her cancer diagnosis, they had been sitting on their deck and enjoying a glass of wine and had heard that familiar song.

"That's a Carolina Wren," Sarah had said.

"Which?" asked Rob, tilting his head to hear better.

"That one. It sounds like teakettle, teakettle."

Rob had listened as the bird repeated its song and turned to Sarah. "Sounds more like cheeseburger, cheeseburger to me."

Sarah had laughed. "Cheeseburger?" she had said with a broad smile. "Are you hungry?"

"Just for you," Rob had said. "Shall we go work on that baby thing?" he had asked with a mischievous grin.

Sarah had smiled, stood, and reached for his hand.

Rob sipped his coffee, closed his eyes, and relived the memory. It had been one of the last truly carefree moments they had shared before cancer shattered their world. A wave of sadness passed over him. If only they had known how little time they had left.

The wren sang again and stole him from his thoughts. He sighed sadly.

He didn't want to admit it to himself, but the pain of Sarah's loss was easing. He found himself thinking more of the good times they had had together and less of her loss. It was a new type of sadness, though, as he felt that he was almost cheating on her memory. Should he not still feel her loss just as strongly? Was it normal? Maybe he would check out that bereavement group and see if talking with others in his situation would help.

He returned to the kitchen, refilled his mug, and made himself a quick breakfast of bread with peanut butter. He finished his meager meal, took a last sip of coffee, and grabbed his coat. Time for a walk.

In his month on the island, he had gotten into the routine of daily morning walks. At first, it had been to think about Sarah, his escape to Nantucket, and try to plan out his time ahead. Now his thoughts focused on Dee, the detective, and of course, Pip. Occasionally he might also run through the latest failed writing attempt with an eye toward understanding where he had gone wrong in his storytelling. He was starting to think, and had little evidence to prove otherwise, that he just sucked as a writer.

He made his way across the bike bridge and into the center of the village. As usual, the streets were empty of people and activity save for a few tradespeople getting needed work completed during the off-season. Continuing up Front Street, he looked out over the water and relished the perspective. His rent was paid for another five months, but the thought of leaving this view made him sad. There was nothing like it anywhere else, especially in St. Louis. He turned right at the end of Front Street and made his way to the Bluff Walk. He took this route several times a week and was now quite familiar with the twists and turns, the old roots that threatened to trip him, and the low-hanging branches that tried to whack some sense into him.

As he approached the old Victorian house, he could just make out a figure ahead of him. It was a woman, and she was dressed in dark slacks and a simple white blouse with a lace collar. She was standing with her arms crossed and staring out across the water. Her brown hair was curly and stopped just above her shoulders. Something about her looked familiar.

Hearing his footsteps, she turned to face him as he approached.

"Good morning," she said.

Rob returned her greeting. "Good morning."

"It's a gorgeous day, don't you think," she said. Her brown eyes turned back to the water.

Rob studied her face intently. Her skin had an almost porcelain quality that seemed to shimmer in the sun. She had high cheekbones and a chiseled nose. She stood confidently, like one accustomed to being the center of attention.

"Absolutely. Stunning, really," said Rob, although he was not sure he was commenting on the day or the woman in front of him.

"I could stare at this forever," she said.

Rob followed her gaze. "It is beautiful." His eyes returned to her, and it clicked. "Are you Lisbeth Hopper?" he asked.

She smiled warmly. "Yes, I am," and offered her hand as if to be kissed.

Rob gently took her hand, his thumb on her knuckles. They were cold. "It is a pleasure to meet you."

"And you," said Lisbeth. "Did you see our show at the Casino?"

"I'm sorry to say that I did not. I wasn't yet on the island."

"Oh, such a shame. It was very well received."

"So I heard," said Rob.

A minute passed as Rob determined how he wanted to proceed. Should he wait for her to say something? Ask her if she is a winter resident? In reality, he really wanted to wish her a good day and get his ass out of there quickly. But he thought of Dee and remembered what this poor young woman had been through.

"I read about you in the paper. I think you stayed in the same cottage that I'm currently renting."

"Oh, you mean the Shanty?" she asked.

"Yes," said Rob.

"We loved that little cottage."

"So that was you that engraved your name in the top drawer of the dresser?"

She smiled sheepishly. "I confess it was. My friend, Percy Barnes, and I wanted to leave a remembrance of our visit."

"But I didn't see her name."

"No. Typical Percy. She lost the nerve after I finished. So it was just me." She turned to walk. Rob followed.

"I hope I haven't disturbed you," said Lisbeth.

"Disturbed me?" asked Rob incredulously. "You mean you've been living there too? At the Shanty"

Lisbeth looked up at him, her big brown eyes wet with tears. "Yes, but I would not call it living. For us, it's really just a portal."

"For you?" said Rob, knowingly. "You mean as a winter resident."

"Yes," said Lisbeth softly. She stopped and looked back out to the water as Rob watched a tear trace down her cheek. She quickly turned back to Rob and said, "Dee said you might be able to help me."

"Dee? You mean Dee Collins?"

"Yes. She said you were helping her go after the man who killed her."

Rob shuffled uncomfortably. "That's a bit strong. I'm really just trying to help the police bring her killer to justice."

"I want justice as well," said Lisbeth forcefully. "For Digby Grey."

"Digby Grey?" asked Rob cautiously.

"Yes. Digby Grey. He assaulted and killed me on Sconset beach, then dragged my body into the surf. He was never held accountable for his actions."

"I understand Lisbeth. But that was over a hundred years ago. Digby Grey is long gone."

Lisbeth stared defiantly at Rob. "Digby is gone. But his seed is still alive."

The light went on in Rob's head. "Jack Reiner."

"Yes. Jack Reiner. He is the last living relative of Digby Grey. And he must pay for the sins of his ancestor as well as his own."

Rob looked back at the old house and saw that there were dozens of faces watching their conversation. A chill went down his spine. He was the only living being in this world of winter residents. He turned back to Lisbeth. Her face was calm, yet her eyes stared intently at him.

"If you can bring him justice," said Lisbeth, "then I'll be able to rest, finally."

Rob was startled. "I thought you would want to stay here," he said, his arms spread, "to enjoy the island, this view."

Lisbeth sighed softly. "This is not my world, Rob. These people," she pointed to the old Victorian, "they loved Nantucket when they were alive, and they choose to be here during the off-season." She paused briefly and looked back out at the water.

"Despite this beauty, it's not for me. I came here for a summer holiday and was murdered. My place is back home at the farm. Iowa."

"I understand, I think," said Rob. "And you can't go there because of this... situation?"

Lisbeth nodded slowly.

"Very well, Lisbeth," said Rob earnestly. "I promise you. I will do whatever I can to bring Jack Reiner to justice."

"Thank you, Rob. You'll never know what this means to me." She smiled sadly, turned, and walked slowly away. Rob watched as she proceeded down the path, her image becoming more and more transparent until it was nothing more than wisps of fog that vanished in the wind.

He let out a long sigh, and feelings of apprehension overcame him. Now he had to deal with two ghosts? Dee had never warned him about this, and it kind of made him angry with her. But nothing he could do about it now. He had made a promise, and he was going to do his best to see it through to the end.

Rob turned and made his way back to the Shanty. It was time to talk with the detective and see what was going on with the case against Jack Reiner.

CHAPTER TWENTY-EIGHT

W hile Rob was walking back from the Sconset bluff, Detective Tuna Fisch was making her way to her desk. It had been a restless night as she continued to turn the case over and over again in her mind. She was desperately looking to find a hook, a gap, something she might have missed that would point to what she knew was the truth; that Jack Reiner had killed his second wife. She had woken from this fitful sleep no further along in the case.

She had just settled in at her desk when her phone rang. It was Mel.

"True to your word, I see," said Tuna, laughing.

"As I said, I'm here to serve."

Tuna sighed. "Please tell me you found something, anything, in that report that I can use to put some pressure on Reiner."

"I'm sorry to say that there isn't much of anything overtly suspicious that I could ascertain from the report."

Tuna heard papers rustling through the phone.

Mel continued, "But, and I want to say this is by no means definitive; there are some signs that she might have been smothered."

"Smothered?" said Tuna hopefully.

"Yes. If you look at the pattern of bruising on the chest as well as the fracture to the left clavicle, combined with the fibers found in her throat, it suggests that someone held her down with their knees on her chest and smothered her with a pillow or another soft object."

Tuna thought for a moment, letting this new theory percolate. "It kind of feels right to me, knowing Reiner. But could we use it to flip him? Would it hold up in court?"

Mel sighed. "That's the problem. It is just one interpretation, my interpretation, of the findings in the report. Others could look at those same facts and come up with a different explanation. So, no, this would never stand up in court. Any good defense attorney would tear it to shreds before you ever got Reiner in the courtroom."

"Damn!" said Tuna. "I was really hoping you might find something."

"Sorry. But you could use this to go at him again. Tell him how you think he killed her. It might rattle him enough to get him to confess. Or at least trick him into inadvertently opening up another area of vulnerability."

"I suppose. But you don't know him, Mel. I think this might just make him feel even more confident that he pulled this off. Like those Chads that always wanted more even after you told them no."

"I wish I could have given you more, Tuna."

"Me too."

"Please keep me in the loop and let me know how it goes with the case."

"Will do. And don't be a stranger. I'd love to see you next time you're on the island."

Mel laughed. "It might be a while. You know my feelings about the current state of affairs on Nantucket. Maybe you should bring that wife of yours and come visit us in Boston. We'll show you both the town."

Tuna smiled, "I like that idea. Maybe this spring before things get crazy here."

"Done. We will look forward to it."

"Thanks, Mel. Take care." Tuna ended the call and put her phone on the desk.

She sat back in her chair, stretched out her legs, and stared up at the ceiling. The familiar pattern of the old tin tiles soothed her anxious brain and helped her think and consider her meager options. The easiest path would be to file the case as unsolved and let it slowly decompose on its own in a file cabinet somewhere. But that would probably mean a death sentence for Emily Reiner if Mel's thoughts on him were correct.

Option two would be to expand the case entirely to try and find this mysterious third-party lover with whom Reiner had claimed she was having an affair. Could he - or she - have been the one that killed her and buried her out at Great Point? But opening up the case meant time and resources she really didn't have. And it went completely against her own perceptions that Reiner was indeed the guilty party.

The final choice, and really the only one in her mind, was to put the whole thing on the line and confront Jack Reiner. If she could leverage the autopsy findings and challenge him with the accusation that he had smothered his wife, maybe he would crumble. But she had to admit the evidence against him was pretty thin. Was there a way to bolster her challenge on Reiner? Convince him that she knew more than she really did? She had an idea that just might work.

Tuna got up and walked down the hall to the sheriff's office, the old wooden floors creaking as she went. She tapped lightly on the door with her knuckles.

"Come in."

She opened the door and stepped in. He looked up from his desk.

"Hey, Tuna. Any news on the autopsy results?"

"They are inconclusive. But there are some interesting bruise marks on her chest and a broken left clavicle."

"Anything else?"

"There were cashmere fibers in her throat."

"What does all that tell you?"

"Do you remember Melanie Thompson?"

"I do. Isn't she a Statey now?"

"She is. I talked to her. I wanted to get some fresh eyes on this, hoping she might see something we've missed."

"And?"

"She feels those marks and the fibers suggest that she was suffocated. Smothered, actually."

"Really?"

"Yes. Her thought is that Reiner probably threw her to the ground, got on top of her, and held a pillow or blanket over her mouth. If he was holding her down like that, it is likely that his knees made those bruises and caused the damage to the clavicle."

"So you think she was smothered?"

"Well, we think so. But as I said, it's inconclusive. There are other possibilities to address the findings. But I'm hoping that if we paint a picture of how we think he did it, then he might just break."

"Knowing him, I think it is a bit of a longshot."

"I agree. But it's really all we have. Unless you want to reopen the investigation and spend valuable resources trying to find the mysterious unknown lover."

Fred shook his head. "That would be a waste of time and money. I've been thinking about the case, and there is one thing that is really bothering me."

"What's that?"

"This," said Fred, pointing to an image in the report. It was of her hand taken while she lay in the morgue before her autopsy. The gray, desiccated flesh was highlighted by a bright gold band on her second finger. It was her wedding ring.

"Yes. What about it?"

"Well, don't you think that's unusual? Reiner said that she was having an affair and was running away. Don't you think she might have taken the ring off?"

"Hmm. Interesting thought. I know I probably would have. But maybe it was just force of habit. I've had my ring on for over fifteen years. Not sure I'd even think about it if I were in a fight with my wife."

"But, if you were planning on leaving her and, say, run away to California to start a new life, don't you think that might be the first thing you do?"

"I see your point." Tuna paced the room thinking. "The bigger question is why didn't Reiner remove it before he buried her?"

"Meaning?"

"He claims she was running away with her lover. If that were true, there is no way she'd keep the ring on. It would remind her too much of the life she was trying to escape. So he should have removed it to reinforce that story."

The sheriff's face went tight in recognition. "That's where he screwed up."

"Maybe. It's an opening we should try to exploit with him. See where it goes."

"Do we have enough for a search warrant? Maybe we can find some evidence at Reiner's house."

"Only if you have a judge in your pocket. There is nothing even remotely strong enough here to support a warrant."

"Maybe we could at least get him on tampering with a dead body or illegal burial," said Boston sarcastically.

Tuna smiled thinly. She wanted to nail Reiner for more than a misdemeanor.

"I need to also brief you on a discussion I had with the chair from the Select Board."

"Oh. What's up?" asked Tuna cautiously. Small-town politics had never served her well.

"She's caught wind of the investigation about Reiner and asked me specifically to back off."

"Back off?"

"Yes. She said he has donated tens of millions to the town and local nonprofits, and unless we had absolute proof that he was guilty, she was hoping we would not take the investigation further. And she adamant that we keep the press out of it."

"So he can get away with murder because he's rich?" said Tuna angrily. "What about the dead wife? Does she not deserve justice?"

"I know," said Boston. "I listened to her but made absolutely no commitments of any kind. As far as I'm concerned, if you think he's guilty, then we need to do everything in our power to convict him."

"Good."

"When are you planning on doing the next interview? Are you bringing him in?"

"Soon, probably tomorrow. But I don't feel we should bring him in. I want him to feel comfortable and not be on the defensive. If we try and bring him in here, he'll probably lawyer up, and we will get nowhere. If he's home, in his domain, he will feel in control of the situation. Hopefully, we can use that arrogance against him."

"Sounds like a plan. Anything else?" asked the sheriff.

"Yes. And it's a bit unusual."

The sheriff looked at her with an eyebrow cocked.

"I'd like to take Rob McGlynn with me on the interview."

"What?" said Boston, surprised. "That's more than a bit unusual, don't you think?"

"It is. But I think you'll agree that, um, McGlynn has certainly known some things about this case that there is no reasonable explanation for."

"You mean he talks to dead people," said Boston acidly.

"I don't know about that, Fred. But you have to admit we would not even be in this position if he had not led us to the body."

"In some ways, I wish he hadn't."

Tuna laughed. "I get that. But we are in it up to our asses now. And I want to see it through. I think he can bring an angle that we, well, um, perhaps don't really understand."

"Have you talked to him about it? McGlynn?"

"Not yet. I wanted to make sure you were aligned first."

"It's unusual for sure. But then again, what's usual for this case. Go talk to him. See if he'll even do it."

Tuna smiled. "Thanks, Fred. I'll let you know how it goes."

* * *

She called Rob the moment she sat down at her desk. He picked up immediately.

"Great minds," said Rob.

"Excuse me?" said Tuna confused.

"Great minds. As in, great minds think alike. I was just getting ready to call you."

Tuna laughed softly. "Okay then. Well, I'm glad we connected. I have a favor to ask."

"Sure. Shoot."

"I'd like you to accompany me when I interview Jack Reiner tomorrow."

"You want me to what?"

"I want you to join me when I interview Jack Reiner," Tuna repeated.

"Um, Detective Fisch, I'm not sure you knew this about me, but I'm not a detective!" exclaimed Rob forcefully. "Why would you even want me there?"

"Because I think you bring an unusual angle to this investigation, Rob. And I'm hoping that you might be able to see something or remember something that will help prove his guilt."

Rob sighed heavily over the phone. "Detective. Please. I'm not a psychic or a paranormal expert or anything of the sort. I will be useless for the interview. More than useless, really. I'll be a distraction that may help him evade your questioning."

"But you know things. You've been instrumental in the discovery of the body. Without you, this would still just be a six-year-old missing persons case."

"All I've been in this case is a messenger. A go-between. As I've told you, Dee Collins appeared to me, and we talked. She's the one that had the information. She's the one you should take on the interview."

"But she's dead, Rob."

"Well, yeah, there is that."

Tuna's fingers tapped her desk as she thought. What if? A crazy idea formed in her mind.

"Could you ask her a few questions for me then?" asked Tuna.

"Dee?"

"Yes. Maybe she can tell you a few things about the murder that only she and Reiner would know. If I had that information, it could totally destabilize him and maybe get him to disclose what really happened."

Rob thought for a moment. He had been pretty successful in finding Dee when he needed her. "Okay. I don't think that would be a problem. What do you want to know?"

"Okay. This is what I was thinking." Tuna read to him a short list of questions to ask Dee.

"Give me the afternoon. I'll call you first thing tomorrow, hopefully with some answers," said Rob.

"Thanks. I really appreciate your help." She ended the call. Now all she had to do was wait.

CHAPTER TWENTY-NINE

R ob hung up the phone with Tuna's questions swirling in his brain. For the millionth time, he wondered how the hell he had gotten himself into this position. It still seemed so surreal and so far removed from his simple life in the midwest with Sarah. Now he was being asked to seek out a ghost to answer specific questions about a murder. Her murder. It felt more like some far-fetched reality show than his actual life.

In truth, he was hoping, planning, on seeing Dee today anyway. He had lots of questions for her based on his unexpected meeting of Lisbeth Hopper. Why was Lisbeth walking the Sconset Bluff as a ghost when she really wanted to be back in Iowa? How did death really work? Was there a heaven? And what about the bad guys? The Jack Reiners of the world, what happened to them when they died?

He left the house and headed down Starbuck Lane towards Dee's cottage, the shells crunching under his feet. Stepping onto her porch, he looked into the windows before he went to the door and knocked softly.

"Hi, Rob," said Dee behind him.

He jumped, startled by her typical sudden appearance. He would never get used to that.

"Agh! Dee, you have to stop doing that!" Rob paused a minute to let the adrenalin in his body settle down. "I was really hoping to talk to you. Do you feel up for a walk?"

"Of course."

Rob stepped down from the porch and led her down Starbuck Lane toward Morey. They were quiet during the first few minutes, just two friends out for an afternoon stroll. As they approached Ocean Avenue with the broad expanse of the Atlantic in front of them, Rob turned to Dee. "I ran into Lizbeth Hopper this morning."

"I know."

"You know?"

"Yes. Lisbeth came to me and asked if I thought you'd help her."

Rob shook his head. "How does this all work, Dee. How are you here? How is Lisbeth? And why the hell have I become ghost central?"

Dee smiled. "I've been waiting for that question from you. I'm a little surprised you haven't asked it sooner. Especially with your, um, wife." Her voice trailed off.

Rob looked at the ground. "To be honest, I think I've been afraid to, for fear of what you might say." He sighed. "I'm such a coward."

"You are absolutely not a coward! A coward would have run away when they first learned the truth about me. You? You've been by my side ever since. You've been my advocate, my savior in some ways. I'll never be able to repay you for what you have done for me."

Rob blushed at the compliment. "I guess." He stopped and looked out again over the sparkling blue waters of the Atlantic. "Please help me understand." He turned to her. "How are you here? How are we able to walk like this together when you are dead?"

"I think the best way to explain things is that time has many, many layers. And sometimes, when conditions are right, those layers can touch."

"But you're dead."

Dee smiled sadly. "Yes, I'm dead. But in other layers of time, I still have physical being. It's not quite the same, but I'm able to experience, to interact, to exist."

"Other layers of time?"

"Yes. Death is just a stepping stone between the layers of time. When your time ends on one layer, it starts on another."

Rob shook his head; it was far too much to take in.

Dee continued. "As I mentioned, sometimes, when the conditions are right, the layers can interact. And someone like me can transit between them."

Rob recalled the event in her cottage a few weeks back. "So that is what you were doing?"

"Yes. If we want, we can sometimes move between layers and interact with people on those layers. People like you."

"But not everybody."

"No. Not everybody."

"But you mentioned there were consequences. What did you mean?"

Dee sighed softly. "Transiting takes energy. We need that energy to survive in our layer of time. When that energy is depleted, then we essentially move to the next."

"The next? What do you mean?"

"A body has a soul. That soul moves from layer to layer through time."

"So you exist forever?" asked Rob, his mind reeling about the possibilities. And does that mean Sarah is still out there?

"In a way, yes. But it's complicated. And to be honest, there is still a lot I don't know."

"Lisbeth mentioned that she didn't want to be here, on Nantucket, that she wanted to be back in Iowa. What was that about?"

Dee smiled. "The layers are most secure when they align with those times in your life when you are most happy."

"So, you go where you were most happy during your life?"

"In essence, yes. But occasionally, a layer can get blocked. Think of it as a wall that can't be breached. Several things can cause these, but the most significant are unresolved life events."

Rob started to understand. "Like an unsolved murder?"

"Yes! In my case, it is Jack Reiner who has killed two women, including me and is planning the death of a third. With Lisbeth, it is knowing that the descendant of her killer, also a murderer, walks freely."

"What about them?"

"Who?"

"Bad people. The murderers. What happens to them?"

"They transit layers, just like me. But unlike me, where I can feed off the energy of my happiest times, their layers align with the times that were their unhappiest."

Jack thought about this for a moment. "So, in a way, they will relive the most unpleasant times of their life?"

"It's a bit more complicated than that, but yes, that is one way of thinking about it."

They had reached the bicycle bridge and stopped together midway to look out over the water. It was a minute or so before Rob broke the silence.

"What about Sarah?"

Dee remained quiet. Rob repeated the question.

"Are you sure you want to know?"

A spike of adrenaline surged through his blood. *What wasn't she telling me? Was Sarah relieving her unhappiest times? Was she cursed?* Rob braced himself.

"Yes, I want to know."

"Then there is something else you need to know about our existence. And by ours, I mean you as well."

"Okay."

"Events in time often have more than one outcome. And each of those outcomes can continue within the different layers of time."

"Different outcomes? I'm not sure I understand."

"Let me explain it in a different way. Do you remember your drive home in the fog last night?"

Rob thought about the impenetrable gray wall he had driven through, taking over an hour to get home when it normally would have been a quarter of that.

"I do. What about it?"

"You remember the pickup truck?"

Rob recalled the huge grill emerging from the fog and steering the Jeep hard to right to miss it. And how the hell did Dee know about that?

"I do. Why?"

"Because that event had two outcomes. In one, you steered your car away from the truck and continued driving back to Sconset. In the other..." her voice trailed off.

"What do you mean, the other?" he asked cautiously.

Dee paused and then spoke. "In the other outcome, you didn't turn in time. Your Jeep hit the pickup head-on."

"What? No, I missed that pickup. I'm here talking with you, aren't I?" His voice was shaky and unsure.

"Yes, Rob, in one outcome, you made the turn and survived. In the other, you didn't. And in that outcome, I'm sorry to say, you were killed."

Dee's words hit him like a hammer blow. He was killed? What the hell?

She saw the confusion on his face and placed a cold hand on his arm. "Yes. In that other outcome, you did not survive the accident."

His mind swirled. What was she saying? That part of me is dead?

"I know it's a lot to take in."

"A lot to take in," exclaimed Rob. "Do you realize what you are telling me? That I'm dead!"

"I know it's hard. But that event caused time to split into two layers. One that we are in now, talking. And one in which you died. But there is some good in that."

"Good? How can any of that be good?"

"Because in that outcome, your spirit has gone to where you were happiest."

Rob let her words sink in. My happiest? That would have been with Sarah. Before her diagnosis when they had their whole lives together stretched out in front of them.

"I'm with Sarah?" he said softly.

Dee nodded slowly.

I'm with Sarah. We are happy.

Strangely the thought brought him comfort, knowing Sarah wasn't alone anymore. Part of him - another him? - was with her. They were once again living their life together.

"Thank you for telling me," said Rob, his eyes wet with tears.

"Of course."

Could his life get any stranger? And were things ever going to return to some semblance of normal? Maybe if he could resolve the situation with Reiner, then Dee would be free to go where she wanted. Lisbeth too. Maybe once he got these ghosts out of his life, his could return to normal.

They turned and made their way back to Starbuck Lane. The silence between them was comfortable, like that of old friends. As they approached Dee's cottage, Rob turned to her and broke the silence.

"Oh, I almost forgot. Detective Tuna wanted me to ask you a few questions about the murder. She is hoping if she has details only you and Jack would know, then maybe that would trip him up. Maybe get him to confess."

"Sure. What does she want to know?"

Rob read out the three questions.

Dee smiled. "She's a clever one, that Tuna."

CHAPTER THIRTY

S o what do you have for me?" Tuna was at her desk when Rob called.

"I saw Dee, and she gave me the answers you were looking for? Do you have a pen?"

Tuna opened up her tattered notebook and found a fresh page near the end. "I'm ready."

"For the first question, she had attempted to attack him. Tried to scratch his face and maybe even damage his eyes. She was hoping to hurt him enough that she could get out of the house and get help for herself."

Tuna was scribbling quickly. ""Okay, what about the second question?"

"It was a cashmere pillow that she had bought at the Ralph Lauren store in town. It had a tan and blue check pattern that she was particularly excited about because it matched their new wall paint color in the kitchen."

"And for the third?"

"Stored it in a large freezer they had in the garage. Kept it there for a month before he buried it."

"This is great, Rob," said Tuna. "Was there anything else she mentioned?"

"Yes. She made a phone call."

"A phone call?" asked Tuna curiously.

"Yes. And I think you'll find it interesting." Rob proceeded to give the detective the details about a single phone call made years before.

Tuna captured the information in her notebook. When she was done, she slapped the notebook shut. "Thank you. This might be just enough to unsettle him so I can pry open the truth. Hell, maybe even scare him into a confession."

"I hope so. And thank you for not making me go with you. As I said, I don't think I would add anything and would probably just get in the way."

"You have been hugely helpful with this," said Tuna clutching her notebook. "And please pass along my appreciation to Deidre when you, um, see her."

Rob smiled at the other end of the phone. "I will. And good luck."

"Thanks," said Tuna and ended the call. She placed the phone down on her desk and laid back in her chair. She now had an impressive arsenal of facts at her disposal that, if leveraged correctly, could finally resolve this case and put a guilty man behind bars. She jumped up and grabbed her keys. It was time. Now or never.

* * *

Detective Tuna Fisch had survived a number of dangerous situations during her career. Despite being a small island, they still had their share of DUIs, burglaries, drug rings, assaults, and on rare occasions, murders. She had been punched, spit on, screamed at, and even shot when she was trying to capture a suspected rapist. She had spent a couple of days at Nantucket Cottage Hospital. The rapist had gotten fifteen years at MCI–Concord. Ten for the rape and an additional five for the assault on Tuna.

Rubbing unconsciously at the scar on her shoulder, she drove up the driveway, the shells crunching under the tires. Even with her experience and training, she felt nervous approaching Gratitude. She was there on her own and had only her wits and her 9mm Smith & Wesson for protection. Sheriff Boston had offered to come with her, but she thought it best to fly solo on this interview. No doubt Reiner would feel superior to her, and she was hoping to use that arrogance to her advantage. But he was a big man, and physics are physics. She was not sure how long her hundred-and-twenty-pound frame would last against his bulk if she had to go one on one with him.

She closed the car door softly and walked to the front door. Above her, hazel eyes followed from a second-story window. Unaware of the attention, Tuna lifted the large brass knocker and let it hammer down on the strike plate. The sound seemed to thunder through the house. She waited patiently, shifting her weight from foot to foot with nervous energy. Silently she prayed he was here. She hadn't bothered to call or set up an appointment, wanting the element of surprise to give her yet another small advantage in the interview.

Emily heard the sound of the knocker and prayed silently that this second visit from the detective might lead to the downfall of Jack Reiner. She was tired of the abuse. Tired of the forced sex. Tired of feeling powerless against his control and ongoing attacks. Tired of living confined to this house unless she was needed to accompany him to some social engagement and demonstrate what a great husband he was. But her feelings of helplessness had turned with the discovery of the secret staircase. That revelation had given her a new hope of escaping this torture. Below her, she could just make out the scrape of Jack's desk chair pushing back and mentally followed him from his desk in the office to the front door.

At the door, Tuna waited. Footsteps approached, and the lock slid open. The doorknob twisted, and the door creaked, the hinges protesting the weight of their burden.

Jack Reiner stood in the door, filling the space. Dressed in jeans and a sweater, he stared down at her with a look of mild disgust in his eyes.

"Ah, Detective Fisch, what can I do for you? he asked irritatedly.

"Mr. Reiner," said Tuna, her voice quavering just a bit. "I was hoping to just get a few minutes of your time to just clarify some questions we had about your wife's case."

"You mean my late wife?" he growled.

"Yes, sir. Can you spare a few minutes?"

Reiner stood in the doorframe, his face twitching slightly as he calculated the risk of engaging in another discussion about his deceased wife with a member of law enforcement. Decision made, he said curtly, "I can give you ten minutes. I'm due at a meeting in town and cannot afford to be late. It's regarding the fundraising plans for the new addition at the hospital." He stepped back from the door, turned, and walked toward the kitchen.

Tuna noted that in that sentence, he reminded her of his importance in the community which he further reinforced by making her follow him like a spring duckling follows the duck. She trailed him into the kitchen where he had taken station leaning against the large island.

"Let's get this done."

"Yes, sir," said Tuna. She opened her notebook. "Thank you for taking the time to talk with me. I will do my best to make this quick. I wouldn't want you to be late to your meeting," said Tuna contemptuously. Two can play this game. She let the silence linger between them as she pretended to look through her notes. Reiner shifted uncomfortably.

"Detective?"

"Sorry. Did your wife drink or use drugs?"

Reiner relaxed a bit. Is this all she was going to ask him? "Uh, yes, but rarely. She'd have the occasional glass of wine at a social event, but that was about it."

"And drugs?"

"Maybe before we met, but since then, absolutely not. She knew I would not tolerate them or allow them here at Gratitude."

Tuna nodded. "The toxicity report showed she had some ibuprofen in her system."

"Okay. Is that unusual?"

"Not necessarily. But do you know why she would?"

"Detective," Reiner said exasperated, "that was over six years ago. I'm not going to remember that. Maybe she had a headache. Or it was her period." He started to relax a bit more.

The questions sounded like they were more for closing paperwork than for any investigative purposes. Softballs. He was going to be okay.

Tuna nodded and jotted down in her notebook. Without looking up, she asked, "Have you thought any more about this possible lover? Any ideas on who that might have been?"

Reiner was a bit taken aback. Maybe not softballs, after all. "As I told you and Sheriff Boston when we talked last week, I didn't know who she was seeing. I have a couple of suspicions," he lied, "but I wouldn't want to cast aspersions without evidence."

Tuna grunted and pulled a picture from her notebook. She handed it to Jack. "I'm particularly curious why your wife would be wearing her wedding ring when we found her."

He took the picture, stared at it emotionlessly, and handed it back. "Why wouldn't she?" he sneered. "We had a great marriage."

"In our experience, women who are running away with a lover tend to remove the ring. So if your story is true, that she was running away with a lover, then we expect she would have removed it and left it here. Maybe on a desk or bedside table."

"I'm afraid I can't answer why my wife wouldn't remove her ring. As I said, we had a great marriage, and her, um, dalliance was nothing more than a diversion. Are we done here?"

"No. I have a couple of questions about your wife's autopsy report."

A shot of electricity shot through Reiner. Had they found something?

"Yes?"

Tuna paused, gauging Reiner's face, looking for a sign of nervousness, guilt, anything that she might be able to hook into. Seeing nothing, she turned to her notes.

"While her tox report was clean, aside from the ibuprofen, of course, her body showed signs she might have been murdered."

"Murdered?" The electricity spiked through his body. "What are you saying?"

"There were some fibers in her throat, likely from a pillow. And there was bruising on her chest as well as a fractured clavicle. Our experts at the State Police believe that this was caused by someone kneeling on her, most likely while they held said pillow over her face." Tuna paused and stared intently into his eyes. "We believe she was smothered."

Jack did his best to keep his face calm and neutral, but inside, his mind was racing, and his body charged. Could they really tell this from a six-year-old body?

"Smothered?"

"Yes, sir. It is easy to do and usually leaves few traces. But in this case, we believe the skin bruising on the chest and the fractured clavicle point to that as the most likely possibility."

"Most likely possibility?" Jack said, trying hard to keep his voice from sounding hopeful. "Do your experts believe this was the only possible explanation for that evidence?"

Tuna paused, again watching him intently. And again, his face refused to belie his internal feelings.

"Um, no," said Tuna reluctantly.

A wisp of a smile spread over Jack's face and then vanished. "So it is not conclusive then?"

"No, it's not."

Jack crossed his arms smugly. Internally he relaxed. They didn't have any evidence. Or at least evidence that they could use to convict him. "So that's it then?" he asked expectantly.

She held his eyes, hoping to make him blink. He didn't. "No, it's not. I received some additional evidence this morning that I'd like to share with you."

Jack stood impassively in front of her. "Can I remind you that I need to leave, or I'm going to be late for a very important meeting."

"Just one more minute, please." She turned back to her notebook. She drew a deep breath. "Here's what I think happened. I think she was trying to leave you. On that night in question, it was the first of November, by the way, she came to your den and attacked you. I think she was trying to hurt you sufficiently so she could escape the house and get help."

He stood still, her words burning through his body like an electric poker. How the hell had she known about the attack? How the hell did she know the date? "What rubbish. What would she need help for?"

"For your abuse."

"My abuse?" asked Jack sarcastically.

Tuna ignored the question. "But you were too strong for her. You threw her down, kneeled on her chest, grabbed the cashmere pillow off the couch, and held it over her face until she stopped breathing. All in all, it probably just took a few minutes."

"I smothered her with a pillow? That is the biggest load of crap. I loved her. I would never have hurt her." He was trying hard to sound angry and insulted but feared his voice would betray him.

"Not just any pillow. The one she had recently purchased at Ralph Lauren. She liked it because it had a checked pattern and matched the color of the kitchen walls."

A fresh wave of adrenaline coursed through Jack's body. How the hell did she know all this?

He tried to quell the inner storm of fear raging through him. "I'm sorry, but that is pure fabrication, pure bullshit. I'm not going to sit here and let you insult me like this. I grieved for my wife for years and made every effort to find her. If she was killed, then you need to be looking for the man she was having an affair with. How is that going, by the way?"

She glanced up at him and, hoping to sound more confident than she felt, said, "And then you dragged her body into the garage and put her in that large oversize freezer you used to keep out there. And then it gets a little murky."

"A little murky? What the hell are you babbling about? I did not drag her into the garage and put her in the freezer! I think you need to leave."

The floor creaked in the living room. Emily had made her way down the hidden stairs and was hovering just outside the kitchen entrance listening to the detective's accusations. It both scared and excited her. Maybe Jack was about to get what was coming to him. Maybe this detective might be the one to save her.

"I think you kept her there for a few weeks and then took her out to Great Point and buried her where she lay for more than six years until we discovered her."

Jack stood silently, his arms still crossed. "I'm not going to justify this garbage accusation with a response. You need to leave. Now!"

Tuna held her ground. "There is just one more thing."

His face red and his body shaking with anger, he said. "What?"

"She made a phone call a week before her death."

"She made a phone call? What the hell does that have to do with any of this?"

"It confirms your abuse and establishes your guilt."

Jack was nearly apoplectic with rage and was using every fiber in his body to resist the urge to punch this detective in the face. He briefly toyed with the idea of killing her but knew that was one murder he would never get away with. Instead, he needed to maintain strategy as best he could; denial and obfuscation.

"This is all bullshit. I don't know why you made up this fantasy story, but it is complete and total crap. Let me tell you what is going to happen now. You are going to leave, and I am going to call my attorney. I will not stand for these blatantly false accusations. And if you try to make any of these allegations public, I will sue you so fast it will make your head spin."

Forcing herself to remain calm, she said, "Don't you want to know about the phone call?"

Jack stood silently, his right foot tapping the floor.

"She called the National Domestic Abuse Hotline."

"She did what?"

"She called the hotline. I talked to them myself this afternoon. Unfortunately, they don't have a recording of the conversation, but they do have the notes the counselor took." She paused, waiting for him to react. He didn't. Turning to her notebook, she read, "The client, who identified herself only as Deirdre R., stated that she had been abused for the past few years by her husband and was fearing for her life."

"Oh yeah, that's a smoking gun for sure," said Reiner sarcastically. "That could have been anyone. Now, I'm going to say this for the last time. You need to leave now! Don't force me to throw you out."

Emily quickly ducked back through the small door in wainscoting and closed it quietly behind her.

"Very well. But I will be in touch." She turned and walked through the living room. Reiner was on her heels. She stepped through the door as Reiner stood in the doorway and shouted at her, "I did not kill my wife. I loved her. Please do not come back here until you can tell me who really killed her!" He slammed the door so hard that the windows on the second floor rattled in their frames.

Tuna stood on the front walk and tried to calm her nerves. She had definitely mucked up the interview. How did she not get him to cave with the evidence she confronted him with? She should be walking him to the car in cuffs right now. Instead, she's going back to the station empty-handed, having shot her entire load. There was no way they were going to nail him now. Jack Reiner would get off scot-free. He was going to get away with murder, most likely for the second time.

Disappointed, she made her way back to the car and drove away.

Reiner watched her leave through a sidelight. He probably hadn't been completely convincing of his innocence, but there was nothing she had that would hold up in court. If there was, he'd have been arrested already. No, she was trying to break him down and make him confess. And there he had done well enough. But where the hell had she gotten that information? How could she have possibly known those details? It was scarily accurate. Especially since all that evidence had been cleared out years before, including the freezer.

The more he thought about it, the more he could explain away. After the death of the First, there had been some police activity at the house. They probably had some pictures or notes from those visits in the file. She could have seen pictures of the house with the couch and pillows and made the rest up. But two things stuck; the date - how the hell had she known the exact date he had killed her? - and the call to the hotline. He couldn't explain those. But since he wasn't in cuffs, he really didn't care. But it was kind of creepy.

Retreating to his office, he poured himself a generous serving of Laphroaig 25 Year and sat by the fire. In the end, he was pretty confident that the Two situation would resolve itself shortly. Give it a few more weeks, and the detective would lose interest. Another month or two, and it would be old news. He might be safe to move on Three in a year, maybe less. So, what would it be this time? He had learned a lot from the first two and wanted to put those learnings to work. This was the type of mental challenge he relished, and he spent the rest of the evening thinking through various scenarios that would end the life of wife number three while leaving himself free and unfettered. He even allowed himself a little fantasizing about Four. Oh, the possibilities! The evening passed quickly.

As Reiner was planning her demise, Emily was safely back into her room upstairs, pondering her next steps. Given how the interview went, she doubted very much that any kind of legal action against her husband would rescue her. And how the hell had Tuna known those details about the murder of Dee? That gave her chills. It was almost like Dee was still alive and feeding her that information.

No. She was not going to get any help. She was going to have to face the situation head-on. She was just going to have to bide her time and strike when the opportunity arose. She just hoped it would be sooner rather than later.

CHAPTER THIRTY-ONE

"What's a nor'easter?"

Pip and Rob were finishing up lunch at the counter of the pharmacy. Located on Main Street, it was an old-school place, and he had fallen in love with it immediately, especially since he could get an egg salad sandwich and a real, old-fashioned, hand-scooped chocolate milkshake. He had started to really enjoy their time together and had missed not seeing her for a couple of days.

"It's the bourbon we drank last week, silly," said Pip smiling.

"Seriously. I've been watching the Boston weather, and they are saying one is going to hit tomorrow. Is that something I should be worried about or need to prepare for?"

"It's just a type of storm we get here, usually in the fall. There will be a lot of rain, strong winds and probably some flooding. But for you in Sconset? I don't think you have anything to worry about except maybe losing power."

"Good."

"So, what's going on with the case? Have you seen Dee lately?"

Rob shifted awkwardly. "I did. Tuna had asked me to talk to her. She wanted to get some specific information that only Dee and Jack Reiner would know. I think she's hoping to use that to make him confess."

"Oh, my god."

"What?"

"It just hit me that we are talking about a real murder. That Mr. Reiner could be a killer. I guess it just hasn't seemed real to me. But when you talk about things like that? It kind of brings it home."

Rob reached out and grabbed Pip's hand. A jolt of electricity shot through his body.

Pip continued. "And I guess I'm still coming to grips with what I saw with you."

"You mean Dee?"

"Yes."

"Trust me, you don't know the half of it."

"What do you mean?"

He paused, not sure how much he really should share about what Dee had told him about death, layers of time, and multiple outcomes. "It's just that I've learned some things that, um, I'm trying to come to grips with as well."

Pip squeezed his hand and grinned. "Enough of this. "What do you say? Split another milkshake with me?"

Rob smiled. "Absolutely."

* * *

"How did it go? By the look of it, I'm assuming not well. Especially since he's not in booking right now."

Sheriff Boston was leaning against the doorframe of Tuna's office. His arms were crossed, and he had a look of sympathy on his face, much like a father would for a daughter who had failed an important test.

Tuna was at her desk, her head in her hands, reliving the interview and wondering how the hell she had not gotten a confession. She had everything but video evidence, and Reiner had danced around it with the dexterity of a principal soloist from the Boston Ballet. She looked up with tired eyes.

"I didn't get it, Fred. I didn't get the confession."

"What happened?"

"The bastard denied everything. I didn't even seem to make him nervous. He is one cool customer; I'll give him that." ¯

"Most psychopaths are, Tuna. If he even felt a hint of guilt or remorse, you would have picked up on that. But he views his late wife as an object, not as a person. Same for his current wife, I fear."

"Still, I should have been able to get something out of him." Tuna let out a growl of frustration and pounded her palms down on the desk. "Dammit!"

Fred walked over and placed his hand on her shoulder. "We knew it was a longshot and that his confession was our only hope of closing this case. We just don't have the evidence we need. And that leaves a hole in the case more than big enough for Reiner to step through."

"Do you think maybe we could depose the ghost?" Tuna said, laughing weakly. "Maybe she could do what I couldn't."

"Don't be so hard on yourself. You've done what you could with what little you had. I think you should set aside that case for a few days. Spend some time with Ellen. Go for some long walks on the beach. Forget about Jack Reiner and this case for a while. Let your mind rest."

"I think I could if I wasn't so worried about Emily. I fear that now that he knows he has cleared himself of Deidre's murder that he might start planning her death."

"Do you really think he'd be so brash?"

"Sadly, yes. And assuming he has killed his first two wives and gotten away with both, he probably has the confidence, and arrogance, to do it again."

Fred paced slowly in front of her desk, his face tight in concentration. "Is there any way to intercede? To, um, for lack of a better word, rescue her?"

"He made it very clear that we are persona non grata at Gratitude. I fear any effort along those lines would only cause him to go on the attack legally. And I'm not sure she would go willingly. Many abused women don't want to leave their abusers."

"Really? I would think she would jump at the chance to leave him."

"Sadly, that is usually not the case. Sometimes the woman feels like it's her fault that she is being abused. That she deserves it. Or she could be afraid that if she tries to leave him, he will react physically, financially, or emotionally. I think if Emily were really trying to escape, she would have made an effort already. Certainly, she has had the opportunities."

"Well, then, there is nothing we can do, is there?"

"I wish I could talk to her."

"Emily?"

"Yes. Get her perspective on things. Warn her about her husband. Maybe I could talk her into getting help."

"I understand your concerns, but my original recommendation still stands. Put the case aside. Take a break. Enjoy life."

Tuna looked up at him. "Thanks, Fred. I will. But I still need to tie up a few loose ends before I can file this one."

"Good."

* * *

Rob was back at the cottage when his phone rang. He glanced at the number and accepted the call.

"Detective Fisch."

"Hi, Rob. Is this a good time?"

"Sure. How did it go?"

Tuna sighed. "I wish I could say it went well, Rob. But unfortunately, we didn't get the confession we were hoping for."

Rob's shoulders slumped. "So those answers from Dee didn't help?"

"It wasn't that. I think my knowing those details really did unsettle him. But when he realized we didn't have any hard, physical evidence, well, he got his back up and essentially walked me out of the house."

"I'm sorry, Detective. So what's next?"

There was silence on the other end of the phone.

"Detective?"

"I've been instructed to set the case aside."

"You mean stop the investigation?"

"Essentially, yes."

Rob felt his cheeks blush with anger. "So that bastard gets away with murder? And everything I have done, from finding her body, being given the third degree, and even getting those answers for you? It's all for nothing!"

"I'm sorry. I can't tell you how much we appreciate what you have done for this case. At a minimum, we will at least be able to give her a proper burial."

"While her killer walks free?"

"I wish I had better news. I'm sorry."

"So am I," said Rob and abruptly ended the call. His body was shaking with anger. All he had been through. All he had done to help Dee. And for what? She was going to be so disappointed. He had really hoped to bring her some form of closure. Now he wasn't sure what this meant. Was he going to be visited by ghosts for as long as he was here? If that was the case, then it was time to go. He was just starting to enjoy the island - especially his time with Pip - but he was ready for his life to return to normal.

And the first step in that process was to let Dee know what was going on. He made his way through the door and headed down Starbuck Lane. He had just arrived at her porch when she called out behind him.

"Hi, Rob." She looked at him intently and saw something was wrong. "What is it?"

"Tuna couldn't get the confession."

"She couldn't get the confession?" asked Dee, shocked.

"No."

"So he hasn't been arrested?"

"I'm sorry, but no. And it looks like they are going to stop the investigation."

"Stop the investigation? So he gets away with killing me?"

Rob stood silently. Dee's image started to shimmer, and then she let out a long wail of rage. "That bastard! That goddamn bastard! I'm dead, trapped in time, while he enjoys life. It is so unfair!" She let out another long scream of emotional pain.

"I wish there was something more I could do."

Dee settled down. "You've done enough, Rob. And I really appreciate it." She paused. "I think it's time that I took matters into my own hands."

"What are you talking about?"

"I think maybe it's time I paid a visit to my husband."

"What? Why didn't you do that before?"

"Because it will be very hard if not impossible for me to make myself visible to him. Maybe if it's dark but even then it's not guaranteed. And those costs I told you about? It will take a toll on me."

"I think I understand."

She continued. "Not to mention I wanted to see him exposed. Arrested. Humiliated in the eyes of the Nantucket community. Knock him and his brutal family off that pedestal so many people put them on."

Rob nodded, "Is there anything I can do?

"No. You've done enough already. Go find Pip. Take her to dinner. Have some fun."

"Are you sure?"

"Yes."

"So what are you thinking?"

Dee smiled sinisterly, "It's time Jack Reiner and I had a chat."

Her tone sent shivers down Rob's back. "Please be careful."

"What's he going to do? Kill me again? No, he can't hurt me anymore. But I think I may be able to hurt him."

"Just be careful," he repeated.

"I will. Now go. And don't worry about me. I will be fine."

Rob walked back to the Shanty, thankful he was on Dee's good side. Seeing the look in her eyes actually made him feel a little sorry for Jack Reiner.

CHAPTER THIRTY-TWO

Jack sat in his study, feeling smug. The interview yesterday had gone well, and he felt quite confident that any attention focused on him around the death of Two would dissipate quickly. He might have to endure another discussion with that bumbling bitch of a detective, but his future freedom was secure. He was celebrating the occasion by treating himself to a dram of Balvenie 50-Year. It had cost him a small fortune when he had purchased it but felt the events of the day were well worth it.

Three was put to bed for the evening, safely ensconced, and locked in her room upstairs. Thoughts of the interview with the detective had strangely aroused him, and he had taken Three rather forcefully. She had protested as she normally did, but in the end, he prevailed as he normally did. She had left for her room immediately after he had finished. His postcoital interlude consisted of turning the key in her bedroom lock to secure her for the night.

Outside the large windows of his study, the nor'easter was gaining strength as predicted. It would be a night of heavy rain, strong winds, and dropping temperatures. But Gratitude had been through much worse over its hundred and thirty-odd years and would weather this tempest as well. Jack put another log on the fire, selected a book from the shelf, and settled into the large leather armchair. Life was good.

A powerful gust hit the house, and Jack could hear the old wooden frame creaking under the pressure. Seconds later, the house went dark. He waited for the backup generator to kick in, but the lights remained off. What the hell? Frustrated, he felt his way over to his desk, pulled open the top drawer, and grabbed a flashlight. Clicking it on, he made his way through the living room and into the mud room, where he put on a heavy yellow slicker. He pulled the hood over his head and, bracing himself, made his way into the storm to see if he could address the problem.

The generator had been put in years before and, to date, had worked flawlessly the few times it had been needed. And it damn well should have, given the cost of its installation and ongoing maintenance. He made his way around the side of the garage to the generator, the rain, and wind lashing at his face, and found it was running as it should. He played his flashlight across the transfer switch and saw that one of the power cables had been worn through. It had done its first job in starting the generator when it sensed the power loss from the grid but failed to route that power to the house because of the worn cable. Why his maintenance crew hadn't caught this and replaced it made him furious. There would be hell to pay tomorrow. But tonight, he was going to have to survive without electricity. Grumbling under his breath, he started back to the house.

In her room, Emily sat in the dark, wondering if the time had come to make her escape. The evening's forced sex had once again made her feel both humiliated and infuriated. He was a selfish partner caring little about what she enjoyed from the experience. No, it was all about him. It was always about him. She was tired of his control, his narcissism, his treatment of her as a sex toy that he could do with as he pleased. She was a person, not an object! Her rage overpowering her fear, she got out of bed and worked her way slowly over to the bookcase and unlatched the jib door. The room was nearly pitch black; the only light was a faint glow from outside where a full moon did its best to shine through the storm. It was time.

She made her way over and quietly eased the small door open. She knelt down and felt for the pipe she had found in her first foray down the hidden staircase. Weapon in hand, Emily made her way slowly down the spiral staircase treading as softly as she could. It took her several minutes before she felt the landing of the first floor and bumped into the wainscoting door. Carefully she opened the latch and, as quietly as possible, pushed the door open. She emerged from under the portrait of Digby Grey just as Jack returned from outside.

Emily scooted over and ducked behind the large sofa, but Jack had seen the movement and played his flashlight over her.

"Emily? What the hell are you doing out?" Hadn't he locked her door? Was something wrong with it?

She stood slowly, her hand hanging firm to the pipe.

"What, you're going to hit me with that?" Jack said, laughing. "You dumb bitch. You just don't get it to you? Give me that." He walked toward her, one hand keeping the flashlight in her eyes, the other outstretched for the pipe.

Emily emerged from behind the sofa and started to edge her way to the front door. "I'm leaving. I'm done with you."

"You aren't going anywhere except back to your room."

"I'm not."

"Yes, my dear, you are," said Jack, approaching her.

Emily turned to run for the door but slipped in a pool of rainwater. He was on top of her before she hit the floor and quickly unarmed her. She struggled underneath him, but he lifted up enough to punch her hard in the gut. She curled up in pain, crying.

"Leave me alone!"

"Such disobedience requires a correction, my dear. Now get up!"

She stayed on the floor, curled in a fetal position, her body wracked by sobs.

"Get up. Now!" he shouted, grabbing her arm and heaving her off the floor. She fell backward and cried out in pain.

"If you don't stop that goddamn crying, I swear I'll use this pipe on you!"

She quieted, slowly getting to her knees and then finally able to stand. Jack put the pipe aside and grabbed her arm forcefully. Using the flashlight to guide them through the darkness, he led her up the stairs to her room. He was surprised to find the door locked, and the key was back in his study. Damn. But a bigger concern came to him.

"How the hell did you get out?"

Emily stood resolutely. She was not going to reveal this one secret. She would probably be trapped forever if she did. But keeping it also might kill her.

"Tell me!"

Again staying silent, Jack slapped her hard in the face. "Tell me, bitch! How the hell did you get out?"

She kept quiet. He slapped her again.

"Jack?" a voice said softly behind him.

He turned to see a faint apparition down the darkened hallway like a small cloud of fog. Emerging from the gloom, it gained density and shape until his late wife stood in front of him, dressed as she was the night he had last seen her over six years ago.

"What the hell?" He played the beam of the flashlight on the image, but it simply passed through, lighting up the wall behind it.

"Hi, Jack. It's me. Deirdre. Don't you recognize me?"

"No, no, it can't be. You're dead," Jack said, his voice quivering. He released his grip on Emily. She backed herself up against the wall, wondering why he had freed her and if she could manage a potential escape down the stairs.

"Yes, I am, thanks to you."

Emily looked back at Jack. Who the hell was he talking to? And who is dead? Was he having some sort of breakdown?

Jack stared intently at the image, his mind trying to reconcile between what he was seeing and what he knew to be the truth. Deirdre Reiner was dead, gone, and buried. Was he really talking to a ghost? He had heard tales of people seeing things and had always dismissed them as rubbish. But here he was, actively conversing with his late wife. Had Emily somehow managed to put something in his drink? Was he having some sort of mental episode? A stroke?

"You are going to let her go, Jack. You are going to let her leave this house as she wishes and give her the life she wants. A life without you."

"I don't think so, my dear. She isn't going anywhere. At least not until I'm done with her."

"Like you were with me? Have your way until you get bored, then kill me and bury me in the sand?"

"You attacked me."

Dee walked slowly around Jack. "May I remind you that it was you who started with the attacks. The physical abuse. I had never struck you until that evening."

"I was only trying to correct you. Constructive feedback, really. To show you where you could improve."

"Improve? You bastard. I was just an object to you. Just as she is."

"Didn't we have some fun times together? Our honeymoon was wonderful," he said, trying to be charming.

Dee softened. "Yes, yes, it was. And I loved you. I thought you were the man of my dreams." She paused, and then her voice hardened. "And then you changed. You went from loving to monstrous, from caring to cruel."

"It's only because you needed correction. I was trying to make you a better person."

"A better person?"

"Yes. I always knew what was best for you. I was only trying to bring that out."

" You knew what was best for me? You arrogant son of a bitch. That is why I was trying to get away from you. And no doubt, that is why Emily was trying to escape your grip tonight."

Jack looked at her and sneered." But you didn't make it did you? And neither will she," he said, pointing the flashlight at Emily. "Either way, that is my decision to make. Not hers."

"The decision is yours to make?" said Dee incredulously and started to laugh. "Well, that decision is most certainly hers, Jack. She should be free to do with her life what she wants."

"That is not going to happen. Now, I don't know what the hell you are or how I'm able to talk to you, but you need to leave. I'm as done with you tonight as the day I buried you."

Dee snorted. "I'm afraid that you are under the impression that you can control things now. Here in your house. With me. That is mistaken. I make the decisions now, Jack. And you are going to let her go."

"I don't know where you get off ordering me to do anything!"

"So what's it going to be for Emily? Are you going to smother her with a Ralph Lauren pillow and bury her in the sand at Great Point? Is that what you are planning?"

Jack laughed wickedly. "That was fun, wasn't it? But I really don't know how they found you. I thought I had taken care of that situation pretty carefully."

"I think you have forgotten how engaging I can be and how clever I am with the, um, resources that are available to me."

"Resources? What the hell are you babbling about. You are dead! Gone!"

"Dead? Sadly, yes. You made sure of that. But gone?" Dee let out a laugh. "You don't know the first thing about death, Jack. And what is possible."

"What the hell are you saying?"

"There is a man visiting the island who helped me."

"Helped you?"

"Yes. He and I became friends. I asked him to help the police discover the truth about what you did to me. He could only do so much, but he did lead them to my body. And what was left of me was enough for them to know that most likely you murdered me."

Jack looked around with his arms open. "That's funny. It doesn't appear I'm under arrest."

"You always were a confident bastard. And even though I fed Tuna specific details about that evening, apparently, you held up pretty well to her questioning."

"So that's how the detective knew those things about that night?"

Dee nodded slowly. "But sadly, there just wasn't enough evidence to nail you to the wall like you deserve. I had hoped that it would go that way - that Tuna would get a confession - and you would be exposed to the world for the abusive bastard you are. I would have liked to have seen how your friends would have reacted to the news. And I would have loved to see you perp walked onto the ferry, hands and feet in cuffs, while the Nantucket community watched."

Jack smiled arrogantly, recalling the interview, and felt a stirring in his groin. "But it didn't go that way. And no one on this island will ever know."

"Unfortunately, your secret will be safe. But a man who kills two women doesn't deserve to live."

"Two women?"

"You pompous prick. You killed Margaret and then me."

"I didn't murder Margaret."

"Filling her full of tranquilizers and alcohol and then slipping her into the water? That's murder."

Jack smiled, recalling that afternoon on the beach. It had gone off nearly perfectly except for the damn ocean currents that brought her body back to shore a few weeks later.

"Okay, maybe I helped a little."

"You son of a bitch. You killed her just as you did me. And I am not going to allow you to kill Emily."

"You? You're not going to let me kill Emily?" he asked incredulously and laughed. "You couldn't stop me if you tried."

Dee smiled threateningly. "If you knew what I know about death, Jack, you wouldn't be so cocky right now. In fact, you should feel frightened. Very frightened. I know where you'll be going. And it isn't pleasant."

"You bitch. You really think you can scare me?"

Emily stood transfixed, trying to understand the conversation her abusive husband was having with himself. He was going to kill her? Who was trying to stop him? She edged her way slowly down the wall, trying to put distance between herself and her raving husband. She thought briefly about escaping down the hidden staircase but remembered her door was locked.

Dee laughed and spoke slowly, as if to a child." Yes, you should be scared, Jack. In a way, it's funny. By successfully avoiding arrest and potential jail time, you've left me only one course of action."

"Oh really? What's that?" he taunted.

"It's simple. I'm never going to allow you to hurt another woman. I've no doubt that you're already planning on getting rid of

Emily. Probably not tonight, but certainly in the next year. And I'm certain you've already started thinking about another woman to replace her. What will it be, Jack, for number four? Blonde? Redhead? Or someone that looks like us," she said, nodding toward Emily. "You have a type, you know."

A chill went down Jack's spine. It was like she was reading his mind.

"No, Jack, there will not be a number four. You have gotten away with this for far too long, and I'm not going to let another innocent woman fall victim to your abuse."

Trying to sound far more confident than he felt, he stared at Dee and said, "You're not going to allow that to happen? Who the hell do you think you are?"

She looked at him, her eyes blazing with fury. As Jack watched, the image began to fade and shift. The long, flowing brown locks were replaced by a rat's nest of matted, dirty hair. The eyes blackened and sunk deeply into the sockets while the skin of her face turned gray and stretched tightly against her skull. Her gray turtleneck turned mottled, and holes formed where the fabric had rotted way in the sand, revealing desiccated skin underneath. She smiled viciously to reveal rows of black teeth, and as he watched, several fell out and dropped to the floor. The once beautiful Dee faded away to be replaced by the Dee as she was now, a dried husk of a corpse that had spent six years in a sandy grave.

Reiner gasped, frightened by the image hovering in front of him. "What the hell is happening to you?"

The image hissed back at him. "Don't you recognize me, you bastard? This is how I look now. This is what you did to me, killing me and burying me in the sand!"

The ghastly apparition raised its arms and slowly approached Jack, its bony hands threatening to curl themselves around his neck. The phalanxes of three fingers on the right hand had broken through the skin, the fleshless white bones pointing menacingly at him.

Jack backed away, his face contorted in fear. Emily watched, amazed, as the man who had been so abusive cowered in front of her. Something was scaring him, but she couldn't see a thing.

Dee continued to advance, backing Jack up until his foot teetered at the top of the stairs. She opened her mouth into an evil grin, her face grossly misshapen. "You are going to die!" The image laughed hideously, its voice in harmony with the roar of the wind outside. And then she rushed at him.

Jack screamed and lost his balance. Tumbling backward, he bounced heavily from tread to tread. His body careened off the wall and sent his head through the railing. One of the white balusters, its shape a traditional spindle handcrafted over a hundred years before, snapped under the force. The bottom half, now a jagged splinter, pierced his fleshy neck severing his carotid artery. Momentum and gravity played their part keeping his body in motion until it landed heavily at the foot of the stairs, a red pool slowly forming on the wood floor.

Emily screamed as he fell and followed him down the stairs as quickly as she could. Dee floated down the stairs gracefully behind her, her image returning to beauty as she did.

Jack lay gasping on the floor and struggling to breathe, choking on his own blood. Emily stood transfixed, watching the man who minutes before had slapped her hard several times after her unsuccessful effort to escape.

"Help me," he croaked. Spatters of blood flew from his mouth. "Please." He extended his hand shakily up to her.

Emily looked down at the pleading desire in his eyes. A part of her wanted to rush into the kitchen and call 911. That would be the right thing to do, and maybe, just maybe, first responders and Cottage Hospital could save him. But another part of her, a stronger part, took quiet pleasure in the knowledge that she had the power, for once, over him. She held his life in her hands and a decision to make. Try to save the man who had been abusing her or let him die and be free of him finally and forever.

But she thought of herself as a good person despite the many mistakes she had made in her life. If she did nothing, she wasn't sure if she would be able to live with herself. And as much as she wanted him gone, she wasn't going to let hate make her a monster like him. No, she would try and save his life, if only for plausible deniability to her future conscience and the authorities. Turning, she walked, albeit slowly, to the kitchen to call the EMTs.

Dee stepped in and looked down at Jack with a grim smile on her face. She could see the panic in his eyes as his life drained away from him. He looked up at her, trying to speak, but no words would come out. Only more blood. As she watched Jack struggle, Margaret appeared next to her, her image shimmering in the darkness. Jack's eyes bulged in shock as he stared up in recognition. The two women he had killed were now watching him die.

His breathing became more labored and slowed as he exsanguinated. His mind, though, was still active, and it was reeling. How could they just stand there and watch? Where was the ambulance? Had Emily managed to screw that up too? Those damn bitches never appreciated me. Didn't they know I just wanted the best for them? Why won't they help me? As he took his final breath, the realization hit him. It wasn't just one of his wives who wanted him dead. It was all of them.

His body hitched and fell quiet as his eyes took on the glassy vacancy of death.

As Margaret and Dee watched in quiet satisfaction, Lisbeth appeared at their side. Together the three women quietly celebrated that the last seed of this despicable family was gone.

Lisbeth turned her attention from Jack's body to the portrait on the wall. The image of the man who had raped and killed her over a hundred years before looked back. Suddenly his eyes began to smoke. His face began to move and distort as if being tortured. His mouth opened, and his head tilted back as if wailing in pain. Thin flames appeared around the edges of the work and quickly crossed the painting ending the silent scream before consuming the rest of the image. Within seconds all that was left was a charred canvas secured in a gilded frame.

The three women looked at each other silently, relishing the moment. Finally, Dee broke the silence. "Our work here is done. And Emily is safe." Margaret and Lisbeth nodded in agreement. Then the images of the three women began to dim, and just as the last wisp of the apparitions faded away, the lights in Gratitude shone brightly, the power restored, the evil gone.

* * *

The EMTs had come and left. There was nothing they could do for Jack Reiner. The baluster had torn a gaping hole in the side of his neck, freeing the better part of three pints of his blood to spill out on the floor. Their only work was to give a mild sedative to Emily, who was now sitting on the sofa, hugging her knees and rocking gently. The events at the top of the stairs had confused and upset her. Who the hell had he been talking to? What had happened to frighten him? And the fall down the stairs? It was almost as if some invisible hand had pushed him.

Detective Fisch and Sheriff Boston had arrived as the medics were leaving and had spent the better part of an hour assessing the scene. It was clear that the fall down the stairs and the collision with the baluster had caused his death. But was the fall simply a matter of losing his balance, or was it more intentional. Like being pushed by an abused wife?

Initial investigation completed, the coroner took control. A large black bag was spread next to the body. Along with her assistant, the coroner lifted the remains of Jack Reiner and laid him in the bag. She pulled the sides up and ran the zipper home.

Emily jumped at the sound. Tuna and the sheriff watched the coroner complete her work and then approached the sofa.

"Mrs. Reiner, I'm very sorry about your husband. Do you feel comfortable answering a few questions?" asked Tuna.

Emily sniffled and patted her eyes with a tissue. "Of course."

"Thank you. Can you tell me what happened tonight?"

"Well, it really started when we lost power. That was at about seven. Jack left to go outside. I'm guessing he must have been checking the generator. For some reason, it didn't come on when the lights went out."

"Okay," said Tuna, taking notes.

"I had, um, made my way down here to check on him."

"And then?"

"He was walking me back to my room. All was okay until we got to the top of the landing, just outside my bedroom. It was like he had some sort of breakdown."

"Breakdown? What do you mean?"

"He started talking to someone."

"Talking to someone?"

"Yes. It was like someone appeared, but I couldn't see anyone or anything."

"What was he saying?"

"At first, he said something along the lines of 'it can't be, you're dead.'"

Tuna glanced at the sheriff and back to Emily. "Who do you think he was talking to?"

"I don't know. I couldn't see anything. I mean, it was dark, but I'm sure I would have seen someone if they were there."

"What else did he say?"

"He said something about a detective knowing things. And then he started to argue. He said she hadn't made it, and I wasn't going to either."

"What does that mean, do you think?"

Emily looked down at the ground before looking back at the detective. She said softly, "I think maybe he was going to kill me."

"Kill you?"

"Um, yes. Maybe not right away. Not tonight. But he was arguing that he could and would when he wanted to. And he also mentioned Margaret."

"Margaret?"

"Yes. Something about how he might have helped a little. I'm pretty sure he was talking about his first wife. Does that mean anything to you?"

"His first wife drowned while she and Jack were at the beach."

"I knew that, but why would he even mention her?"

"You probably don't know the full story, but it was likely that Jack played a role in her demise."

A look of shock came over Emily's face. "You mean he killed her?"

"Nothing was ever proven. It was considered an accidental drowning, although she had tranquilizers and a lot of alcohol in her system."

"Oh, my god. I didn't know. I thought it was an accident."

Tuna let Emily process that news before continuing. "Then what?"

Emily gathered her composure. "Well, then he said something like, 'what the hell is happening to you' then he got scared. Really scared. He started to back away. I don't think he realized he was at the top of the stairs, but he lost his balance and fell backward. I heard him falling, and then there was an awful splintering noise. It was the..."

Tuna placed her arm on Emily's shoulder. "It's okay. I know it must have been a terrible experience for you."

Emily nodded.

"Is there anything else you can remember?"

"After he fell, I ran down the stairs to him. When I saw what had happened, I rushed into the kitchen to call 911. That's when the lights came back on. And then I saw him, lying there in all that blood. It was awful."

"I am sorry for your loss," said Tuna again.

"What is this?" said a voice.

Tuna turned to see the sheriff holding up the short length of galvanized pipe. They both looked at Emily.

Looking confused, Emily said, "I don't know what that is. Maybe Jack took it with him to look at the generator?"

Tuna and Fred shared a quick look.

"Can you please excuse me for a minute? I really need to use the bathroom."

"Of course."

Fred walked over with the pipe. "What are you thinking?"

"I'm wondering if maybe we wouldn't find Emily's prints on that pipe. Maybe she was going to attack him. Or self-defense? Or maybe he did need it for the generator."

"Hmm"

"But there's no evidence it was used on him. Clearly, it was the fall - and the baluster - that killed him in the end. The bigger question is whether or not she pushed him. Or was it accidental?"

"Good question. What or who do you think he was talking to?"

"To tell you the truth, Fred, I have absolutely no idea. But from what I've seen so far with this case, I wouldn't be surprised if he was talking to Santa Claus."

Fred laughed. "It's definitely been a strange one for sure."

"So what do you think we should do?"

He thought for a moment. "Over twelve thousand people die a year from falling down the stairs. It sounds like he was confused. It was dark. I think we can add one more to that statistic."

"I was thinking the same thing. I'm glad we agree."

Tuna nodded and surveyed the room. Her eyes fell on the charred remnants of the portrait.

"Oh, my god."

"What is it?" asked Fred.

Tuna nodded at the wall. "It looks like the portrait of Digby Grey has been torched."

The sheriff walked up to the portrait to make a closer inspection. The frame appeared sound except for some light scorching on its inner edge, but the canvas was completely burnt. Whatever image had been painted was long gone. He turned back to Tuna. "That's weird. What would have caused this, I wonder?"

"I think I have an idea," said Tuna.

"Care to enlighten me?"

Tuna put a hand on his arm. "Trust me. Ignorance is bliss."

Emily returned. "Do you have any more questions for me?"

"I think we are done. Again, I'm so sorry for your loss. If there is anything you need, please don't hesitate to call me," Tuna said and handed Emily her business card.

"Actually, I do have a favor."

"Of course."

"Would you give me a ride to the Nantucket Hotel? I don't want to stay here tonight."

Tuna smiled, "We'd be happy to."

CHAPTER THIRTY-THREE

It had been a week since the nor'easter and the fall - quite literally - of Jack Reiner. Rob had talked with Tuna the following day and gotten a full report of what had happened at Gratitude. Tuna suspected that Reiner hadn't lost his balance but rather had been pushed but didn't have the evidence or the will to pursue criminal charges. Rob had been shocked to learn that Reiner was dead but silently agreed with Tuna that he had probably been pushed. He just doubted that Emily had been the one responsible.

When he had last seen Dee a few days before, she had a murderous look in her eyes. But could she have physically pushed him? He recalled she hadn't even been able to open a car door, so that seemed unlikely. Maybe just her appearance to Jack would have been enough to upset his balance. Or could she have said something to scare him? In the end, it didn't matter. Jack Reiner, the bastard husband, serial abuser, and murderer of two women, was dead. Emily was safe. And the case was now thankfully closed. Maybe now his life could return to normal.

The only lingering question for him was wanting to know about Dee. He had to laugh to himself. He was worried about her like a close friend, yet she was a ghost. But with his time on the island, he had become quite fond of her. She had been the first person to really welcome him to Nantucket with a brief wave the night he arrived. He thought back on their meeting on the bicycle bridge - certainly not by chance knowing Dee - and how he had shared his goal of wanting to write a novel with her. What was it about her that had made him open up to her?

And what was it about her that had made him put his reputation on the line to get her justice? He thought back to what he had shared with Pip, with Tuna, and even with Sheriff Boston, and it made him cringe. What they must have thought about him and the stories he was telling. But at least Pip had seen her or at least believed she had seen her, so he knew he wasn't completely crazy after all.

But where was she now that Reiner was dead? Was she gone forever, released from this burden to a happier place, on what was she called it, another plane on the space-time continuum? It made his head spin, just trying to reconcile it all. But he did hope that wherever she was, she was happy. He would just have liked to have said goodbye.

Rob had spent the better part of the morning on his laptop, struggling to get a paragraph or two written. He had yet to find a groove with his writing, and the events of the past few days had stifled any creativity he might have had. And mentally, he just didn't have the capacity to write, his mind too full of thoughts of Dee, of Pip, and of the death of Jack Reiner. As had been his past remedy to free his thoughts, he went for a walk.

Walking to escape writing had become his daily ritual and further confirmation of his failure as a novelist. That regret, though, was greatly offset by the enjoyment he derived from walking through the neighborhood. Despite the approach of winter, the beauty and charm of the little village still shone through. Gray shingled cottages, their roofs covered in the bare skeletons of climbing roses, huddled side-by-side in the cool and foggy air. The

Atlantic, its blueish-gray expanse, still stretched to a perfect line on the horizon. The shells paving many of the lanes still crunched under his feet, and when not hidden by the all too frequent fog, the azure blue sky still blazed brilliantly above.

He turned onto Atlantic Avenue and smiled when he saw the three deer grazing on a lawn. With the seasonal residents gone, they seemed quite comfortable roaming through the village, nibbling leisurely at window boxes, hydrangeas, and, surprisingly, roses. Many homeowners had covered their landscaping with netting to discourage the behavior, but the deer still had ample choices for their daily buffet.

Rob stopped and looked out over the Atlantic. The nor'easter had created some very large waves, and despite the day's calmer winds, the impressive swell remained. He could see the white foam of the breakers and hear the roar as they approached and then crashed onto the beach. The thought of being out on that ocean, caught in the storm, sent shivers through him, and again he marveled at the men and women who made their lives at sea.

As he approached the bike bridge, he saw two women standing in the middle. As he got closer, he realized one was Dee. The other he didn't recognize. Dee turned and gave him a broad smile as he neared. She looked radiant and stunningly beautiful. Her long brown hair floated gently in the breeze, and her pale skin shined luxuriantly. She looked happy, relaxed, and free.

"Hi, Dee."

"Hi, Rob."

"I'm so happy to see you. I thought that maybe, you might have, um, gone away forever."

"You know I wouldn't leave without saying goodbye, don't you? After everything I've put you through?" She smiled warmly. "I can't thank you enough for everything you did for me, for us."

"Is this…?"

"Yes," She turned. "Let me introduce you to Margaret. Jack's first wife."

Rob turned to her and smiled. "Margaret, it is so nice to meet you."

"And you. I just wanted to thank you for everything you did to help Dee bring justice for us."

"I'm just glad it worked out for you both. Although I was a bit surprised to hear that Jack was dead."

Dee looked pained. "You need to know that his death was not my intention. I had wanted to scare him enough to confess. I'd rather see him rot in jail. But you also need to remember that man killed both of us."

"So where is he now?" asked Rob, remembering their earlier conversation.

"I'm not sure," said Dee. "But wherever he is, I hope he is suffering. He was an evil man."

A seagull cried in the distance. Rob followed the sound and noticed a thick wall of fog approaching. Typical of fall weather in Sconset, the fog hovered just off the beach and was threatening to come ashore to embrace the village.

"So what's next for you?" asked Rob, turning his attention back to the two ladies.

"I think we will be moving on. Nantucket is a wonderful place, but both of us have some unpleasant memories of our time here with that man."

"I certainly understand. Where will you go?"

Dee smiled. "Even if I could explain it, I'm not sure you'd understand it. But you remember we talked about layers within time?"

Rob nodded.

"Let's just say we are moving on to another layer."

Rob smiled. "As long as you will be happy wherever you go."

"Thank you."

Delivering on its threat, the fog bank swept in, enveloping them. Rob realized he could no longer make out the water.

"Will I ever see you again?"

"Perhaps. Life and time are funny things. You never know when our paths might cross again."

"I would like that. I'm going to miss you."

"Oh, Rob, you are too sweet. I will miss you as well. I can't tell you how much I enjoyed our walks and talking with you. You are the man I had hoped Jack Reiner would be."

He blushed.

"Do you remember when you wanted to give me a hug?" asked Dee.

"I do. But I thought…"

Dee opened her arms. "Things have changed since then."

Rob relished her embrace. He could feel energy rippling through her warm body. She smelled of lavender and rose. Her soft hair fell across his face and tickled his skin. He didn't want to let go.

After a few moments, Dee pulled away, her image dulled. The hug had cost her.

"Goodbye, Rob. We will meet again, I promise you."

"I hope so," said Rob, a tear in his eye.

Margaret looked at him, nodded, and smiled.

The two women turned and walked slowly away, heading back toward the center of the village. Before they had reached the end of the bridge, their images dissolved into the fog.

Sad, Rob stood on the bridge and looked toward the water. He could still hear the roar of the waves but could no longer see the few hundred yards to the beach. Gazing into the fog, he thought he could make out images of people walking, kites flying, and children playing. The fine mist danced and swirled around him, playing tricks with his eyes and his mind.

Reluctantly he turned and started to back to the cottage. Making his way up Ocean Avenue, he could just discern a figure approaching him through the fog. The shape of the body and the gait of the walk looked very familiar. No, it couldn't be. It can't be. A jolt of adrenaline shot through him.

Sarah?

She emerged out of the fog, her features gaining definition. She was just as beautiful as the day he met her.

"Hi, Rob," she said, smiling, her green eyes sparkling in the fog.

"Sarah," said Rob, his voice shaking, ready to cry. "Oh my god, is it really you?"

"It is me, sort of. We are lucky that our layers are close enough that I can visit you."

"I have missed you so much, Sarah; you have no idea."

"I think I do, Rob. I've missed you too."

"Can I touch you?"

Sarah shook her head slowly. "I don't have the energy to solidify, hon; I'm sorry."

"Will you be able to stay awhile?" he asked hopefully.

Again, Sarah shook her head slowly. "I'm sorry, but I can't stay. But because of what you did for Dee, I've been granted this time."

Unable to control his emotions any longer, Rob started to cry.

"Please don't cry."

"Oh, Sarah, I just want to be with you."

"In some ways, you are, Rob."

Confused, Rob looked at her. "What do you mean?"

"Don't you remember what Dee shared with you? That you had an accident driving home in the fog? Fog kind of like this," said Sarah, her arms up.

Rob recalled the conversation. Dee had explained to him how things had worked just a few hundred feet from this spot. And she had also told him that some events in time had multiple outcomes. She claimed his near collision with a pickup truck on Milestone Road had had two outcomes.

"So I'm with you?" he asked, confused.

"Yes. A part of you is."

"I wish that were me. I wished I had died that night and could be with you."

"No. No, you don't, Rob. You still have a long life to live. And this layer," said Sarah pointing at the ground, "this layer is the most important for your happiness."

"But will we ever be together again?"

"I know this is really hard to understand, but we are together again, on another layer of time."

Rob shook his head. "But that's not me."

"It is you, Rob. It's another version of you that took a different path through time. And that path reconnected you to me."

"I wish I had been on that path. To be reconnected with you."

"You have many, many years left on this layer, Rob. On this path through time. You must take advantage of them."

"Take advantage of them?"

"Yes."

"How?"

"Pip."

"Pip?"

"Yes, Rob. I have seen you two together. I know she can make you happy."

"Oh, Sarah, I couldn't."

"Yes, you can, hon. And besides, you still have a promise to fulfill."

"A promise?"

"You have a dream. A novel to write. You first confessed it to me right after we were married. I want to see you achieve that dream. It would make me happy."

"I don't know, Sarah. I don't think I can."

"That's not the Rob I fell in love with. You are not a quitter. And you have the talent; I know you do. You just need to believe in yourself."

Rob nodded sadly. "I will keep trying. For you."

"And Pip?"

"What about her?"

"She is perfect for you, Rob. Go get her. Marry her. Have children. Live a long and wonderful life together."

"But what about us?"

Sarah smiled sadly. "Cancer took from us the life we should have had, Rob. But you can have that life with her. If you'll welcome it."

Rob looked down and then back to Sarah. "Okay, I will try."

"That makes me happy. And unfortunately, Rob, now I have to go. I'm sorry."

"Please don't go!"

"I must, Rob. It really is not up to me. And these few minutes with you? They have been a gift. The best I have ever received."

Rob was crying, the tears chasing down his cheeks. "God, I miss you."

"I miss you too, Rob. Just remember I will always love you with all my heart."

"I love you too, Sarah. More than you'll ever know."

"Goodbye, Rob. I promise you that we will see each other again." She started to fade.

"Sarah!" Rob reached out with his arms just as her image swirled away like droplets in the mist.

Rob stood alone on the street, sobbing like a child. After a while, he regained his composure and reluctantly started to walk back to the cottage. He thought he would never be happy again.

CHAPTER THIRTY-FOUR

Two months later

Rob woke refreshed. The dreams of Sarah, which seemed to have plagued him when he first arrived on the island, had faded away. Instead of having them nightly, now he would dream of her once or twice a week, if that. He felt guilty, as if he were forgetting her, but knew from his meetings with the bereavement group at the Unitarian Church that it was a perfectly normal part of the grieving - and healing - process.

Grabbing his phone off the nightstand, he sat up in bed and checked his messages. He had a couple of texts, one a confirmation of an upcoming dinner reservation and another from her thanking him for a fun evening and wishing him luck on his writing. He looked out the window. The day was going to be gray and cold.

Sighing, he swung his legs out of bed, pulled on some thick socks, jeans, and a heavy sweatshirt, and padded down the hall to the kitchen. Winter was in full swing, and despite the temperance of the Atlantic helping to keep temperatures warmer than the mainland, it still got cold. Nights were now frequently in the twenties and, during the day, struggled into the low forties. Thankfully the little oil heaters had worked, keeping each of the rooms comfortable, while the fireplace had proven to be a godsend both in warming the front of the cottage as well as providing a cozy atmosphere.

Life had settled into a comfortable routine. Days were spent reading, walking, and struggling at the laptop. Evenings were spent watching television by the fire or enjoying dinner out at one of the few restaurants still open in the off-season. Several of his favorites closed between New Year's and March, so his options were pretty slim. And on those occasions went they went out together, he certainly enjoyed her company. He was also thankful that she was giving him the space he needed. She was sensitive to his feelings and knew he wasn't quite ready. Not yet.

As he waited for the coffee to brew, he thought of the other people he had met during his months here. Despite being a midwestern boy, he had been accepted by the year-round community on the island. New Englanders had a reputation for being surly and unwelcoming, but he had experienced none of that on Nantucket. Instead, he had found a diverse group of people that shared a communal bond as they dealt with many of the challenges of living on a speck of sand thirty miles out to sea.

He poured himself a coffee, added a dab of creamer, and walked into the front room. Although he had stoked it heavily before retiring, the fire was now nothing more than a bed of smoldering ash. He grabbed the poker, stirred the coals so that the hotter ones were brought to the top, and laid some kindling on them. He blew on the embers, and soon they caught and roared to life. Satisfied, he grabbed a few logs from the carrier next to the hearth and added them to the grate. Soon he had a blazing fire that was quickly taking the chill out of the air.

He sat on the couch to enjoy his coffee. He clicked on the flat screen and navigated to the local weather. The meteorologist was predicting a potential snowstorm to hit the Cape and Islands later in the week. A further reminder that he was here in the off-season.

359

He had yet to experience summer on the island with warm weather and the influx of tens of thousands of seasonal residents. Would it change how he felt about Nantucket? Would he embrace it? Hate it? He wasn't sure but thought he might like to find out.

When he arrived, the plan had been to spend six months, and he had secured the cottage through March. But for the past few weeks, he had been toying with the idea of extending his stay indefinitely. Although he missed his friends and family in St. Louis, he had found something here that had been missing in his life since he had lost Sarah. Nantucket and its people were filling a hole in his heart, and the thought of leaving overwhelmed him with sadness.

The realtor had quoted him the cost of staying in the Shanty for the summer, and it had shocked him just how much more expensive his rent would be. Technically he could afford it, he still had most of his savings, and his investments had done fairly well, but he thought he might just find a job instead to offset the increased cost. Home repairs and remodels were in high demand, so maybe it was time to buy some tools and hang out his handyman shingle again. Certainly, he wasn't going to be able to pay the increased rent with his novel, especially since it was nothing more than a handful of unfinished and barely literate pages.

The writing - or rather lack of it - had been his biggest frustration with his time on the island. He had made a promise to himself and to Sarah that he would be successful. And he thought that this time on Nantucket would have been the perfect opportunity. But for whatever reason, the words just hadn't come. He had explored a dozen different storylines, but none of them seemed to resonate creatively. He would start on a new idea, flesh out an outline, knock out a chapter or two, and then hit a dead end. He didn't think it was the story but rather something in his brain that was the culprit.

But today, this morning, for the first time, he felt different.

She had played a big role in turning the tide. Her support and positive feedback on what few chapters he had written had helped bolster his confidence. And that support brought with it a new energy, a new excitement, an optimism that he hadn't felt before. For the first time since he had confessed his wish to Sarah about writing a book, he knew that he really could. It was as if all the frustrations, the doubts, and misgivings had faded away.

When he had first started writing, the idea of sitting at the keyboard had scared him. But now it excited him, and he couldn't wait to get back to it.

But first things first. One thing he knew was that he couldn't write on an empty stomach. Rob went back to the kitchen and made a quick breakfast of eggs on toast. He refilled his coffee, ate mindlessly, and then put his dishes in the sink. He looked out the kitchen window at the hedge, still green despite the cold, and saw a bright red cardinal perched on a limb. It cocked its head from side to side, ruffled its feathers, and stared at him. Rob smiled. The Northern Cardinal had been Sarah's favorite, and he felt that it must be a sign. She was watching over him.

Hunger satisfied and emotionally content, Rob made his way to the office. He put his coffee on the desk and opened the laptop. Navigating to his favorite streaming site, he put on some Ludovico Einaudi to get him in the mood. He closed his eyes and leaned back in the chair, and let the beautiful music wash over him.

A smile crept slowly over his face.

His book, his novel, his lifelong dream lay stretched out in front of him. He could see every chapter, every twist of the story. He could hear the characters speak, their dialogue loud and clear. In his mind, he had a straight path from prologue to denouement. All he had to do was to take the movie that was playing in his imagination and convert it into words on his laptop.

He opened his eyes, settled up against the desk, and laid his fingers on the keys. This was it. He took a deep breath, exhaled slowly, and started to write.

It was a beautiful evening to bury a body.

Author's Notes

I must first thank you for reading Not All Bodies Stay Buried. I really hope you enjoyed reading it as much as I enjoyed writing it. Thank you. But before you go, I have two requests. The first is to please leave a review and let others know how much you (hopefully) enjoyed the book. The second is to join my mailing list at www.garthjeffries.com so we can stay in touch on future projects.

I also wanted to touch on the tragedy of domestic abuse. The fictional character, Jack Reiner, is an abuser. Sadly, domestic abuse and domestic violence are all too common in the real world. This pattern of coercive and controlling behaviors is used by one individual to establish power and control over another person in an intimate relationship. This can manifest in various forms, including physical, emotional, psychological, sexual, or financial abuse. Murder is not uncommon. It affects individuals of all genders, ages, races, and socio-economic backgrounds.

If you or someone you know is a victim of domestic violence, please know there are resources available to help including:

National Domestic Violence Hotline (NDVH):
- Provides 24/7 confidential support and assistance
- Call: 1-800-799-SAFE (7233)
-Visit their website at www.thehotline.org

Help is also available through local domestic violence shelters, legal aid and advocacy organizations, mental health professionals, and community-based support groups.

If you or are in immediate danger, please call emergency services (911) to ensure your safety and seek legal protection.

I also wanted to ensure a word of thanks to our men and women in the military, our first responders, and all our healthcare providers. Thank you for all you do in keeping us safe, healthy and free.

Garth Jeffries
Kansas City
March 2024

Made in the USA
Las Vegas, NV
19 August 2024

93977606R00215